*PRAISE FOR THE DANG[...]*

*NAUGHTY STRANGER*

"A steamy and emotional romance with a generous dose of intrigue and suspense...The unpredictable twists and turns of this story will keep you on the edge of your seat and rooting for Peyton and Boone every step of the way."

—Frolic

"An entertaining thriller hidden in a sizzling small-town romance."
—*Fresh Fiction*

"From the very first page *Naughty Stranger* will have you hooked, once I got started I just couldn't put it down. Its sultry and suspenseful story line and captivating characters drew me in and had me teetering helplessly from the edge of my seat!"
—Reds Romance Reviews

"I really enjoyed this story, and I loved watching two broken souls find hope, and love, in each other. Especially amidst a crazy murder plot, and all their friends' nosiness!"
—Alpha Book Club

# Wicked Sinner

### Dangerous Love #2

*USA TODAY* Bestselling Author

# STACEY KENNEDY

FOREVER
YOURS

New York   Boston

Copyright © 2019 by Stacey Kennedy
Excerpt from *Ruthless Bastard* copyright © 2020 by Stacey Kennedy
Cover design by Yoly Cortez. Cover copyright © 2019 by Hachette Book Group, Inc.

Forever Yours
Hachette Book Group
1290 Avenue of the Americas, New York, NY 10104
read-forever.com
twitter.com/readforeverpub

First published as an ebook and as a print on demand: October 2019

Forever Yours is an imprint of Grand Central Publishing. The Forever Yours name and logo are trademarks of Hachette Book Group, Inc.

The publisher is not responsible for websites (or their content) that are not owned by the publisher.

The Hachette Speakers Bureau provides a wide range of authors for speaking events. To find out more, go to www.hachettespeakersbureau.com or call (866) 376-6591.

ISBNs: 978-1-5387-4696-7 (ebook), 978-1-5387-4694-3 (print on demand)

*For everyone who believes in second chances.*

# Wicked Sinner

# Prologue

"You promised me forever."

Remy Brennan barely processed the words that left her mouth, but she felt every single one of them down to her bones. The world was silent around her. Not a sound breaking past the steady thumps of her beating heart. The streetlights cast a soft glow across the old, historic area of Stoney Creek. The coastal town in Maine was known for its fresh catch restaurants and picturesque coastal views, but to Remy, Stoney Creek was home. And that home suddenly looked abruptly different. Nothing was recognizable now, everything seemed hazy, far away, as the love of her life said, "The FBI has offered me a job. I'm leaving for Washington tonight."

Her eyes watered as she stared into Asher Sullivan's light emerald-colored eyes. Tall and fit, Asher had the power to make Remy melt, even after five years together. She'd known Asher for as long as she could remember. She'd been a freshman when they'd gotten together, but he was already a senior at that time, being three years older. The age difference had mattered to just about everyone but her and Asher. Nothing could have stood between their love. They'd stayed together through his high school, his college graduation, and his time at the police academy. He'd only gotten hired by the Stoney Creek Police Department a few months ago. He'd been her first date. Her first kiss. And on her eighteenth birthday, Asher had been her first *everything*. Her entire world. And now that world was crumbling, and she was racing to find a way to solid ground again.

"I never planned for this, Remy," Asher said softly, not meeting her gaze, putting his final boxes into his Ford pickup. "But how can I turn down a job with the FBI?"

"Easy." She hugged herself against the bitter chill. "You call them up and say that you don't want the job. You tell them that your family and friends are here, and that you refuse to leave them."

Asher planted his palms against the gate of his truck and bowed his head. "Why are you punishing both of us? The decision is made. It's done."

"Why am *I* punishing us?" She gasped, angry tears filling her eyes. "You're breaking my heart, Asher. You said we'd get married. You promised me *everything*. And what…with a snap of your fingers you're taking it all away?"

"I don't want to hurt you." He finally faced her, his typically dazzling and playful gaze now dark. Haunted. His baseball cap covering his blond hair was low on his face. His good-hearted was nature nowhere to be found now. "The very *last* thing I want to do is hurt you, Remy."

"Then stay here with me." Desperate not to feel this iciness between them, she closed the distance and ran her hands up his muscular arms, feeling them trembling. "I don't understand any of this. You already have a job here, a good job. Your family is here." Her voice blistered. "I'm here."

A foreign coldness flashed across his expression. "My mom is gone."

Remy's hands tightened on his arms to keep him from leaving, and her heart reached for him to ease the pain he endured. His mother had committed suicide two weeks earlier. The strong and flirty Asher she knew had died that day too. "I know she's gone, but your friends are your family too. We need you here, Asher. Boone and Rhett"—his childhood friends—"they all need you."

"They're both moving away," Asher said, his jaw set. "Boone to New York City. Rhett to the army."

"But they'll come back eventually," Remy implored. "This is home for them too." He turned to face her again, but his shoulders pulled back. He had already decided. "And what about me?" she whispered, cupping his face, frantically trying to reach the man she knew and loved. "I need you here."

He jerked away and stepped back, putting cold distance between them she didn't understand. "This is my dream career, Remy. The FBI. Jobs like this don't come around often, especially for a small-town cop." He slammed the gate of his truck closed before addressing her again. "I need to think of myself right now, with Mom gone. What's good for my future."

"Then ask me to go with you." Hopelessness began to claw at her throat, tears making him blurry. "Take me with you to Washington. I'll go. Just ask me."

He stared at her. Hard. Then he shook his head slowly. "I can't do that to your nana. You need to be here. Kinsley's here." Kinsley was her best friend since they were in kindergarten, and Boone's younger sister. "And you're still in college." She was getting her business degree to eventually open her own shop. "You need to stay here."

Her breath caught deep in her throat, the world somersaulting around her. She held on to her stomach, pain cutting through her. "Everyone will understand if I go with you."

A beat.

Then his voice was as sharp as a knife. "No."

Remy went rigid, taking a step back at the finality in his voice.

"Dammit," he said, softer this time, still keeping his distance. "I don't want this to hurt you, but it's better this way."

"But what about *us*?" Remy shot back, her pounding heart growing louder in her ears. "What about all the dreams we had together? What happened to getting married? What happened to the children we talked about having? About the house we wanted to live in?"

Sudden emotion flared in his eyes. "You don't want those things from me."

"I do," she said, raising her voice. "I've wanted those things the day you first kissed me under the big willow tree. I have forgotten nothing, and nothing has changed for me. I don't understand where any of this coming from."

The sky suddenly opened, rain falling down from the heavens.

"I don't want this life, Remy." He took a loaded pause, then the Asher she loved was gone. In his place was a stranger she didn't even recognize as he said, "I don't love you anymore."

Her breath caught again at the pain splitting her chest wide open. She squeezed her hands, trying to wake up from this nightmare, her fingernails digging into her palms. "Asher, don't do this."

"It's already done." He moved to her, and alongside the fresh rain, his earthy cologne infused the air as he pressed his lips against her forehead.

All the love, sadness, and fear suddenly vanished, replaced by cold, hard rage. "No." She shoved him, and he took a step back. "No! You don't get to do this. You don't get to make yourself feel better before you go. I'll never forgive you for leaving me, Asher. *Never!*"

His shoulders were high and tight, tension radiating off him. The rain beat against them, the drops of water dripping off his baseball hat. His chest rose and fell with his heavy breaths. For a single second she thought he was going to gather in his arms, kiss her, and tell her he'd stay.

He didn't. Instead he said, "Some sins should never be forgiven."

Without another word, Asher got into his truck. Time slowed for Remy as the headlights faded away, the icy rain hammering down, and then the dark night enveloped her.

# Chapter 1

*Present Day*

"Today we are gathered here to celebrate Damon Lane and Remy Brennan as they proclaim their love and commitment to the world."

Asher Sullivan wasn't sitting in the church in his hometown of Stoney Creek to celebrate. He was in the fifth pew back from where the only woman he ever loved stood, ready to marry someone else. She wore a strapless gown, fitting her five-foot-five frame to pure perfection. Her long, blond, wavy hair flowed down her back, and every time he looked into her big light green eyes, she took his breath away. She'd been with him since she was a freshman, and even back then, she'd been beautiful. Only now she was breathtaking and no longer *his*.

The bastard standing next to her, about to become her husband, Asher could do without. Especially considering Remy had no idea she was about to marry a con man. Or that this impending marriage was a sham to get Remy's half-million-dollar inheritance that her beloved nana left for Remy when she passed away. Remy's sweet grandmother who raised her from six years old had stipulated in her last will and testament that Remy would only gain her inheritance once she married.

Asher thrust a hand through his sandy-colored hair, ready to crawl out of his skin. There was no doubt the sweat trailing his spine showed through his white button-up. A pair of handcuffs poked his thigh through the pocket of his dark gray slacks, all but teasing him with anticipation to wrap them around Damon's lowlife wrists. But Asher couldn't act, not until the chief of police sent word that they'd received the arrest warrant.

"We are gathered to rejoice, with and for them, in the new life they now undertake together," the minister called out in a smooth, nearly rhythmic voice.

Asher snorted. "What a load of shit."

Heads turned and a few glares came Asher's way, telling him he wasn't as quiet as he'd hoped. Remy was meant to marry *him*, until Asher's life fell apart when his mother committed suicide. Everything changed after that. *Asher* changed after that. At one point in his life, his mother was the mother everyone loved. She was cool and funny and had done everything right for Asher. That's what made her death so hard. She deserved a good life, but what she got handed was a life married to an abusive alcoholic. Too many times, Asher wished he could go back to that day she downed a bottle of pills when his father left. Asher would have shown her she wasn't as small and worthless as his bastard father made her feel. And he'd always regret that the only time he punched his father was the day of the funeral, telling him to never come back.

From that day on, Asher decided to never let love control him like it had controlled his mother. Love made people foolish.

It made people forget the things they wanted out of life. And Asher couldn't have given Remy what she wanted. She deserved the life his mother didn't have. The life Asher had no idea how to give her. He'd left to give Remy the chance to find the life she deserved, and to salvage any strength that he had left in the darkest moment of his life. Only that's not what happened.

Ten years later, he felt more lost than ever. That's why he'd come back to Stoney Creek five years ago. He needed his hometown roots. His friends. The life he knew. Except that, for the first four years he was back, Remy barely acknowledged his existence. Of course, he understood. He'd heard while in Washington that she'd gone into a deep depression after her nana passed away soon after Asher left. Something Asher hadn't learned until much later. She'd dropped out of college and had ended up working as a bartender. She hadn't dated anyone. She'd given up completely on all the dreams she'd once had about opening her own New Age shop. And Asher knew that most of that was his fault. He'd set the crumbling of her life into motion the day he left her.

After he'd come home, he'd taken it slow, never pushing, giving her the time she needed to forgive him. They might never have a relationship again, but he wanted her as a friend. No, *needed* her as a friend. It was a selfish want, but nothing made sense without Remy in his life. It took her a year to stop avoiding places he went. It took another two years for her to have a conversation with him. When she finally seemed herself around him, she'd begun dating. And this past year, when things were good between them, Asher watched Remy fall in love with someone else.

At first, he was happy for her. Until he met the bastard and knew Damon wasn't who he said he was. A full investigation revealed the truth about the con man. As much as Asher didn't want to hurt Remy, he would protect her. Always.

"You need to calm down," Boone Knight said in a clipped voice, breaking into Asher's thoughts. Boone was a powerhouse of a guy with neat dark hair who was usually quick to smile. But right now, Boone turned his head and set his hard blue eyes on Asher. "You're drawing attention."

On Asher's other side was Rhett West. His features had always been hard, and Rhett carried heaviness and darkness with him. The man was lethal, both in the military and out of it. They were both Asher's closest childhood friends and fellow detectives. "Where is the goddamn arrest warrant?" Asher bit off.

"Remy will never forgive you if you act before having it," Rhett shot back quietly.

Asher restrained the curses sitting on his lips and glanced back at his phone, his leg bouncing a mile a minute. Rhett wasn't wrong. Asher had broken Remy's heart once. He couldn't act rashly. His instincts had gotten him through the police academy, then hired at the FBI, and now back in Stoney Creek working alongside his buddies as a detective. Those same instincts were what had him investigating Damon Lane. It only took days to realize something was wrong, but it took weeks to gather enough evidence against Lane to go to the prosecutor.

And Asher knew Remy needed that proof too.

One call. That's what they waited for. The month-long investigation had finally delivered Damon Lane's real name, Kyle Fanning. And Remy wasn't his first victim either, she was his fourth. Three previous marriages, and Fanning went by all different names.

The minister continued, "The relationship you enter into today must be grounded in the strength of your love and the power of your faith in each other."

Asher held his tongue this time. For the briefest of glances, Remy turned her head, her gaze connecting with his. And held. Asher felt the intensity in the air between them. That had never faded, no many how many years had gone by since he last touched her. But Asher understood why she wanted to get married. For as long as he knew Remy, she had dreamed of her wedding. She told him every single detail. From the ceremony being at night under the stars, with torches lighting up the grounds. She'd shown him the exact wedding dress she wanted. He noted that this ceremony was in a church and her dress was not the one she'd dreamed of wearing. But he knew why she did this. She wanted to open up a New Age shop she'd call Black Cat's Cauldron, and her inheritance would help make that happen. Remy believed in magic. She believed teas could bring positive energy. That herbs could heal. That burning incenses could chase away evil.

He ground his teeth and glanced down at the black screen of his phone, waiting for the damn text message to stop this wedding. Asher hunted criminals—that was his job. Most crimes he solved dealt with theft, domestic violence, and, only recently, murder. The first one to happen in town in years. But right now this crime was personal.

He came here to save Remy, but he knew he'd be stopping this wedding today. And that would devastate her. But when the time came, he'd object with or without the evidence. He just really hoped, for his life and well-being, that he had the arrest warrant and the photograph of Kyle Fanning's last wedding.

A flash on his phone caught his attention.

*Get him.*

Asher jumped to his feet and growled, "Stop. I object."

Remy turned to him, eyes huge, but for one split second,

Asher swore he caught a hint of a smile. A smile that she once only gave to him. The shock of seeing her look at him with such warmth and affection stuttered his mind, until he spotted the prick next to her shift slightly. Damon still held her hand and a ring. Yeah, he was a good-looking scumbag. But Asher saw Damon for what he saw, a slimy bastard who didn't just break hearts but left a trail of shattered women behind him.

Determined to ensure Remy wasn't one of them, hot adrenaline pumped through Asher's veins as he charged forward, the crowd in the pews a blur around him. Damon went to take a step back, but Asher was there a second later, grabbing him by the arms and taking him down swiftly to the ground.

"Asher!" Remy bellowed. "What are you doing?"

"Saving you from this fucker." Asher dug his knee into Damon's back while he reached for his cuffs. As he grabbed Damon's wrist, he snarled, "You want to tell her the truth. Or am I going to do it?"

"What the fuck is wrong with you?" Damon snapped. "Get him off me."

Around Asher, and in the deep silence of the church, he felt the weight of everyone's gaze. After he got on the second cuff, he glanced back over his shoulder, finding Boone frowning and Rhett grinning from ear to ear. With a moment to breathe, Asher cursed softly. Perhaps he hadn't handled this well, but he wouldn't apologize for shit. He blew out a slow breath to steady himself and then rose, bringing Damon to his feet.

Rhett grasped Damon's arm, pulling him back away from Remy. "And here I thought I was the one who always fucked up," he said quietly to Asher. "Good luck dancing your way out of this."

Next to him, Boone cringed, staring over Asher's shoulder.

*Fuck.* Asher knew he had to face the inevitable, so he turned around. Tears flooded Remy's pale face. Beside her, her bridesmaids—the blond-haired woman was Boone's fiancée, Peyton, and the dark-haired one glaring was Boone's sister, Kinsley. They were both wearing light purple dresses and holding Remy's hands tight.

"You better explain yourself, and pronto, buddy," Kinsley spat.

Peyton looked from Asher to Boone rapidly, her hazel eyes unable to find whatever they were looking for. Probably an explanation.

Asher's heartrate began to slow. He took in the minister, Remy's coworkers and friends in the pews. *Shit.*

"Asher," Remy snapped.

He turned back, finding a thousand questions in Remy's pretty green eyes. While he wanted to give her all the answers she needed, this was also his chance to fix the past. Asher's leaving her was part of the reason she'd given up on all her dreams, and nearly married a con man. She'd lost everything, all because he was a stupid kid full of fear and despair.

He wasn't that kid anymore.

Though the truth remained as it had all those years ago. Asher couldn't give her his heart. Remy was safer and would be happier without him. But he had this one chance to right his wrongs and set her life back on the right track. No missteps this time. "We don't have to do this here."

She dropped Kinsley's and Peyton's hands and stepped forward. "Tell me. Now."

To keep the conversation private, Asher sighed and closed the distance, becoming more aware of her trembling body. His fingers twitched to grab her, bring her close, and keep her safe until she remembered all the things she once wanted for herself.

"This man isn't Damon Lane," he explained gently. "His name is Kyle Fanning. He's a con man who has swindled more than three million out of his past three wives, all under different aliases."

Before Remy could even respond, Kinsley lurched at Damon. "You motherfucker."

Gasps came from the pews as Boone caught his sister by the waist, holding her back while Kinsley did her best to murder Damon with her bare hands. Kinsley and Remy had been best friends since they were both ankle biters, and Kinsley had distrusted Damon as much as Asher had.

The minister's skin had turned ashen at some point, and he raised his hands to the crowd. "Please, everyone, let's calm down."

Remy slowly stepped closer to Damon. "This can't be true. Damon, tell me this isn't true."

Asher glanced back and found the bastard's head hanging, shoulders slumped.

"You were only after my inheritance," Remy squeaked, tears welling in her eyes.

Asher ground his teeth against the pain in her expression and reached for her, desperate to take her away from all this shit. "I'm so sorry, Remy."

She blinked, wobbling slightly. "Don't be sorry," she said to Asher without looking at him. Her gaze wasn't focused on anything specific, so far away from there. "I'm sorry for all this. I'm sorry I believed that you loved me," she said to Damon, and then she glanced over the crowd behind Asher in the pews. "Most of all, I'm sorry I wasted all your time today." She took one final look at Asher, her heartbreak seeping into the air between them, and then she grabbed the hem of her dress and ran down the aisle.

Asher cursed and chased after her, meeting her by the big oak tree outside. He grabbed her arm. "Remy."

She whirled around, tears flooding her face. "Why did it have to be you? Boone or Rhett could have stopped the wedding, why did it have to be *you*?"

Asher released her arm slowly. "Because this is what I do."

"Hurt me?"

The bitterness in her voice took his breath away. And yet, he deserved her wrath. "No, Remy," he countered gently, "I protect you." He took a step forward.

She shook her head, stepping back. "Just don't. Stay away from me. Just leave me alone!" Her dress rustled and brushed across his legs as she ran away.

It occurred to him then that even though he *knew* he did the right thing by stopping the wedding today, he'd forever be remembered as the guy who broke her heart, not once, but twice.

# Chapter 2

"You can't hide in your wedding dress forever."

"Watch me," Remy called to Kinsley from beneath her blanket on her queen-size bed. They were best friends, but not even Kinsley could get her out of where she'd been hiding all morning. The sunlight shone through the thin sheet, promising a gorgeous day. There was nothing beautiful about it, and Remy wouldn't be fooled.

Life sucked.

And she wasn't just wallowing in finding out her fiancé was trying to con her out of her inheritance, even if her heart currently felt like Damon had put it through a cheese grater. First of all, she thought she'd wake up this morning married to a man who was as close to perfect as he could get. Damon had been sweet, thoughtful, and romantic. He'd given her foot rubs without her having to ask. He'd listened to her problems and offered gentle advice. He'd even planned perfect dates. *Lies! All lies!*

Second, she thought she would finally put working as a bartender behind her, would finally have her inheritance to open her long-awaited shop, Black Cat's Cauldron, a New Age witch, herbal medicine shop, mixed with some good old-fashioned voodoo, spell making, and tarot card reading. All things she'd learned from her nana, whom she'd lived with since she was six years old after her mom decided she didn't want to be a mom anymore, and instead went on tour with her country folk band. Only days ago, Remy had figured it all out. She planned on buying the empty shop beneath her rented loft apartment. A shop that was beside Peyton's lingerie shop, Uptown Girl, with Kinsley's bar, Whiskey Blues, on the other side. But that dream was now gone. And so was her inheritance. Not that she blamed her nana for putting in that stipulation into her last will and testament. Her grandmother thought Remy would marry Asher. She couldn't have anticipated that Remy would have still been single at the age of thirty.

The other—*biggest*—problem was Remy's unexpected reaction to Asher objecting to the wedding. In those long seconds after he called out, her heart skipped a full beat, hoping—hell, begging—that he had come for *her* because he still loved her. She hated the hurt that followed when she realized that wasn't the case. She'd spent *years* getting over Asher. She'd spent even more time pulling her life together after he'd left. She was supposed to be over him. Asher was behind her.

Apparently, her heart didn't get that memo.

No wedding. No shop. Still renting. Total failure.

And now on top of all that, she felt broken. Clearly she had nothing together if she couldn't have spotted Damon for what he was, and she obviously hadn't gotten Asher out of her heart.

Somewhere between waking up and when Kinsley and Peyton entered her bedroom, Remy decided to live under the blanket with her black cat, Salem, the biggest bottle of wine she could find, and a gigantic tub of cookie dough ice cream.

"What is that smell?" Kinsley asked, breaking into Remy's thoughts with a tight voice. "Seriously, Remy, I know you believe in magic and spells and all that jazz, but your room smells like a mix between a fart and a very spicy dead thing."

"It's called 'I'm fixing my wrong' incense," Remy said, giving Salem a scratch on the head. He sat on her chest, purring away like life was great, with his bright green eyes on hers.

"What wrong?" Peyton asked.

"Damon…or Kyle…"—Remy hesitated and then winced. "Nope, I can't do it. I'm calling him Damon. Anyway, Damon didn't like all the witchy stuff, so he asked me not to do anything magical at the wedding, so I didn't." And boy, did she regret that now. "Hell, maybe that was the first red flag. He feared all the *light*, that damn evil bastard."

"I agree with the evil bastard part," Kinsley said. "But I can do without whatever shit this is that you're burning."

"Touch it and lose a finger," Remy said calmly as Salem lifted his chin for more scratchies. "I need all the help I can get. That incense will cleanse me for abandoning what my nana taught me—for abandoning magic at the wedding."

Heavy silence filled the room. Until Peyton broke it with her sweet, soft voice. "Your mom has called a dozen times now."

Peyton had only moved to Stoney Creek a few months ago after losing her husband in a tragic car accident. The worried tone of Peyton's voice was endearing, really, considering only a month ago the man who'd caused her husband's murder had set out to kill her too. All in order to take full ownership of Peyton's husband's multi-million-dollar real estate company. Sad as that was, Peyton found love with Kinsley's brother, Boone, and they were engaged now, so at least there was some good in the world still.

Compared to everything Peyton had been through, Remy's problems seemed tiny. Even if her life was less than picture-perfect, with a father she never knew and a country folk singer mother who had less money than Remy did in her bank account, Remy felt like an asshole for hiding when Peyton faced everything with strength. She lowered the sheet, meeting the gentle stares of her two closest friends. Salem rose, yawned, and dug his paws into Remy's chest as he stretched. The strong one, Kinsley, was sitting in the chair in the corner of the room. Her long, dark brown hair was straight today, with little makeup around her blue eyes. Not like she needed any. She looked beautiful first thing in the morning. The sweet one, Peyton, stood at the end of the bed, worrying her bright pink lips, her honey-colored hair in a side braid, looking perfectly put-together in her cream-colored sundress. "If my mother is really so worried about me, she would have actually come to the wedding yesterday instead of sending me a text," Remy pointed out. She sat up in bed against her light gray fabric headboard, sending Salem moving off, only to return a second later to curl up in her lap. "She sends a fucking text to wish me well on my wedding. Who does that?"

Peyton cringed. "Okay, you're right, that's shitty, but she's calling you now. Wouldn't talking to her help?"

"Doubtful." While Remy mentally understood that her mother couldn't leave the tour, her heart didn't. Especially considering it's not like her mother was selling out huge stadiums. Playing small gigs was worth more than coming to her daughter's wedding, apparently. Remy knew that shouldn't surprise her. Her mother had never been the nurturing type; that's why her nana had raised her when Mom decided to hit the road. And thank God she had her nana, or Remy's life would have likely been filled with drunk and stoned adults.

"All right," Kinsley finally said, breaking the silence with a scrunched nose. "You're burning whatever shit this is to cleanse the bad energy; what else can we do to get you out of this bed?"

Remy took in what Kinsley said and then covered her face with her hands. God, she was pathetic. Seriously, pathetic. "Wine," she mumbled, beneath her hands. "All the wine."

"I don't think that's a good idea," Peyton said. "You need to face this."

"Which will be much easier with wine," Remy said, dropping her hands.

Kinsley mouth twitched as she sat down on the bed next to Remy. "Dude, we got loaded with you last night, remember?"

Yeah, Remy remembered everything. She remembered curling up in her bed, sobbing until she had no tears left. She remembered chugging the wine straight from the bottle, while Kinsley and Peyton drank from their glasses. "Yes," Remy stated, "and we should do that again. Right now."

Kinsley gave a knowing look and patted Remy's leg beneath the sheet. "You can't keep drinking this away, babe, no matter how much you want to. Peyton's right—you've got to face this." She reached out and petted Salem, who hissed at her. "All I want to do is love you," she snapped at Salem. To Remy, she said, "And you can't run from this. Everyone is calling to check on you."

Peyton agreed with a nod and then, being her sweet self, she added, "Damon—and I'm on board calling him Damon because it *is* totally weird to call him Kyle—is at fault here."

"Exactly," Kinsley agreed, nodding quickly. "Once all this is said and done, you'll see that he's an asshole who doesn't deserve another thought. He deserves to have his nuts squeezed in a vise or ripped from his body, but not anything else."

Remy considered that and then gave a firm nod. "Yes, to the nuts part." The truth was, she wasn't *only* hiding from what Damon had done to her; the girls simply didn't know that. But there wasn't a chance in hell that she would tell either of them what her heart did when she thought Asher had come to make her *his* again. In fact, there would be no facing that at all since she'd decided to pretend it never actually happened.

Once, she forced her heart to forget Asher. She could do that again, as she'd forget Damon too. But she couldn't ignore that she had embarrassed herself in front of everyone she knew. She'd been so desperate to move on, to finally get her shop, and to show Asher that she had moved on, she'd found herself a con man.

Perfect.

Remy realized that her thoughts must have showed on her face when she caught the pity in both her friends' expressions. So she went right back under the sheet again. "Please just let me die in peace."

Kinsley snorted. "Can't do that, babe."

Sure, a part of Remy wanted to stand up and fight back, be the strong woman she was. But for this one second, she wanted to do none of those things. She was so damn tired of fighting this same game to find happiness and always meeting brick wall after brick wall.

Her heart hurt. Her head hurt. Hell, *everything* hurt. And while the tears were dry now, her soul felt empty, exhausted.

A sudden shuffle sounded outside her makeshift tent, obviously another set of feet entering the room, and just like that, the air thickened, and the hairs on her arms rose. Great. Just what she needed. "I don't want to see you," she told Asher. She hated being so in tune with him, but back when they'd dated, she was convinced they'd been in love in their past lives. The tarot cards told her as much, as did her nana. But there was no denying that whenever he got close, the air became electrified. On a spiritual level, her soul knew Asher's intimately.

"I'm not leaving until you come out of there."

His voice, both strong and smooth, almost tripped her heart. That was if she didn't hate him. And right now she hated all men, especially men who broke her heart. "Unless you have wine, ice cream, or an athame"—a black-handled knife used in rituals—"that is blessed in such a way that I can use it on Damon, leave me alone."

Four feet exited the room, but not the ones Remy wanted.

Heavy weight sank the bed next to her. "Remy."

"No," she snapped.

Asher's heavy exhale filled the room before he grabbed the sheet and yanked it back as she tried desperately to hold it into place. Salem hissed and then jumped off the bed. Not a surprise. Salem only loved Remy.

"Missed you too." He grinned at the retreating cat.

Remy became utterly lost in the view. With the sunlight beaming on his sculpted face, and with his perfect hair, perfect lips, perfect *everything*, Asher was a damn near god. "I want to punch you," she told him seriously. Not for interrupting her, but for being so handsome. Men were devils.

Asher's eyebrow lifted—his signature move. "Would that make you feel better?"

She considered it for a good few seconds. "No," she finally admitted. Hell, she'd probably feel worse because she hated any kind of violence. Nana had raised her to walk in the path of light. Sometimes she really hated the promise that she'd made as a child to never use what she'd learned from Nana to harm. She had been taught a few spells by Nana that made people violently sick to their stomachs, but she learned those for protection, never to seek revenge.

Asher stared at her for what seemed like a lifetime, his expression unreadable before he rose and headed for the adjoining bathroom. She frowned at his back, and his great ass in his jeans, rethinking her decision not to use one of her spells. He deserved one night of pain for the pain he caused her, didn't he? Maybe she needed to drive over to Damon at the jail and bring him a drink. What Nana didn't know wouldn't hurt her…

Asher disappeared into the bathroom and then she heard the water running. When he returned to her, she told him straight up, "I'm not having a bath."

Obviously having a death wish, he stepped next to the bed, yanking the sheet off completely. "It'll do you good."

"Bossy much?" she growled.

He gave her an answering grin that made her belly flutter. "No one's perfect." She glared at that damn irritating smile while he grabbed the clothes off the chair. Kinsley had set them out last night when Remy dove under the sheet still in her wedding dress. "Come on. Up you get."

She gave him the finger.

Asher's mouth twitched and then he gave her a level look. "You've got two seconds to rethink your decision before I'm putting you in there myself."

He didn't bluff. Ever. Asher would deposit her in the bath, dress and all. Years of dating him had taught her that, and truthfully, that was probably the cop in Asher too. All he wanted to do was help, and he knew her better than anyone. Baths put her mind back together every time. Of course, he knew that. Asher thought things out. He didn't act rashly. He'd probably considered his steps a thousand times before coming into her bedroom today. But that had also been one of their *issues* back in the day too. He took charge of everything, all the time, including when he decided to move away without including her in that decision.

Regardless that she didn't want to follow *his way*, she did want to keep her dignity and realized she had to stop mopping and clear these negative thoughts from her mind. She shoved off the bed and stormed into the bathroom. "I'm doing this for me, not because you told me to, just so we're clear."

"We're all clear, Remy," he said behind her.

She scowled at how she warmed at hearing her name from his mouth. He said it with all the history they had between them, thousands of memories and moments that linked their souls together. When she reached her small bathroom with a claw-foot bathtub, she realized something. She nearly turned around, but Asher was there, right behind her.

"I'll help you," he said gently.

Surely, she should feel *nothing*, but when his fingers brushed across her back as he began unlacing the corset of her dress, seemingly lingering longer than necessary, heat tingled through her and spiraled low in her belly.

She shut her eyes, forcing herself to forget how warm and safe Asher's touch had always been. That was what took the longest to get over. No one touched her like Asher. No one kissed her like Asher. No one held her like Asher. No one loved her the way he loved her.

Until he broke her heart into a million pieces, of course.

The memory of that touch remained, even though she knew Damon was the best next choice. Until, *again*, he wasn't.

The dress slowly fell away to pool on the floor, revealing her bridle lingerie that was meant for Damon, not Asher. And somehow, as the dress fell, it felt like her guards fell with it. All the walls she'd kept up against Asher since he'd come back home were suddenly *gone*. She felt bared. As if Asher knew it, he quickly wrapped a towel around her. There was a long pause, and then Asher said softly behind her, "You're going to be all right, Remy."

Something came over her then, an emotion she couldn't really place. She turned around and said before she thought about it, "I know. I'm always all right. That's what I do. I survive. But I'm so damn tired of surviving. I thought for once I was going to be happy. Truly happy."

Sadness darkened Asher's eyes, his expression turning to stone. His second signature move. He never expressed *anything*. He never said *anything*. He'd never apologized for breaking her heart. He simply came back.

And then he did his last signature move. The one he excelled at doing. He walked away, shutting the door behind him.

She did what she was good at. She grabbed some banishing bath salts out of the small metal container on the wicker shelf and tossed them into the hot water. She might not have her shop, a husband, or her sanity at the moment, but she'd always have her magic.

Magic never lied, never hurt, and never broke promises.

# Chapter 3

The pipes groaned and complained, taking the water from Remy's bath away, while Asher sat on the end of her bed. He rested his elbows on his knees, staring at the closed bathroom door, trying to not inhale the disgusting aroma coming from the incense on the bedside table. He *should* feel terrible for what happened yesterday, but he finally felt like he was doing right by Remy. Once, he'd failed her terribly. He'd never fail her again, not if he could help it. He'd made mistakes. Big ones. And he couldn't help but feel at fault now. He should have never left, should have stayed and not run like some coward. When he realized that, the damage had been done and there was no going back. But watching her fall for someone else this past year made him realize something worse than his own fears. He could lose her. *Really* lose her.

He had this one chance again to get this all right. He hadn't helped his mother when she'd most needed him. He'd never let Remy fall into another depression, not if he could help it. Asher was well aware now that one wrong move and Remy would cut him loose permanently, but he wouldn't make a wrong move.

Not this time. Not with her happiness on the line. And not when he knew this woman and what made her heart tick. She'd recover from this, and he'd be there alongside her. Until he'd fixed his mistakes.

He owed Remy that. He owed her so much.

When the bathroom door finally opened, Remy exited wearing a T-shirt and black leggings, her wet hair around her fresh face. He couldn't find a spot of the black mascara that darkened her eyes when he'd arrived.

Damn.

She looked more beautiful than ever. When he'd left all those years ago, she'd been a girl. When he'd come back home, she'd turned into a woman with curves in all the right places—curves he couldn't ignore.

"Who called you to come here?" she asked, walking past him with her wedding dress in her arms.

"Who do think?"

Without looking back at him, she said, "Kinsley."

There was a hint of annoyance in her voice. Of course, he understood. "She's worried about you, Remy. *Everyone* is worried about you."

Remy grabbed a metal garbage bin from next to her vintage whitewashed bedside table and stuffed the wedding dress inside before she took something else out of the drawer. She opened the balcony door and headed out. Confusion racked Asher as he followed her out, leaning against the door frame, studying her as she placed the garbage can on the metal floor. "What are you doing?"

She dodged his question. "Let me guess: Kinsley called in backup to drag my ass out of bed by someone who would literally do it."

Asher watched her closely, considering his next move. He wisely said, "There's no answer that won't paint me into a corner."

"That's probably true," she replied with little emotion in her voice.

When she knelt in front of the garbage bin, he clenched his fingers, tempted to drag his hand through those soft strands and then bring her into his arms to make her feel all better. Yeah, he was no saint—he still wanted her, even if he knew she'd never give him her heart again. And he agreed with her 100 percent. With her body, Asher knew what he was doing. With her heart, he'd always fail her. But they could do friends. If he helped her get her life straight again, he hoped that would lead to forgiveness. Trying to understand her headspace, he asked gently, "Do you hate me for objecting at the wedding yesterday?"

She fiddled with something in her hands. "Hate, no. I'm just…mad, and not at you specifically, just the entire situation."

"Anyone would be, Remy," he said in relief. He could work with mad. "I realize there were subtler ways of stopping the wedding than arresting him, but Damon was going to hurt you. That's all I saw, and my only thought was protecting you."

"Yeah, well, men hurting me seems to be my forte in life, so you're off the hook." She rose then, stepping away from the garbage bin, right as it went up in flames.

Asher deserved the dig and let it roll right off him. He had hurt her. He'd made promises to her. He was her first kiss, her first *everything*. He said they'd be together forever. Then he'd abandoned her. Her life had once been happy and easy and free. Her soul had been that way too. He'd heard from just about everyone over the years after he left Stoney Creek, including Boone and Rhett, that nothing was easy for Remy after Asher left. Asher knew Remy's anger toward him wasn't only about his breaking things off with her, but it was about how his leaving her set off a chain of events that slowly made her world fall apart.

For the past five years, Asher had been trying to rectify that. The path had been slow and torturous, and he deserved every single bit of wrath she threw at him.

With a heavy sigh, he took in the flames, black smoke and odd scent similar to burning leaves coming up from the garbage bin. He arched an eyebrow and gestured at her burning wedding dress. "Should I be worried about you?" She seemed stable enough, but perhaps she'd been pushed over the line, and the next step would be setting her loft on fire.

"Nope, I'm good." She crossed her arms, shutting her eyes and lifting her face to the sky. "First of all, I don't need the dress, so why keep it? And second, to rid myself of the dark energy Damon created, I need to spiritually cleanse myself." She lowered her head again, obviously finished with her prayer to Mother Earth, and then pointed at the flames. "Burning the dress is an effective cleansing."

While he understood, he also didn't want the fire department getting a call. "How about we keep you in your landlord's good graces and not burn the place down." He quickly returned to her bathroom, grabbed a large glass off her sink, and filled it to the top with water. When he returned, he tossed the water into the garbage bin, dousing the flames, sending thick, black smooth billowing in the air. He kicked the garbage bin, making sure the fire was all the way out, and then turned to face Remy, finding her gone.

When he reentered her bedroom, he spotted the big lump under the sheets again. "Remy," he said gently, placing the glass on her dresser and then taking a seat on the bed next to her.

"How could I be so stupid?" she asked beneath the blanket.

"How did I not see the signs that this guy was just after my money?"

Asher pulled away the sheet, meeting her sad eyes. "Because you've got a big heart. You don't see that darkness."

"But you must have, since obviously you were investigating him?"

Asher gave a slow nod. He hated the prick from the second he met Damon, and not just because Remy had fallen for him. "Something seemed...*off*. No one has all the right answers all the time. But he fed you all the right lines and seemed very rehearsed to me."

She glanced up at her ceiling and let out a long, slow breath before addressing him again. "When did you start suspecting something was up?"

"The moment I met him."

"Seriously?" She placed her hands on her bright red face, though the heat rose equally into her ears. "Right away?"

Asher could sugarcoat all this, but he'd been a coward in the face of hard times before when he'd left Remy. He couldn't give her everything she wanted, but he could give her the truth. "My instincts—"

"Are never wrong," she finished for him, finally dropping her hands.

"Not usually," he agreed.

Another sigh and then she began twirling her hair around her finger, her one tell that she was contemplating heavy things. "Damon said his groomsmen were old college buddies. I take it that's a lie."

"From what we've learned, they were paid actors."

Her eyes went huge and a deeper flush crept across her cheeks before she yanked the sheet back over her head. "Just kill me."

"I'm afraid I can't do that," he told her seriously, staring at the lump beneath the sheets. She'd recover from this. He'd see to that himself, even if he didn't quite know yet exactly *how* he'd help her.

When she didn't remove the blanket, he gently tugged it away again. Her gorgeous eyes—so much more guarded than he ever remembered—held his.

"There is something wrong with me," she eventually said.

"There's nothing wrong with you." No, she was perfect, only he kept his mouth shut, afraid if he told her that, he'd scare her away. One step at a time and he'd inch his way closer to being a memory for her that wasn't drenched in pain.

"Oh yeah?" she retorted sharply, her fingers clenching the bedsheet tight. "I *almost* married a con man who was going to drain my bank account."

"You're the fourth woman he's done this to," Asher countered. "Damon was clever and cruel and chose sweet women who didn't deserve this."

Remy considered this a moment, then shook her head slowly. "I don't even get how he knew about my inheritance. I never told him."

"I doubt we'll ever know that answer unless Damon tells us himself."

"God." She released the sheet and her hands curled around her middle, all the color draining from her face. "I just feel so stupid. You know this is going to end up in the newspaper, all over town."

That was the shit-end of living in a small town: Everyone knew everyone's business, but Asher had already considered this and thought up a good next step. It occurred to him that this was how he could help Remy move forward. From his years spent with the FBI, he'd honed his skills of thinking outside of the box and always being one step ahead of the media and criminals. Remy needed to turn this situation on its head, and he happened to know exactly how to do that. "The way I see it," Asher explained, "you have two ways of handling this. One, hide away in your bed and hope that everyone just forgets this and moves on. Two, take control of the narrative and give the town something to talk about. Let everyone know that you're not a victim."

She went still. "How exactly do I do that?"

Asher gave slow smile, hoping to send his confidence her way. "Face him. Let the town talk about that."

"Face him?" she repeated, tilting her head to the side, obviously mulling over the idea.

"Go to the police station. Let the townsfolk see you out and about. Word will spread, you know this. Give them something to talk about."

A twinkle lightened her eyes. "I've got to say, I don't hate this idea, but I also can't go in there unarmed." She shoved off the blanket and grabbed a perfume bottle and sprayed herself. "It's a homemade protective and purifying blend featuring patchouli, frankincense, and dragon's blood, which all help to feel grounded and prepared."

It smelled good, that much he knew. He rose from the bed, and he watched her pupils dilate a little as he ended up right in front of her, very little space between them. "You ready?"

"Ready." She gave a firm nod, looking a little like the Remy he used to know.

"Good." He smiled softly. "When this is all said and done, we'll see about that wine you wanted."

She smiled back. "Well, I'd much rather Damon's nuts served on a platter, but hey, wine will work too."

* * *

The walk of shame was so much better than the walk of embarrassment. Remy hadn't quite figured out why Asher was there by her side, totally cool and calm walking down Stoney Creek's historic Main Street, but she was glad to not have to do this alone. They left her loft and then grabbed coffee at a shop a block away from the station, and the entire way, Remy had to fight to keep her chin up. Boutique shops lined the skinny road where cars were parked, and mature trees hugged the road. Burnt orange and dark red leaves scattered the sidewalks as autumn had settled into town. She wrapped her sweater tighter, telling herself that was from the chill in the air, not from insecurity. The last thing she wanted was to allow Damon to make her feel shamed in *her* hometown.

"Oh, my dear, Remy."

Remy cringed at the soft, sweet voice. "God, please, no."

Asher chuckled and hastily turned to face Heather Longfield, their old principal from Stoney Creek's high school. "Hello, Mrs. Longfield, how are things?" he asked gently.

"Doing just fine," she said to Asher. Then to Remy, she gave sad, pitiful eyes. "I was so very sorry to hear what happened. That Damon is just an awful man." She turned back to Asher and her lip curled. "I hope you will ensure he is punished to the full extent of the law."

"Yes, ma'am, I will," Asher said with a firm nod.

Mrs. Longfield's brow wrinkled as she reached out to touch Remy's arm. "If there's anything—"

"I'm really sorry to interrupt you," Asher interjected softly, taking Remy's arm and tugging her forward, "but I'm afraid we're on our way to the station and are already late."

"Oh, yes, of course," Mrs. Longfield said, taking a step back. "You must have things to do."

Remy booked it forward, never taking her gaze off the police station up ahead, wishing she could blink and get there. When they were a few feet away from Mrs. Longfield, Remy said, "Thank you for that. I don't think I could handle her pitiful looks for another minute."

"She always was a bit dramatic," Asher said with a smile, finally releasing his grip on her arm.

Maybe another day that would've made Remy smile too. Or maybe she'd think about how her tummy filled with butterflies at Asher's touch. But now she didn't want to think about anything or draw more attention to herself, so she kept her head down and didn't give anyone else eye contact.

A few minutes later, when they entered the station, Remy sipped her coffee. Every single police officer, dispatch, detective...*everyone*...turned their curious gazes onto her before quickly looking away. A glance up revealed the reason. Asher had upped his glare game. She sighed away the tension in her shoulders and fell into the feeling of weightlessness that stole away the dread in her chest. One thing Asher did well was protect her. She'd always felt safe with him. Until he broke her trust.

She followed him into his office, and he gestured to the client chair in front of his desk. "Give me a minute. Let me see where we're at with Damon."

"Okay," she said, and then promptly dropped down into the hard plastic chair. Voices and chatter sounded behind her from the cubicles in the middle of the police station. She scanned the plain office with the dull pale blue walls and just the bare necessities on the desk, trying to keep herself busy. When that didn't work to ease the nerves, she crossed her legs, then uncrossed them, and finally sighed, trying to slow her heart rate.

Her gaze fell to a picture on the wall where a window should have been to let in light. Instant warmth rushed through her tingling limbs. She'd taken the photograph. It was of Acadia National Park, where she and Asher had gone camping to celebrate her eighteenth birthday. That night Asher had taken her virginity under a blanket of stars. The next morning she'd woken early and there'd been a fog that had settled over the lake, making it picture-perfect. She could hardly believe that he'd not only kept the photograph but framed it and put it in his office.

"Interesting couple days."

She gasped and jerked away from the photograph and the memory, finding Boone's warm blue eyes regarding her carefully. "That's one way of putting it," she said with a snort.

Boone wasn't blood family, but he'd always been there, watching over her as much as he watched over Kinsley. Not like they appreciated that fact very much when there were teenage girls. "How are you holding up?" he asked, propping his shoulder against the doorframe, hands stuffed in the pockets of his jeans, which was detective attire in Stoney Creek.

A lie sat on the tip of her tongue, but she quickly swallowed that back. "I have no idea what I am at the moment, other than I'm still breathing, so I guess that's good."

"It is," Boone said with a firm nod, and blessedly there was no hint of pity in his gaze. "It's good you came today to face Damon. This is the right step forward to getting this situation behind you."

She figured he was probably right, but nothing about any of this felt good. She shrugged as her answer, not really sure she had anything to say. In all honesty, she wasn't even sure what she had to put behind her anymore. Sure, the fact that Damon wanted to steal her inheritance needed to be put to bed, and that her shop was gone for the foreseeable future. Then there was that she was messed up enough to nearly marry a con man, and that when Asher objected, her heart craved *him*. But all of that seemed so impossible to put behind her, she didn't even know where to start.

Boone watched her a moment, obviously misreading her messy emotional state. "You're not in this alone, Remy." His voice was as comforting as a bowl of hot stew on a cold day. "I hope you know that. Whatever you need, we'll be there."

She wanted to thank him, to say that she knew that, but her throat got clogged up. Her friendships weren't something she questioned.

Boone gave a soft, sad smile like he knew exactly what she needed. He opened his arms. "Come here." She rose, then stepped into his big warm arms and comforting embrace. "He'll pay for hurting you, Remy. Do not doubt that."

"Thank you," she finally managed to squeeze out of her tight throat. She leaned away, fighting tears. "Now stop trying to make me cry with all your love and support. I'm already way too emotional."

Boone chuckled, right as Asher stepped into the doorway. "We're ready," he said.

Heaviness returned to Remy in a flash. She exhaled slowly, lifted her chin, and then straightened her shoulders. "All right, let's get this over with."

When she went to walk away, Boone stopped her with his hand on his arm. "Stay strong."

"Always do." She forced a smile.

He frowned. Damn. Maybe she looked worse off than even she thought.

Putting that aside for now, she followed Asher down the thin hallway to the back of the station, where Rhett waited near a door. Rhett had always been a hard guy to figure out, his expression usually unreadable, and most times he looked pissed off. But today, she swore she could see hints of concern in his dark eyes.

When she reached him, he watched her closely a moment. "You good to have this talk?"

No matter how much all of this sucked, she wouldn't forget all the love around her. She could do this. Face Damon, then put this hell behind her. "Since I doubt that you'll let me castrate him, then yes, I guess I have to be okay with just a talk."

Rhett's mouth twitched and then he leaned in, keeping the conversation private, and said quietly, "You know I'd vote to castrate too."

She barked a laugh, a surprise even to her that she could find anything amusing now.

Rhett gave a long look to Asher over her shoulder, having some kind of male private conversation where one look seemed to explain everything, and then he opened the door.

She entered the room, spotted Damon sitting there in his orange jumpsuit, and heat radiated through her chest.

Asher shut the door behind her with a heavy slam and addressed Damon with a low, steady voice, "Remy is here to talk. You're going to listen to what she has to say. If I don't like how you talk to her, you won't like what I'm going to do to you."

Damon snorted.

Remy didn't. Damon obviously thought Asher was joking. The firmness in Asher's voice, the carefully controlled rage in his gaze, told Remy he was dead serious. And she knew, after years of being together, that while Asher prided himself on being a good cop, he was also insanely protective of his friends. Maybe his limit had been reached.

She tried not to think about that too much; she was too emotional as it was.

Asher pulled out the seat across from Damon and then gestured for her to sit. She drew in a long breath and sat down, while Asher stood in behind her. Obviously, a show that he had her back. One she oddly found herself appreciating.

Damon's gaze held Asher's before zeroing in on Remy. She searched for any sign that he was some guy out to steal away her inheritance. She didn't see anything but the warm man that she'd planned on sharing a life with. Maybe that's where she'd gone wrong. She never *really* loved Damon, not like she had loved Asher. But love lied and hurt, and Damon had been a solid in her life. He had made her happy. He was sweet and gentle and affectionate. He didn't hurt her ever. They never fought or disagreed. Hell, he was perfect. Until, of course, he wasn't. And maybe that should have been a red flag. When was any person perfect?

As much as anger boiled beneath her skin, her heart shattered as she stared at Damon. She still had a hard time believing he could do this to her. All the memories they shared, the long walks in the park, the dinners over candlelight, the nights snuggled up watching movies together rushed through her mind, reminding her that none of those would ever happen again. And…and this was a big *and*…he was only there for her inheritance.

Emotion tickled her throat, and tears threatened to rise, when Damon finally broke the silence. "Can we talk alone?" he asked.

"Not a chance in hell," Asher stated firmly.

Remy caught Damon's glare, figuring Asher's probably looked the same. Then she cleared the emotion from her throat and spoke up for herself. "Yes, we can talk alone," she said directly to Asher.

He frowned. Deeply. "Remy."

"Asher." She held her ground.

He finally let out a long sigh, his lips pressed into a thin line. "I'll be right outside." His gaze turned hard as he set his stare on Damon. "The warning remains."

Again, Damon snorted.

Remy watched Asher leave before turning back to Damon, finding him staring intently. "What do you have to say to me that you couldn't say with Asher here?"

Damon's expression softened as he leaned forward, reaching his hands out to her across the metal table. "You owe me nothing, I get that. But I've got something at your house and I need you to do a favor for me."

She parted her lips to respond, then they shut with an audible *pop*. Of all the things she expected Damon to say, that was certainly not it. Her vision suddenly went cloudy, adrenaline rushing through her body, and any sadness she'd felt a moment ago was suddenly ripped away and replaced by red-hot rage. Anger that no longer boiled beneath the surface of her flesh rose, cutting through all those good memories they shared. "You cannot be fucking serious."

Damon cringed. "Remy, I—"

He couldn't finish that statement. Her fists tightened and she shot up and slugged him in the nose. Hard. His head flew back, and blood started dripping.

The door slammed open and Asher rushed in, grabbing Remy

by the waist just as she lunged forward to claw out Damon's eyeballs.

Boone shot toward Damon, grabbing his arm. "Move and you'll regret it."

Her vision tunneled on the man she had planned to spend her life with. "Of all the things you could have said to me. 'Hey, Remy, I'm a psychopath and have problems, but I'm sorry for using you to get your money.' Or maybe 'Don't worry, it's not you, it's me.'" Her hands shook and she gritted her teeth as she went on. "Even, 'I'm a total asshole, but whatever.' You could have said *anything*, but the first thing you do is ask for a favor." She struggled against Asher's tight hold, desperately clawing to get her hands around Damon's neck. "I'm going to fucking kill you," she yelled at the bastard who'd tried to swindle all the money her nana worked so hard to have.

Behind her, Rhett laughed. "I'm so happy I stayed for this."

Boone had a bloodied Damon back in handcuffs.

Asher finally managed to get her out the door and kicked it shut. Her blood felt like it was boiling, pumping too fast through her veins. Her fists were clenched, ready to hit anything to make herself feel better.

But then suddenly as she met Asher's gaze, she realized she was in his arms. Those emerald eyes held hers, intensity rushing through them. Now her heart rate spiked for another reason entirely. Asher lowered one hand to her hip, pinning her to the wall in a move that seemed more for pleasure than a need to keep her from attacking anyone. Her hand was moving without her say-so up his strong biceps, her lips parting.

"You've punched one guy today," Rhett said, voice well amused, as he'd obviously opened the door and neither of them noticed. "Probably shouldn't make out in the hallway too."

At that, she realized what she was doing and stepped back. *Sweet Jesus.* What was wrong with her?

Maybe she *was* having a total breakdown.

"I'd say you succeeded."

She glanced up, finding all the intensity gone from Asher's eyes, his solid front back in place. "At what?"

He grinned. "Giving the town something to talk about."

# Chapter 4

After a good twenty minutes of having an icepack on her hand, Remy left Asher at the police station while he finalized paperwork on having Damon transferred to the larger jail in the neighboring town of Whitby Falls. She didn't ask questions after that. What she did do was walk the few blocks back down Main Street and entered Kinsley's jazz club, Whiskey Blues, needing her best friend. From the bar's original flagstone walls and restored burgundy velvet chairs to the gold accents, Kinsley had turned this once dingy dive bar into pure class. Four large crystal chandeliers gave the space a warm, inviting feel, and round tables surrounded the black shiny stage, where bands performed, but this morning, the stage was empty, and the bar was quiet. Kinsley always opened early in the day, as she thought a bar needed to be open in case someone desperately needed a drink. Her tell-it-like-it-is attitude seemed to make her part therapist, part bartender for most of Stoney Creek's townsfolk.

Behind the bar, Kinsley wore a tight black T-shirt with WHISKEY BLUES written across her chest. She studied Remy as she approached and then moved to the bar fridge. By the time Remy slid her butt on the stool, Kinsley placed a chocolate bar and a glass of red wine in front of her. "I take it you knew I'd be coming by today," Remy said.

"Boone told me to have the reinforcements ready," Kinsley said with a soft smile. "How did it go with Damon?"

Remy reached for the chocolate bar. She opened it quickly and broke off a big piece before taking a bite. "I punched him in the nose."

Kinsley's eyebrows shot up. "Seriously?"

The cell phone set next to the liquor bottles was tuned to Whitby Fall's rock station, and Remy wanted to punch the current love song too. She shoved more chocolate into her mouth. She savored the sweet smooth goodness against her tongue, feeling immensely better already. "He asked me for a favor."

"That's an odd request. What kind of favor?"

Remy shrugged. "Got me. I didn't give him a chance to ask. That's where the punch came in."

"Weird," Kinsley said, dropping an elbow on the bar and resting her chin on her hand. "Did he say anything else?"

"Nothing at all," Remy replied with a heavy sigh. "No apologies. No explanations. Nothing."

Kinsley watched Remy, and then Remy watched the chocolate bar as she ripped another big piece off and shoved it into her mouth. She washed it down with the biggest gulp of wine of her life.

"I'm sorry, Remy," Kinsley said gently, drawing Remy's full attention again. Her eyes looked as sad as her voice sounded. "I can't imagine any of this. I mean, I never liked Damon, but I never guessed he'd do something like this."

No one liked Damon, except for Remy, who'd thought he

was the bee's knees of boyfriends. "I just don't know how I could have been so wrong about him. Or how I couldn't have seen what you all saw. It's like I had blinders on, only seeing what I wanted to see." Her chest felt so hollow and empty, and her body depleted of all its energy. She'd have to research a spell later in her nana's book of spells to find something powerful to bring her back from this hell. "Most of all, I hate that I keep repeating the past. It's like I fall for these guys who are just not who they say they are. I am so done with love it's not even funny."

Kinsley snorted a laugh. "Keep dreaming on that one, babe. You're all about love, sorry to break it to you."

"Well, that's got to change," Remy declared firmly. "The old me is getting me nowhere but heartbroken. Repeatedly." She glanced down into her wineglass, staring at the deep crimson color, and sighed, wishing her nana were there. She'd have all the answers to make everything better. She really missed her wise advice and warm, gentle smile. Her throat tightened and she glanced up into her best friend's eyes, finding tears in them. "I'm not so sure how much more my heart can take. I quit here a week ago thinking I was about to have it all." She'd been waitressing and bartending ever since she dropped out of college to support herself after Nana died. When Kinsley bought the bar after she'd gotten her business degree—the same degree Remy was meant to have—Remy came on board immediately. But bartending had never been the dream. She felt her chest hollow even further as she went on. "I thought that I'd finally have the perfect husband and eventually be the mom I always wanted to be. I could nearly taste it. I was finally going to have my shop, one that would've made Nana so happy. I saved for it, planned it out. And now...there's nothing."

"There's not nothing," Kinsley said, reaching for Remy's hand and giving it a hard squeeze. "You can have your job here until you figure out what to do next. I know that's probably not what you want to do, but it's your first step in starting over again."

Regardless that taking her old job back felt like a gigantic step in the wrong direction, she squeezed Kinsley's hand back. "Thanks." She'd liked working at the bar. Kinsley paid her well, and the tips were great. The people who came in were awesome. But it wasn't her own shop. She didn't feel like she was doing what she was meant to do—help people like Nana had helped people—though what choice did she have? "Is it okay if I start back in a couple weeks? I think I need to just—"

"It's fine," Kinsley said quickly. "Take however long you need. You don't have to figure all this out now. Just know the job is here, if you want it."

"I love you," Remy said, and gave a smile she knew probably looked really sad.

"I love you back." Kinsley returned the smile and then her gaze shifted to something over Remy's shoulder.

When the air shifted slightly and the hairs on her arms rose like static, Remy sighed. She was a step away from grabbing that wine bottle behind the bar and hiding in the closet until he was gone. Keeping her gaze on Kinsley, she said to Asher, "I really appreciate that you took me to the police station, but I can't deal with you right now. Honestly, my emotional limit is reached."

"I'm sorry I hurt you."

Kinsley's eyebrows shot up and her mouth dropped open. She glanced rapidly between them and then she quickly sprinted away.

Remy shut her eyes and breathed deeply in order to not lash out. Her heart felt battered, and her mind utterly exhausted. When Asher didn't move away, she grabbed her wineglass and chugged the entire contents back and then turned to face him.

He stood directly behind her, his hands shoved in the pockets of his jeans, and his gray T-shirt was stretched across a thick chest. "What in your mind has you thinking that *now*—out of any time that you've had in the past five years—is the appropriate time to apologize to me?"

He didn't even hesitate and gave an easy shrug. "Seemed as good as time as any. You're finally letting me talk to you. And you're no longer getting married, so I'm not feeling like I'm treading on ground that I shouldn't be."

Maybe it was his blasé attitude, her emotional state, or just her heartbreak paired with red-hot anger, but she closed the distance to poke his chest. "I have already punched one guy today. Want to be number two?"

"If it'd make you feel better, then yes," he stated.

She stared into Asher's eyes, not seeing any emotion, just strength. And all of that was just a reminder of the day he walked away. The day that changed the course of her entire life. And it was a reminder that when Asher objected at her wedding, it wasn't out of love. "I'm going home now," she told him dryly. "Do not follow me." She charged out the door, heading down the street until she met the alleyway that led to the back parking lot of the row of shops.

Just as she reached the metal steps that led to her loft, a firm grip grabbed her arm. She whirled around, her fist clenching, when suddenly a different Asher stared at her now. One torn apart with guilt.

"I know that I fucked up and hurt you." His voice blistered. "And I know you have every right to hate me." He slowly released his hold, obviously realizing she wasn't going to run. "But you don't have to face all this alone. Let me help you through this."

"Why should I?" she asked, desperately wanting to know.

"To mend this between us. Don't you think it's time for that?" He drew in a long, deep breath before addressing her again. "I've made mistakes. Big mistakes, I know that. But I'm not that fucked-up kid who left you all those years ago. We were good friends once, Remy. I want that again." Intensity flared in his gaze. "No, I *need* that. I've missed you. I've missed the laughs and the fun we had together. Don't you?" She felt the ground drop out from under her as he went on. "I know there will always be a part of you that can never forgive me. I accept that and can live with it. But I'm done sitting back quietly and pretending that I don't miss having you in my life."

There were a thousand things to say or do in this moment, but all she could do was burst into tears and yell at him, "I'm just so fucking angry. I'm angry at you for leaving me. I'm angry at Damon…Kyle, whoever the fuck he is. I'm angry that the life I thought I was going to have—the marriage, the family, my shop…it's all gone. And I'm angry that every time a man offers me the world, he takes it away just like that." She snapped her fingers.

"You should be angry," he said softly, pain etched into his features. "You deserve better."

For years there were things she wanted to say but never did. Now that she had her chance, she couldn't quite stop herself. "After you left, everything, and I mean *everything*, fell apart for me. Nana died. College was no longer a reality since I needed to support myself. I needed you so bad, and you weren't here."

He visibly swallowed. "I know."

She stopped short, not expecting him to take all the blame. He didn't give an excuse or explain it, just accepted his blame in hurting her. It made her remember the Asher she once loved deeply. "I don't know if I can be your friend."

He glanced down for a moment, then looked up, and in that one second, she saw his desperation that he hid well. "We were very good at that once."

They were, she knew that. No one made her laugh like Asher. No one made her feel as alive as Asher had. In that empty hollowness of her chest, a part of her wanted to feel a little piece of that again. "One chance to be friends, Asher. That's it. Mess this up, and we're done. Forever."

"I understand what's on the line here."

She caught the darkness in Asher's eyes that had never been there when she was with him before, and she knew, she hadn't been the only one who suffered in the past. Asher had his pain too. Maybe he was right. Maybe it was time to heal what was broken. "If you really want to help me, I know one thing you can do."

"Name it."

"Erase that fucker from my life."

Asher gave a tight smile. "My pleasure."

\* \* \*

Three hours had ticked by since Remy coldcocked Damon. Since Asher couldn't physically erase Damon from Remy's life, he did the second-best thing. He packed up Damon's belongings in her loft. Worried that if he didn't, she might set her apartment on fire and then retreat under her bed fort. He shoved the final box into the back of his truck to take to Goodwill. It dawned on him then that the last time he was with Remy and packing boxes away, it was when he left her for Washington. Pain clawed at the back of his throat, and even wearing only a T-shirt in the cool autumn weather, his skin felt flushed. Had he been a better man, she wouldn't be hurting right now, but he was done living in the past. His chest felt lighter than it had in years. The last thing Remy wanted from him now was marriage, and she wasn't looking at him as the man who'd failed to make those dreams comes true. He could earn her friendship back, help her discover new dreams, and he'd finally free himself from the crushing guilt for destroying her life. Now all he had to do was not screw it up. And not fall back in love with her.

"Is Remy okay?"

Asher glanced over his shoulder, finding eight middle-aged women holding plastic containers filled with food. They weren't strangers. Asher and Remy had grown up with some of their sons and daughters. And now that many of the millennials in Stoney Creek moved away wanting the taste of the big city, those that stayed became second children to the moms in town. "She's doing much better," he told them with a smile. "I see you've been cooking."

MaryJane Abbott, the leader of the bunch, and the one who knew just about everything about everyone, said, "We've got two weeks of meals here for her." She had a head full of purple curls, bright red lipstick covering her thin lips, and deep laugh lines. "All she needs to do is freeze them, then heat 'em up in the oven when she's ready to eat."

"That's so very generous of you, ladies." Asher held out his hands. "I can take those up for you." The last thing Remy needed was a group of women in her loft pitying her, no matter how kind they were.

"Oh, you'll take them up to her, hmm," said MaryJane, her bright blue eyes twinkling. She shared a look with the other ladies around her.

Great. He had no doubt he'd just joined the gossip train.

"Yes, yes." MaryJane shoved the containers at him, then handed him three plastic bags full of more containers. "You're exactly who should bring these to her." She grinned from ear to ear, nudging him forward. "Please let Remy know we're all thinking about her. Damon is just horrible. A terrible human being."

Asher nodded, not disagreeing with her. "Enjoy your day, ladies, and again, thank you for taking care of Remy." He left the giggling women behind and strode with purpose toward the stairs at the back of the building. If he hung around any longer, he'd get cornered and questioned.

On his way up the creaky metal stairs, he spotted the back doors to Kinsley's bar, Whiskey Blues, and Peyton's lingerie shop, Uptown Girl. They were both working today, and Asher figured a drink at the bar later sounded like a perfect end to the day.

When he finally made it up the stairs and reentered Remy's loft, he got a waft of a spicy scent mixed with something pungent that he couldn't identify. All very typical smells coming from Remy's kitchen. Back in the day, her nana had been a sweetheart, and she always had some concoction she was teaching to Remy. There was never a time when Asher came over that they weren't either praying to Mother Earth, or creating some kind of tea, cream, or drink to fix people's problems. Asher had many regrets, but right up there with breaking Remy's heart was leaving Stoney Creek without telling Nana goodbye. He'd just...*left*. Not letting that regret drown him, he shut the door behind him, then kicked of his boots, hearing Remy's voice as he got closer. The galley kitchen was tiny and set underneath her bedroom loft above, with the living room furnished with gray couches leading to floor-to-ceiling windows, letting in natural light. On the live edge countertop were small glass containers spread out all over the counter filled with herbs and liquids. Sitting next to her on the counter was Nana's book of spells, which basically was an old scrapbook with dark brown paper and a leather case. Asher never believed in the New Age magic Remy and her nana did, but over the years, he'd grown to miss Remy's quirky ways. She could fix everything, or so she believed, and he liked that nurturing side of her.

She stood at the stove with a phone pressed between her ear and her shoulder, using a big wooden spoon to stir *something* that had a slightly nutty aroma. Her kitchen was a disaster, but at least she wasn't setting anything on fire. Salem sat at his food bowl, enjoying his fresh cooked chicken. "Yes, Mom, I'm fine." Remy paused, obviously listening to her mother talk. "Well, if I knew he was a money-hungry prick, then I wouldn't have dated him." Another pause and then Remy's voice tightened. "Yes, Mom, my inheritance is safe. Please stop worrying, I'm okay. Sure, I'm a bit sad and angry, but I'll be fine." She added a spice to the pot and kept stirring. "Yup. Yup. Perfect. Love you too. Bye." She ended the call, then without turning around, Remy said, "She's worried about me, apparently."

"Understandably so," Asher replied, setting the containers and bags on the kitchen table. "Is she coming to visit?"

Remy snorted and glanced into the pot. "Yeah, right. That would involve thinking of anyone but herself."

That was something her mother, Joni, never did. The only unselfish thing she'd ever done was leave Remy with her nana when she decided to hit the road with her band. And even that hadn't been entirely unselfish. "Where is she playing now?" he asked.

"Nashville," Remy said, tension in her voice. "She invited me to come travel with her for a while, but where's that going to get me? Further from where I already want to be."

*A shop owner* was what she didn't need to say. "You'll find a way to make the shop happen," he said.

"Oh, I know." Her shoulders lifted and fell with her heavy breath as she continued to stir the pot. "I'll just go back and bartend at Kinsley's and keep saving. It'll happen, one day."

Asher's gaze fell to the way her ass wiggled a little with every stir of the pot. She'd never had *this* body when he'd dated her. A woman's body. He ached to take a nibble out of that ass. Hot and hard now, he forced his gaze up to the soft strands of her hair, and when Remy still didn't look back, focused on whatever she was making, he said, "The gossip train brought you dinners for the next two weeks."

Remy piped up then, glancing over her shoulder, gaze scanning the items. "Really?"

He nodded. "They're worried about you too."

"Or they're just nosy and this was a good way for them to get the deets on my life." She glanced over each container, her expression warming immensely. "Still, that's incredibly kind of them. I'll make sure to send thank-you notes. Do you mind shoving it all in the freezer for me? I've got to keep an eye on this."

Asher grabbed the containers again, and on his way to the fridge, he strode by Salem, who hissed, fur sticking straight up. "I can't believe he still hates me," Asher said, glaring back at the cat.

"He doesn't hate you," Remy countered. "He just doesn't trust you. Two very different things."

Probably much like Remy felt about him. Asher began

putting away the containers in the freezer and decided to leave that subject alone. "What are you making, anyway? It smells...*interesting.*"

"I've been thinking about what to do all day, and I've come to the conclusion that I must be cursed." She poured a small vial of something into the pot on the stove. "So, I'm going to break the curse."

"You're not cursed." He adjusted a few containers, the cold air brushing across his face. "Want to leave the lasagna out for tonight?"

"Yeah, sounds yummy." She paused, then went on. "And as for the not being cursed, you can't have an opinion because you broke my heart once."

"That's fair," he said, shutting the freezer door and turning back to her. "But you can't possibly think that potion you're making is actually going to help."

She slowly turned around, a wooden spoon in her hand. "Asher Sullivan, take that back right now."

He didn't really believe in this voodoo shit the way she did. But he respected that Remy believed in it. And he'd seen some of her teas do remarkable things for colds, but a curse? "I take it back," he said.

"You bet your ass you do!" She waved the spoon at him. "You, for one, should know how much my stuff helps. You've seen it." She reached for another vial and dumped in some herbs.

He took in the swelling on her knuckles. "You need to keep icing your hand," he said.

"Ice is a terrible thing, and I only did that to make you all shut up about it back at the station. I put a salve on it and it will be just fine." She finished stirring, turned down the stove, then came over to the kitchen table and sat down, opening up the wooden box on top. She took out crystals, placing them near a small candle, which she then lit. She shut her eyes, exhaled deeply, then reached for her tarot cards wrapped in silk.

Asher watched the ritual she'd done a thousand times before. Some women followed their instincts. Others talked to their friends and sought advice. Remy used tarot cards to decide her fate.

Asher smiled, moving to the kitchen table to sit across from her. "What's the question today?" he asked.

"Oh, this and that," Remy said, shuffling the cards.

Salem jumped up on the table and lay down next to Remy. Asher couldn't be sure, but he'd bet the cat was glaring at him.

Remy went quiet and began shuffling the cards, her eyes fluttering shut. When she opened them again, she began laying out the cards—three side by side, then a card on top and on the bottom of the middle card. He'd never believed in psychics, but Remy was definitely intuitive, as was her nana. He'd never admit it aloud, but there were more times that Remy's tarot cards were right than wrong.

"Hmm," she said, frowning down at the cards. "Is that so?" Her gaze lifted to his and she gave him a measured look. "See." She pointed at the card. "Totally cursed."

He glanced down at the cards, finding what appeared to be a grim reaper, before arching an eyebrow at her. "Remy, I have no idea what I'm looking at."

"An epic disaster, that's what." She picked up the cards again and then passed them all through the flame, doing what Asher knew to mean she was cleansing her deck. In no time, she packed her things away and then rose. "I need to get this curse off me."

"Okay, who do you think cursed you?"

She moved toward the kitchen cabinet. "If I knew that, then I'd deal with them, but since I don't, this will have to do." She grabbed two scotch glasses and used a ladle to pour dark liquid into each glass.

He knew where she was going with this before she even handed him a glass. "I'm not drinking that," he told her seriously.

"Yeah, you are." She set the drink down in front of him.

"Care to enlighten me on why I would do that?"

"Because as much as you don't believe in all this, you have also been cursed." He frowned as she nudged his glass closer to him. "Stop looking at me like that. I'm not wrong. Are you happy with all aspects of your life?"

He stared into the depths of her eyes, finding the answer all too easy. "No, I'm not entirely happy with every aspect."

"See." She picked up her glass to *cheers* him. "Also cursed. Bottoms up."

Against his better judgment, and to do and be whatever Remy needed him to be, he grabbed the glass and clanged hers, then he drank the shot back. And coughed like hell.

She wheezed, "I know, curse breakers taste terrible."

# Chapter 5

Remy's laughter filled the air as she danced her way back into the living room after grabbing herself another glass of her potion. An hour had gone by since they'd *cheers* their drinks, and they'd already had one more of Remy's concoction that apparently was similar to homemade moonshine. Born from an alcoholic father, and ensuring not to become him, Asher had a two-drink rule that he never broke. But whatever she put in that drink was the strongest alcohol he'd ever tasted. While Asher knew without a single doubt in his mind that he was the closest he'd been to drunk ever in his life, Remy was most definitely drunk. With the help of the homemade booze that Asher suspected her nana created to explain away getting loaded whenever things got bad, Remy had opened up, reminding Asher of the Remy he once knew. They'd talked about everything over the last hour, almost like they were the same people who once loved each other. Laughed like they used to. And then everything changed, becoming flirty and sensual, just like old times, and Asher knew he was in trouble. He remembered the heat, the passion, and he wanted to taste that again.

Now he couldn't take his eyes off the way Remy swirled her hips to the Queen song playing through the speakers. Her arms were in the air lifting her shirt just enough to show the creaminess of her skin. He felt the warm hum of the alcohol running through his veins, alongside the desire driving him wild. "You should come sit down," he told her, noting her glass coffee table was a disaster waiting to happen.

She spun in a little circle and then gave him a smile of pure unadulterated sex. "It always did make you hot watching me dance, didn't it?" she practically purred.

"You were always a very good dancer." She'd taken years of dance growing up and she was the type of person who danced freely, loving music. He rose, offering his hand. "Come sit. That shit you made us is guaranteed to make you fall on that table."

"It's got Devil Springs vodka and Sunset rum." She rolled her hips, her eyes darkened with lust. "Apparently, I put in a little too much." Her lips parted as she caressed her hands slowly down her body. "How about now? Am I still a good dancer?"

He watched the slide of her hands until they moved into her hair and she flicked the gorgeous strands teasingly. Feeling tense, and *hot*, so damn hot, he cleared his throat. "You know you're incredible at most things you do."

She smiled playfully back. "You're right, I do." Cocking her head just enough to let her hair fall beautifully across her cheek, she nibbled her lip.

*Jesus Christ.*

"We both need coffee." Hot and growing harder as the seconds passed, he nearly tripped over Salem, who *again* hissed at him and then ran away as Asher took a step toward the kitchen.

"I know exactly what I need." She suddenly leaped into his arms. He stumbled back before quickly righting himself and held her tight. "And it ain't coffee." Then her lips crushed again his.

For a second—the tiniest little second—he nearly broke away. Until she gave a soft moan. Every touch and every second of pleasure filled his mind again, and he hadn't realized how much he missed kissing her until her tongue dipped into his mouth. With an arm around her waist, keeping her close, he took control of the kiss. He fisted his other hand in her hair and spun her around until her back pressed against the wall. She moaned and he devoured every sound she made with his kiss.

When she reached for his shirt, lifting it up, somewhere in his brain, reality kicked in. He broke away, breathless. "Fuck, we can't do this."

"Sure we can," she said, pushing on his chest until he was walking backward. "If I recall, you used to excel in this department. I can only imagine you've gotten better these past ten years."

"Remy," he said firmly, but a push sent him down on the couch.

"Asher." She climbed onto his lap, sliding her hands up biceps flexing beneath her touch. "I know you want me." She brought her heat tight against his erection, threading her fingers into his hair. "I can feel it." She ground against him and her fingernails dragged against his scalp. "I can see it in how you watch me sometimes."

He slid his hands to her sweet ass. A low sound came from deep in his chest, finally feeling *her*. "I do want you," he told her. She lowered her mouth closer to his, and he quickly added, "But you're drunk, and I'm pretty damn close to it."

She laughed softly, looking a lot like the woman he once loved. "I'm not *that* drunk. I'm just happy. I also totally know what I'm doing."

Her mouth got closer.

"You're going to regret this tomorrow," he told her, squeezing his hands onto her hips, holding her still.

"Am not," she rebuked, then kissed him. Hard.

He let her play a while, teasing him with openmouthed kisses and a little tongue before he needed to point out the obvious. He rested his head on the back of the couch, watching her carefully. "This is a dangerous thing you're starting. You know what happens when we touch each other." *We only want more* he left unsaid.

"It's only dangerous," she said, her breath against his lips, grinding her heat against him, "if we're not grown-ups and can't handle this. *I* can handle this. Can you?"

He ground his teeth against the pleasure and played with the hair by her face, taking in her dark, aroused eyes, and then tucked her hair behind her ear. A few hours ago, she finally decided to be his friend again, and he didn't want to screw that up. He knew this was a dangerous road he should not take, and yet, the stronger part of him wanted her—that had never faded over the years. In fact, his desire only grew when he'd returned to Stoney Creek, finding the girl he once knew had become a gorgeous woman. He simply never thought it was a possibility she'd ever let him close, considering it took her years to talk to him again. Now with the possibility there in front of him, he hungered to feel the *good* that Remy made him feel, and to watch her fall apart in his arms in the way only Remy did. But most of all, he wanted to make her happy, to be everything she needed until she no longer looked at him like the biggest mistake of her life…even though he knew it was wrong. Knew he couldn't ultimately give her what she wanted. "I can handle this, and you," he told her seriously. "That is not the problem here."

Instead of answering him, she reached for the hem of her

shirt and pulled the fabric quickly over her head, revealing a black bra, and his brain failed to comprehend anything but *her*. Her skin, both creamy and smooth. Her body was so familiar to him, and yet he wanted another full introduction to what made her wiggle, moan…and what made her scream. Yeah, he wanted that most of all. Still, his mind stuttered. "Should I remind you that you nearly married someone else yesterday?"

"Believe me." She planted her hands on either side of his head on the back of the couch, giving him full eye contact. "I fully remember that fact. But here's the thing: I'm done feeling like shit. This night has been so much better than I even thought possible. It's made me remember how good you used to make me feel. And most of all, you're a safe bet."

He arched an eyebrow. "A safe bet?"

"I won't fall in love with you," she said firmly, then grabbed his face. "Asher, shut up and have sex with me already."

She didn't need to ask him twice. Any further objections failed to enter his mind. He wanted her friendship, but he was all in for friends with benefits. He gathered her in his arms and strode them up the stairs next to her kitchen leading to her loft. He tossed her onto the bed, sending her laughing and the mattress bouncing. She was so damn sexy. He grabbed his shirt over his head, tossed it to the ground, then reached for a condom in his wallet before shedding his boxer briefs and jeans.

"You've gotten big. Most definitely became a man." Her gaze traced over his shoulders, his chest, down his abdomen, which all flexed under her examination. When her gaze hit his erection, she grinned and looked into his eyes. "There, you were always big."

"I'm glad I don't disappoint. Get over here." Feeling like no time and no pain had passed between them, he grabbed on to her foot, yanking her closer toward him. He reached around and removed her bra and then dropped his mouth over her rosy nipple, sucking while he reached for her leggings. With quick fingers, he pulled them off, finding her exactly as he remembered her.

*Sweet. Perfect.*

Primal need had him grabbing her thighs and he yanked her ass off the bed, sending her squealing. Desperate to get the taste of her he'd been wanting, he spread her wide and slid the flat of his tongue across her wet and hot heat, remembering how sensitive she'd been. He moaned against her flesh, over-whelmed by *her*.

"Yes. Damn. Yes," she drawled, threading her fingers through his hair. She held on to him, slowly grinding her hips as his tongue worked over her clit. His body flushed and muscles flexed against the intensity surging through him. He knew this body. He had loved this body. He'd been the one to teach her about lust, about sex, about how to let go and lose your goddamn mind.

And she obviously remembered too. She rode his mouth, searching for her pleasure.

When her moans shortened and legs trembled, he slid one finger inside her and then another, and in a few fast pumps, she was shuddering, coming beautifully against his mouth. His muscles were quivering, hot desire pulsing through his veins with every moan she gave. When she gasped, sensitive, he drew away, finding her head tilted back, her chest rising and falling, her eyes closed to the orgasm.

He grinned at how boneless he made her and sheathed himself quickly in a condom, unable to wait another second to have her. He grabbed her waist, pushing her farther onto the bed while sliding between her thighs. Her hands rested on his arms while he pressed his tip against her wet slit. He entered her in one swift stroke, and her fingernails dug into his skin when she finally looked at him with wide eyes. Needing all of her, and desperate to make her finally feel good again, he dropped his mouth to hers and he kissed her with everything he had to give. He moved slowly, gently, allowing her to become accustomed to him. He went nearly cross-eyed at the squeeze of her, the beautiful feel of her. *His Remy*.

"Make me come again," she breathed again his mouth.

He shifted his weight onto one arm, threading his fingers into her hair. "Been a while for you?" he asked with pure masculine satisfaction, giving a hard thrust forward.

She gasped. "It's been a while since I've come like that."

*Because it wasn't me touching you…* He kept his thought to himself and leaned up on his arms, staring into eyes that he both lost and found himself in. "Whatever you want, Remy. I'll give you it all." He thrust slow and hard, building up the pleasure, enjoying the feel of her around him, all for himself. Years he'd not had her. He'd take these moments to feel the sweetness of her body hugging his until he reminded her how well he knew her body.

Her lips parted but only a moan escaped.

Overwhelmed by finally being close to her again and feeling like—for this one moment—nothing had ever come between them, he pumped his hips harder, knowing just how she liked it. That's where he wanted her. Right there, beneath him. Safe. Staring into his eyes—only his. He slid a hand under her soft bottom, lifting her to him, determined to give her all that she needed and more.

Her breath hitched, muscles clenched, and she moved with him until she was falling into pleasure. Captured by her beauty, and in that sweet second of bliss, where they became united fully and completely by the passion between them, he gave in to the warmth in his chest and followed her into hot intense pulses of pleasure.

# Chapter 6

Early the next morning, Remy jolted awake in her bed. Her head pounded with every pulse of her heart, and her mouth was dry, reminding her she'd had way too much alcohol last night. She forced her eyes open, glancing out her window and finding a blue sky with big fluffy clouds. All that was fine. What wasn't fine at all was the warm, familiar, deliciously hard body next to her. She wanted to move closer, yet she also itched to run away.

"No, no!" she exclaimed, removing herself from Asher's arms and snapping up in bed, covering her bare chest with the blanket. She blinked once, then nearly drooled when she caught sight of Asher naked, the sheet sitting low on his body, revealing his near perfect form with all those beautiful muscles, including the V at his waist. Every detail about last night came back in an instant. Heat flushed to her cheeks, spilling all the way down to her chest. "I totally jumped you last night."

Asher peeked an eye open and said in a low, gravelly voice, "I liked it."

"No. No. No." She lurched out of bed and then grabbed her head. "Ow."

Asher gave his low sexy chuckle. "Climb back in bed with me. I'll make that headache go away."

She looked through her fingers. Yup, the sheet was even lower now, showing a little bit of his groomed pubic hair. "Oh, this is so, so bad," she muttered. Especially considering he looked *delicious*, and she really, *really* wanted to take him up on his offer.

His chuckle deepened, and he leaned up on one arm, displaying his incredible six-pack. "I recall you yelling out last night that I was oh, so, so good." Damn him, his eyes twinkled.

She dropped her head into her hands. "Oh my God, I threw myself at you," she grumbled into her fingers. "This is so embarrassing." Drunk Remy was always so much braver and sexier than sober Remy. "What is wrong with me?"

"Absolutely nothing," he said huskily. "Come here, and I'll prove it."

She dropped her hands, her headache pushed to the side now that her embarrassment had stolen the show. She tried to think up one of Nana's spells that could somehow make all this better, but she failed miserably. Memories of last night began drifting in, and her pushy seduction followed. She needed to hide under that blanket, which meant he had to get out. "If I got back into that bed with you, that would be the second"—she counted on her fingers—"no, like the fifth mistake I've made this week, if you include my almost getting married to a con man."

"Last night wasn't a mistake," Asher said softy in a tone she supposed was meant to be reassuring. "You needed something. You took it. And I happily gave it." He grinned and then his gaze did a full once-over on her body before those sexy eyes rose to hers again.

Instantly reminded she was naked, she crossed everything, "Don't look at me."

His easy grin widened. "I kissed and touched every inch of you three times last night. Why can't I look now?"

"Ugh. Stop it!" She beelined it for her closet, stopping short at the emptiness on the right side, where all of Damon's clothes had been. Dear God, she was going to marry another man two days ago and she'd slept with the love of her life last night. *Bad, Remy. So, so bad!* She hurried into a sports bra, T-shirt, and yoga pants before returning to him.

Asher hadn't moved an inch. The shit.

"Okay, you have to go," she said, crossing her arms. "Right now."

He laced his hands behind his head on the pillow. "Why?"

"Why?" She moved closer, put her hands on her hips. "Are you kidding me? Two days ago I was wearing a wedding dress and was about to marry someone else."

"A wedding dress you burned," he gently reminded her. "And your groom is in jail and will likely stay there for a very long time." Asher's gaze basically ate her up, promising things, making her nipples pucker.

She went to turn away. "I cannot even talk about this."

"Talk about how you ravished the hell out of me last night. Three times," Asher said, drawing her attention back to him. "Well, twice"—he winked—"I did the ravishing that third time." He smiled, a playful grin.

Her body froze in place, her face and neck and ears all feeling impossibly hot. *Oh, my God!* A quick glance around revealed Asher's clothes scattered on the floor. She scooped each thing up, then hastily handed them to him. "You've got to go. We need to forget this ever happened."

Asher stretched, and in his easy manner, he slid out of bed. He rose to his full height, staring down at her, displaying his spectacular body with muscles on top of muscles. "I can go." His voice was low and smooth, and sent heat straight between her thighs as he went on. "But I won't forget last night happened."

She blinked, momentarily stunned by his hefty erection. Did every inch of him have to be so damn perfect? She put on her game face and looked him in the eye. "Put that away."

His grin melted her bones. "There's definitely a place, or two, I'd like to put this. And it's not back in my jeans."

She squeezed her legs together against the hot pulsing need.

His grin widened.

She rolled her eyes and gave him a gentle push. "Stop flattering yourself. You're hot and you've got a perfect dick. I can't help but *notice* you." She turned her back to him, folding her arms. "But that changes nothing. Get dressed."

His low laugh that echoed with heady masculine amusement rose goose bumps on her arms. Damn, she was in so much trouble.

When she heard the zipper, she turned back to find him wearing only his jeans and dog tags. She shouldn't have turned around. Emotion flooded her, making her move toward him and touch those dog tags. With all *that* body on her mind, and maybe her shock, she hadn't seen those on him last night, or been sober enough to realize, but those belonged to his mother, who had been in the military. "You still wear them, huh?"

He moved away, pulling the tags from Remy's hands as he slid his T-shirt quickly over his head. "They never come off."

For all the heat that had been there a second ago, all the confusion and fear pulsing through her, now the air only seemed to hold thick emotion, pulling her forward. The memory of the last time she'd felt that emotion slammed into her.

*The steady beep of the monitor was the only indication that any life remained in the woman lying in front of them. Remy stayed back as Asher sat on the chair next to the hospital bed, holding his mother's hand. Remy's heart reached for Asher, but it also reached for his mother. She couldn't imagine being so wrapped up in any man, or having such low self-esteem, that when he left her she'd seen no way to continue on, so she took her own life. Maybe downing the pills had been a cry for help. Or his mother hadn't meant to actually go through with it, hoping it would bring her husband back to her. But more likely, years of abuse suffered by the hands of a drunk had rendered his mother broken. Too broken to carry on.*

*"Mom, can you hear me?" Asher asked, breaking into Remy's thoughts.*

*Tears welled and emotion clawed at Remy's throat. She wanted to stay next to him and hold him, but she knew he needed time with his mom. The curtains were drawn in the room, only a sliver of sunlight casting into the room.*

*"Mom," Asher said louder. "Mom."*

*Each second felt like a lifetime. Asher should have everyone here. His family. All his people. But he refused to call the people who loved him most. The only person he called was his father, who answered his cell phone completely inebriated. He'd shown up to the hospital after driving drunk to get there, made a spectacle of himself, and then was arrested. Remy wished so hard she could cut the man from Asher's life, as much as wished she could have given his mother the strength she never had.*

*The beeping slowed and slowed until his mom flatlined.*

*Remy closed her eyes and let the tears fall. For his mother. And for Asher.*

*A second later, the nurse turned off the monitor. "I'm sorry." She pressed a hand to his shoulder. "I'm sorry, Asher. I'll give you a minute with her."*

*When the nurse left the room, Asher dropped his face into his hands. His body shook with his silent cries. Remy shot forward, wrapping one arm around his neck, the other hand threaded through his hair. He turned into her, gripping her so tight. And she held on, pressing her lips to the top of Asher's head as he cried into her shirt.*

She blinked out of the memory, staring into the same eyes, and yet they were so different from back when they were younger. Harder. Darker. Wiser. They'd been through so much. Gains. Losses. Death.

Asher's brow furrowed as he took her hand, tugging her forward into his warmth and strength. "We don't need to overthink this. I can be what you need right now." He tucked a finger under her chin. "Let me be that for you."

Maybe this was a big mistake. Maybe Asher was trying to fix walking out on her by being there for her now. But what Remy knew for certain was that she didn't want to become the woman she was after Asher left. A shell of what she once was. Broken and shattered into a thousand pieces. She couldn't fall into that depression again, hiding under the blankets, refusing to live. She stepped back. "Right now, I need to think about me, and figure out how I got myself into all these messes." Most of all, she couldn't get hurt again.

And her heart felt unsteady with Asher. Her body, obviously not so much.

"Whatever you need, Remy." He gave a sweet smile that touched places that her heart didn't want him touching, then headed down the stairs. "Lock the door behind me."

She followed him, watched him slip back into his boots, then he was gone.

She dropped her head against the locked door and breathed

deeply. She needed to call Kinsley and Peyton to get her head straight, but first, she had to figure out how to word all this exactly. *I slept with Asher. Asher and I kinda did it. We totally had hot sex all night long!*

With a deep sigh, she moved away from the door. There was no way that she told them and it wouldn't have a huge impact. Even Remy couldn't quite wrap her head around last night. She couldn't even blame it on the booze. Her desire for Asher had never left; the booze simply made her heart shut up with all the warnings and red flags.

Needing the only thing that made her feel better, she hurried back into her bedroom, fell back in bed, and then promptly hid under the blanket. Salem meowed, then instantly joined her under the sheets, climbing onto her chest. "How do I always seem to make things messier?" she asked the cat.

Salem yawned as his answer.

She slowly stroked his head, half thinking she made life more complicated, and half thinking a good night of hot sex might be the best thing she ever did for herself.

Though her heart still remembered Damon, even if anger lived there too. Was it all lies? Every smile, every gentle kiss…was none of it true? She guessed if she looked back throughout their year together, Damon never kissed her like Asher kissed her last night. With heat and passion. Damon held her hand on long walks, said all the right things to make her feel special, but he never set her body on fire and made her laugh like Asher did. With Damon she felt safe and content. With Asher she felt alive.

She sighed as Salem began snoring, and now she contemplated if anything she felt for Damon was truly real. Could it be real if Damon wasn't real? Or did she make herself believe everything was rainbows and sunshine so that she could move on from Asher and salvage some sort of happiness in her life?

Truth was, she didn't know, and she wasn't sure she ever would.

She stared up at the white sheet with the sunlight flickering outside and felt her body relax as she stroked Salem's soft fur, when her mind traveled back to Damon and all the messiness going on there. His odd request yesterday came to mind again and what *I've got something at your house and need you to do a favor for me* meant. There had to be something there that he wanted. The only question was, what?

\* \* \*

After a hot shower and a quick breakfast, Asher grabbed his car keys off the kitchen counter in his two-story redbrick childhood home. His mother had paid for this house with blood, tears, and hard work at a diner downtown after she got medically discharged from the military for mental health when he was young, and from the money left to her from her parents when they passed away. His father had never come back to Stoney Creek to claim any part of the house, though Asher knew he wouldn't. His father was a drunk coward. The house remained unchanged. The cherrywood table still sat in the dining room. The dark green countertops and oak cabinets were still ugly. The only thing Asher changed was the furniture in the living room. Brown leather couches, with a big-screen television to watch the game, and he was good. The rest felt like home.

He locked the front door behind him, hopped into his black Chevy Camaro, and made the ten-minute drive to the police station. He parked next to Boone's motorcycle and then hurried out. Fall was officially here, and he zipped up his black leather jacket, wearing his black beanie, fighting off a chill. He headed down Main Street in desperate need of another coffee. The one at home didn't cut it today. And it was also his day to bring in coffees for the team.

Most of Main Street was original; the buildings, including the police station, had been there since the 1800s and had been restored to showcase the charm of the small-town village. The shop owners had done their best to modernize the town too, making their signs a bit flashy. There were a few coffee shops in town, but none better than Flaming Pie. Set in between a chocolate store and an art gallery, the shop was busy most times of the day.

Asher entered through the front door, finding the place stuffed full of customers. Some people settled into casual conversation. Others were working on their laptops, already well into their workday.

"Asher, buddy, what can I get ya?" Danny, the owners' son, asked as Asher reached the front counter.

"The team's usual," he said, his gaze sweeping the glass display of every pie imaginable.

"Heard about Remy," Danny said, drawing Asher's focus back to him. He poured the first cup of coffee. "Shitty deal."

Asher reached into his back pocket, taking out a ten-dollar bill from his wallet. "Very." Danny had been in the same graduating class as Asher and the guys. He knew Remy well—the whole town did.

Danny added sugar to the coffee before putting on the lid. "Is she doing all right?"

Asher nodded. "She's hanging in there."

Danny finished up the next coffee. "That guy, Damon, or

whatever his name was, he came in here all the time." He added the coffee cups to a tray. "I never would have guessed he'd con anyone."

"Which is what makes him so good at it," Asher explained when Danny moved back to the register. "Criminals prey on nice people and act like they're nice too."

Danny frowned. "Sometimes I really hate human beings and wish there were more dogs in the world."

"I can't disagree with you there." Asher laughed dryly and handed Danny the bill before grabbing the tray of coffees. "Thanks for these. See ya soon."

"Later," Danny said with a wave.

Asher strode through the coffee shop, catching two pretty twentysomething-year-olds making eyes at him. When he'd returned to Stoney Creek after leaving the FBI, he would have been all over that. Everything changed now. Remy getting back on her feet was all that mattered. And hopefully, finding his way back into her bed too. Last night remained on his mind. Every moan and every shudder she gave seemed imprinted on his brain. He could smell her, taste her. She was *everywhere*.

In quick time, Asher made it to the station. When he entered, he found a couple people in the waiting room. He waved to Doreen, their receptionist, and then headed into the back. The station's halls were a pale dull blue. Cubicles were outside of Asher's office, but most desks were empty now, with only a couple of the street cops working on their paperwork. The two jail cells were in the back of the station, which mainly housed those in need of sobering up before they were cut loose. Just like Damon was processed, then shipped off to the larger jail in Whitby Falls to be housed until his trial.

Asher passed the cubicles and headed into the command

center, where all the investigatory cases were handled. Boone and Rhett were already there, sitting around the long rectangular meeting room table. When they were working a murder, the table was set aside, and the big white boards came out. Boone liked to pace while he thought. Rhett typically stood in front of the boards, staring at the photographic evidence. But today there was none of that; the last murder they solved had been when Peyton found a dead body in her lingerie shop. Asher was glad all that was behind them now, and that Boone and Peyton were planning their destination wedding for some time this winter. A vacation sounded damn good. Especially if that vacation included Remy in his bed. "Anything interesting happen last night?" Asher asked, placing the coffees on the table.

"Debbie Brown knocked out her husband's tooth," Rhett said, reaching for his coffee. "She's still sleeping it off in the back."

Debbie and Jon were regular troublemakers who drank too much, hated each other too much, and Asher was pretty sure that one day one of them was going to kill the other. "Nothing major, then?" He took his seat next to Boone, taking off the lid of his cup, revealing steam coming from the coffee.

"Nothing major," Rhett confirmed. "The night was quiet."

"Good." Tourists typically caused the most trouble with their drunken adventures, especially when those adventures included the beach or rowdy nights at either Kinsley's bar or the nightclub, Merlots, farther down Main Street. Feeling better than he had felt in years, Asher took a long sip of his coffee, thinking of his own rowdy night, and assuming he needed three times the amount of caffeine to get through this day.

When he set his coffee down, Boone narrowed his eyes slightly.

"What?" Asher asked

Boone's fingers rhythmically tapped against the table. "You either got laid or won the lottery."

"Neither." Asher snorted, having no intention of telling either of them about last night. His only thought was to protect Remy, and damn, that felt a whole lot better than the guilt that had been riding him for the past ten years.

Rhett cocked his head, regarding Asher intently. "It's not the lottery. He's got that stupid-ass grin."

Asher stopped smiling, not even realizing he had been. Sex always increased his mood. Sex with Remy. Damn. He felt lit up.

"Was it that chick from the bar the other night?" Rhett asked.

"No," Asher said, desperate to get the focus off him and onto their day. "What's on the agenda for this morning?"

Boone's body posture perked up. "It's the new girl that works at the bakery?"

"Definitely not." Asher sighed, shaking his head in exasperation. "Again. What's the job today?"

Rhett crossed his arms. "I'll figure it out, just give me some time."

"Good for you." Asher reached for his coffee again and took a long, deep sip, trying to think of a way out. The downside to his life-long friends being detectives was that secrets were hard to come by. He finished his sip, then said bluntly, "Now can we move on?"

Boone stared a little harder for another minute, then blinked. "Yeah, all right." He finally succumbed and grabbed a file off the table before tossing it at Asher. "The chief"—who also was Boone's father, Hank Knight—"had us look deeper into Damon, aka Kyle Fanning."

Asher's back straightened like a stiff rod had been shoved down his spine. "And?"

"And nothing," said Rhett, leaning back in his chair and stretching his arms. "He appears to work alone. We found some connections between him and some pretty heavy hitters in underground crime in Portland, but from what I got from the local PD there, nothing about that case seems related to what's going on here with Remy."

Asher felt tension he hadn't known was there leave him with a long exhale. "Good, then nothing more will come back on Remy?"

"Doesn't look like it," Boone said.

Voices coming from the cubicles filtered into the room as Asher flipped through the file, spotting a photograph of Fanning. His fingers twitched to crumple that bastard's face. "It's too bad we don't have him on anything more than fraud."

Rhett coughed a little on his coffee and then laughed. "Looking for more time to add to his sentence?"

"He deserves that and worse," Asher said, hearing the venom in his own voice. "Remy shouldn't have to worry about this prick walking the streets ever again."

Boone's eyebrows shot up, then he exchanged a long look with Rhett, and Asher immediately regretted his words.

Rhett slammed a hand down on the table. "Remy? Are you out of your fucking mind?"

Most days Asher thought so. He nodded. "Quite possibly."

Both his friends stared at him for what felt like a lifetime with shock on their faces. Of course, Asher understood. A year ago, Remy barely talked to him. A week ago, she tolerated him. This was a big jump in a direction no one expected, most of all him.

Boone finally broke the silence. He slowly whistled and laced his hands behind his head. "That is a dangerous line you're walking there."

"Don't I know it," Asher said. Most times, he liked danger. With Remy, he knew the risks there.

"Was this her decision or yours?" Rhett asked.

Asher flipped another page, seeing the police report on Fanning's first marriage. "Remy owns this show, I'm just along for the ride." When heavy silence greeted him, Asher glanced up, finding frowns. "Got something to add?"

"You're being far too blasé about this," Boone said firmly. "I'm sure I don't need to remind you that when you left her, Remy was destroyed. She's an emotional mess right now and not thinking straight."

Asher didn't need the reminder. He had only ever seen Boone furious once. And that was when Boone showed up in Washington the day after Asher left, and he'd returned to Stoney Creek leaving Asher with a shiner. Boone loved Remy like a sister. "I've never forgotten what I've done to her," Asher said firmly. "She wanted me last night, and I let her take what she wanted. I'm treading carefully." Boone had only forgiven Asher when he explained why he left. To protect Remy from the dark shit swirling inside him. She would have been worse off had he stayed, and Asher refused to destroy a woman like his father destroyed his mother. Love was just all types of fucked up.

Rhett slowly shook his head. "This sounds like an explosion waiting to happen."

Asher scoffed, "Only if I let it fall apart, and I won't."

Heavy silence filled the room again. Rhett and Boone both stared at Asher in a way he knew he deserved. They doubted him where it came to Remy. She wasn't the only person Asher needed to prove himself to.

Boone finally said, "You've got your head on straight here?"

"I do." Asher nodded firmly. No missteps. Not this time.

"Good, keep it that way," he told Asher.

Asher slid his glance to Rhett. "Anything left to add?"

"Nope," Rhett said with a quick smile. "This shit sounds complicated, and you both know that's not my style." No, Rhett liked his ladies to be of the one-night variety. When things got serious, Rhett ended it.

Not at all bothered that two men who cared very deeply for Remy called him out on his shit, Asher jabbed his finger on the file on the desk, curious about something he'd been wondering. "Do we know how Fanning found Remy in the first place?"

"Her grandmother," Boone said.

Asher felt the cold shock roll over him. He leaned forward. "Explain."

Boone grabbed the corner of the file, turning it back to him, and flipped through a dozen papers before finally handing Asher one. "Edward Matthews used to be Remy's grandmother's lawyer. Remember him? He had his practice in the main floor of his old house near the cliffs."

"Yeah, I remember him," Asher said, glancing over names that included Remy's on the list. "Go on."

"Those names there are Fanning's victims," Boone reported, flicking the page with his fingers. "The connection between the women was that all their grandparents' last will and testaments were handled by this lawyer, who eventually moved to Portland about ten years back now. Fanning likely got his hands on this lawyer's files."

Asher stared down at Remy's name, wishing he could scrub it off that list. He considered what he heard, reaching for his coffee again. He took a sip, letting the hazelnut flavor sit on his tongue. While Boone and Rhett had done the legwork, Asher would follow up on this report for the rest of the day, making sure every line was crossed and no detail was overlooked. He couldn't risk that somehow Remy would find herself in more trouble. "So, from what you've seen so far, this all ends here with Fanning and Remy is safe."

"Well, she's safe from Fanning," Rhett said with a smirk, leaning his chair back on two legs. "But from you? That's another story altogether."

Asher snorted and threw the coffee tray at him, sending Rhett falling backward with a loud laugh.

# Chapter 7

Hours had gone by since Asher left this morning. Long hours. Excruciating hours. Remy paced her living room after tying together a piece of palo santo wood and a selenite crystal and placing it on her glass coffee table. The bundle was basically a spiritual punch that cleared away lingering negativity and safeguarded against bad vibes, but the bundle did nothing to calm Remy down after she finally went looking for the *thing* that Damon had left at her house. Desperate to clear her head, she pulled out the big guns, and within minutes, smoke billowed up from a ceramic bowl, the burning amber infusing musk and floral into the air for wisdom. Salem had been watching her pace back and forth for the last half hour while he sat on the windowsill. Remy nibbled on the side of her nail, her heart racing and beating hard in her chest when *finally*, there was a knock at the door. Before she could even get there, the door whisked open and Kinsley strode in wearing jeans and a black T-shirt with WHISKEY BLUES written across her chest. Peyton wore a dark purple dress and black tights with a black cardigan.

It occurred to Remy then that she'd been so worried to talk to them about what happened with Asher last night, and now, sex with Asher seemed miniscule in comparison to the reason she'd called them.

"Thank God you're here." Remy grasped their hands and pulled them inside quickly, having called them minutes ago after finally gathering her courage.

Kinsley rolled her eyes. "Oh, yeah, because the two seconds it took us to get here from downstairs was brutally long."

Yes, Kinsley owned the bar next door. Yes, Peyton owned the lingerie shop. But that was precisely why Remy called them here. She needed wisdom since her spells were doing nothing to help her. "It was *forever*," Remy drawled, hands plastered to the door behind her.

Peyton gave Kinsley a long look, then asked, "Has something happened?"

"Okay, first, did you close your shop for me?" Remy asked, suddenly feeling not only wildly on edge but also a hot burn of guilt. Kinsley managed her bar, sometimes worked the bar for fun. She could leave whenever she wanted. Peyton, on the other hand, couldn't. "Do you need to get back soon?"

Peyton smiled and moved to lean on the back of the couch. "My new employee is doing great on her own. Coming here was a good excuse to give her some time by herself in the shop." Peyton had worked the lingerie shop herself since she'd moved to town, but now she and Boone spent more time in bed than out of it. Remy figured a baby wouldn't be too far off in their future once they got married. "Stop stalling. What's going on?"

God, where to start? Remy sighed and then resumed her pacing, nibbling on her nail again. Kinsley and Peyton watched her closely. She finally stopped and huffed. "I have no idea how to begin, so I'll start at the beginning. After Asher left this morning—"

"Whoa." Kinsley held up her hand. "Stop right there. Asher stayed the night?"

Remy's entire body, right down to her toes, flushed red hot. She waved off the question. "That is not why I called you here."

"Um, excuse me," Kinsley countered, moving closer until she had Remy by the hand and led her to the couch. "That's the reason you *should* have called us here. Did you sleep with him?"

Peyton took the chair across from them as Remy explained quickly, "Yes, we slept together, but there was a curse breaking involved where I might have added too much booze." She was no fool. She'd complicated an already complicated situation, but there it was, in all its complicated glory. "Please, let's not make this out to be a bigger deal than it has to be." Both Kinsley's and Peyton's mouths dropped open, and Remy itched to grab her shirt and pull it over her head. Instead, seeing no way out, she forced herself to face the situation. "Yes, that happened with Asher. Yes, we did things that would make my nana roll over in her grave. No, it's never going to happen again."

Kinsley blinked rapidly, her gaze flicking between Remy and Peyton. "Dude. I think this *is* a pretty big deal."

Peyton picked her mouth up off the floor and nodded firmly. "Like, a really, really big deal."

"Well, it's not," Remy countered, not even wanting to go there. Hell, maybe she wasn't even prepared to go there. Last night happened. Whatever. "We got drunk and did something stupid. And now we're forgetting all about it." Or at least she was. "Let's not lose focus. There is an even *bigger* reason I called you here."

Kinsley didn't even miss a beat. "You've murdered Asher and need us to help you bury him."

Remy rolled her eyes. "No."

"You want us to help you burn Damon's stuff?" Peyton asked.

"No." Remy sighed.

"Just a minute," Kinsley said, waving her hand in the air like she had the biggest question of the day. "There is a reason bigger than you not calling us here because you slept with your ex-boyfriend who shattered your heart ten years ago, then objected at your wedding and arrested your fiancé." Her expression got serious, real serious. "What in the hell has happened? It's got to be bad."

"It's not bad...but not good...or maybe it is." Seeing she was getting nowhere *still*, Remy huffed and hurried up the stairs to her bedroom, coming back downstairs carrying the black duffel bag she'd found an hour after Asher left. She dropped it onto the coffee table, and the bag feel open, wads of bills spilling out.

"Holy shit," Peyton exclaimed, jumping to her feet.

Kinsley gasped, wide-eyed. "Oh my God, one of your crazy-ass spells worked!"

Remy burst out laughing. "Yeah, sure, just call me Harry Potter." Then she put her hands on her hips. "And what the hell, Kinsley? My spells aren't crazy."

Kinsley gave a blank stare at the money and then slid her gaze to Remy's, eyes suddenly intense. "Explain how you got this money." Her dad was a cop, and so was her brother, and being around cops her whole life, Kinsley had the hard cop look and voice nailed down.

Remy sighed, trying to settle the butterflies in her belly. "Yesterday, Asher took me to see Damon—"

"Boone told me you punched him in the nose." Peyton smiled.

"I did, it felt awesome." Remy returned the smile, remembering the satisfaction of hearing his nose crunch and seeing the blood.

"Um, hello." Kinsley snapped her fingers and said firmly, "You have a giant bag of money here. Focus."

"Right." Remy turned back to the task at hand, gathered her focus, and explained, "When I was there, Damon said that he needed a favor with something here at the loft. Which had me thinking—what could he possibly need me for?" She drew in a quick breath, staring at all the bills. "Asher packed up Damon's stuff yesterday and got it out of here, and he didn't find anything then, so this morning after Asher left, I went looking."

Kinsley voice rose in pitch as she pointed at the bag. "And you found this?"

Remy nodded. "In my air duct."

Peyton slowly shook her head like she couldn't quite believe it. "Wait. How did you even find it there?"

"From a movie I saw once," Remy said with a dry laugh, trying to cut through the heavy tension in the room. "People always keep stuff in air ducts, so I looked there after I checked everywhere else, and, yup, Damon wasn't even original."

"Wow," Peyton breathed.

Kinsley leaned forward, snooping in the bag. "How much is in here?"

Remy had counted twice. "Two hundred thousand. Give or take."

Silence descended into the room. Heavy silence. Until Remy couldn't take it anymore. "I guess I should call Asher and report this, right?"

Peyton nodded. "It's the right thing to do."

Kinsley slid off the couch to grab wads of bills. She lifted them to her nose and smelled them. "If we call Asher, he'll tell you to hand it in."

"Which is exactly what I should do," Remy said.

"Yes. Definitely," Peyton agreed with a firm nod.

Kinsley paused, sat back on her legs, and exhaled deeply, pondering. She eventually said, "I've heard something before from my dad. If you turn in Damon's money, the money goes in for evidence and it might be stored for years, even decades. Then it'll go to the Treasury to be destroyed." She picked up a wad of cash in both hands and shook it at Remy. "This will buy you your shop."

The thought had crossed Remy's mind the second she opened the bag. When her fingers first grazed the money, she knew the freedom the cash would buy her. She'd finally have the life she wanted, sharing all the things that Nana had created. Healing people. Bringing them happiness. Remy wanted that too. But…and there was a big *but*…"Yeah, good and all if I don't want to go to hell and spend the rest of my life burning in misery for being a terrible person for spending money that doesn't belong to me."

"Who says the money's not yours? It's in *your* house," Kinsley countered. "You haven't committed a crime. You're just not giving Damon his money back. As far as I see it, this is a way to take what's gone wrong and make everything right again. You deserve this, Remy."

Unsure about that, she nibbled her lip and glanced at Peyton.

Peyton stared at the money for a long few seconds, then shrugged. "I don't know. What if it's money that belongs to the other women Damon married?"

"But what if it's not?" Kinsley interjected. "What if it's just Damon's cash from investments or something like that. He was a smart guy. He's got nearly four million in his bank account, from what my dad told me."

Peyton's eyes widened, her hand covered her mouth. "That's how much he took from those women?" she mumbled.

"Obviously, this was some sort of addiction," Kinsley said with a nod. "Greedy sonofabitch. His first wife lost the most—two million dollars. Second wife lost a half mil. Third wife lost a few hundred grand before he took off running. The rest of the money he got from making smart business investments." She turned to Remy and said softly, "Boone and my dad told me that his accounts are currently frozen, because the women he stole from are going to receive all their money back once things settle. Even once that is figured out, Damon will still have a couple million in his account." She reached for a wad of money again and held it up. "Everyone is getting what they deserve. You deserve that too, Remy."

When Remy turned to Peyton again, looking for answers from the sweetest and most honorable one of the bunch, Peyton sighed. "You do deserve this," she after a beat. "After all you've been through, I, out of anyone, know that finding a bit of happiness in the darkness can change everything." Peyton did understand—she'd lost her husband in a car accident arranged by his murderous and greedy business partner in Seattle. "I moved here because I needed that new *something*. I found that here. I found you both. I found Boone."

Remy smiled, her heart thundering in her ears.

"So…?" Kinsley asked, bright eyed.

Peyton's lips pursed as she glanced between them. "I was never here. This conversation never happened. I saw nothing." She moved to Remy and gave her a big hug and then strode out the door.

"I guess that's as good of an 'okay' as we're going to get from her," Remy said, turning back to Kinsley.

Kinsley nodded. "She's marrying a cop, goes against the grain not to tell him."

"Are we totally horrible people?" Remy asked, moving to zip up the bag.

"Hell no," Kinsley snapped in an instant. "Damon is a horrible person who did horrible things to people but was smart to invest his money. You're simply getting your due for the shit he put you through."

Remy took the bag off her coffee table and it landed with a *thud* on the floor. The confusion and guilt seemed to disappear with Peyton's approval. If the good one out of all of them didn't see anything wrong with this, then how bad could it be? "What if Damon comes back for the money?"

Kinsley considered that and then shook her head. "Not going to happen. My dad told me that they have him on identity theft, fraud, mail fraud, and who knows what else. He can put be away for twenty-four years in prison." She paused, then shrugged. "But if it's really worrying you, then we could also drive to Whitby Falls and tell him that you found the money and turned it in."

Remy nodded. "Yes, I'm worried. I want to make right decisions, not wrong ones." The only reason she was even considering this was because Kinsley nudged her toward it. Remy *always* made bad decisions. Kinsley seemed to always make the right ones.

"Okay, later today, let's pay him another visit," Kinsley said, then wiggled her eyebrows. "So, are you in or are you out?"

Remy stared at the bag. The bigger part of her thought she did deserve this. The money was in her house. Damon's past victims were getting what they were owed. She had the chance to change her life for the better, and she wanted desperately to take it. To finally have the shop she'd always dreamed of having. But big decisions like this were not handled rashly. "I'll tell you tomorrow morning if I'm in or out."

Kinsley hopped up from the couch and then slid her arm into Remy's. "Dude, can't you just decide for yourself, without doing some voodoo shit?"

"Take. That. Back." Remy frowned.

Kinsley rolled her eyes. "Fine, I take it back, so what ritual happens tonight?"

"I'll do a cleansing spell before bed, then ask Nana what I should do," Remy explained. "By the time I wake up, I'll know."

Kinsley gave her the most exasperated expression Remy had ever seen. "Because she'll tell you in your dream?"

"That's right." Remy pinched Kinsley's arm. "And stop looking at me like I've lost it completely."

"Actually," Kinsley countered after a moment. "I stress drink and binge eat over huge decisions. Your way sounds healthier."

Remy smiled, reached for the bag to bring back upstairs, and then considered what Kinsley had said. "Um…so about the drinking and binge eating, can we do that too?"

Kinsley was already walking toward the kitchen. "On it!"

# Chapter 8

Two weeks later, Remy's life wasn't only back to normal, her dreams were coming true. Above her, standing on a ladder, Asher hung the new sign for Remy's shop. The dark wood sign hung from a wrought iron hook and had her new black cat logo with BLACK CAT'S CAULDRON written in calligraphy with vines growing out of the words. With the help of the entire gang, they'd renovated quickly and painted the walls a deep cream color after she'd bought the building that included her loft. Remy loved the worn hardwood floors and left those as is. There was already a counter from the shop that was there before, so they simply sanded the old wood and painted it black. The shop was everything she'd hoped for, and she could hardly believe two weeks had flown by since she woke up from her dream and got the go-ahead from her nana. It hadn't exactly been a yes, but Nana had been smiling as she walked down Main Street toward Remy. That's about as good of a thumbs-up as Remy could hope for to use Damon's money to buy her shop. Which, of course, Damon didn't know, because she and Kinsley had driven to the larger jail in Whitby Falls. In privacy from the hovering Asher and Boone, Remy had told Damon that she'd turned his money in. The scowl on his face told her he believed her. Free and clear, she was taking the little help fate had given her to turn her life around.

"How's that?" Asher asked, glancing down at her. Today he wore jeans and a leather jacket around a gray T-shirt, looking mighty fine this chilly afternoon with a brisk west wind cutting through the town.

"Perfect." She smiled, holding on to the ladder. "It's just perfect."

Everything was perfect, really. Considering her life two weeks ago was in complete shambles, things had taken a turn for the better. Except for the Asher part. She'd tried over the last couple weeks to keep things very platonic, not thinking about him too much. But he came around, *a lot*, obviously worried about her. Only she wasn't in bad shape. She wanted him…*all the time.* Asher wasn't helping matters, considering she was trying to stay out of his bed, and he seemed determined to get her back in it, always getting *very* close and doing his best to keep the heat burning between them. Which he seemed to do without much effort. He had yet to kiss her again, but all the teasing he'd done lately made her want to grab that T-shirt and drag him close until those lips met hers. For that reason, she had made sure someone was always with them. Being alone was a big no-no, just in case that urge to rip his shirt off took over.

When he slowly came back down the ladder, she quickly moved away, knowing that if he got near her, all that energy between them would electrify her. Ever since she woke up after their night together, there was this weird back-and-forth thing going on. Her body trusted Asher, but her emotions didn't. And right now, her emotions were at a high risk, because with every hot spike of desire also came the clench of her heart.

She couldn't forget that he'd broken her heart into a million pieces. No matter how much growing up Asher had done these past ten years.

His feet hit the pavement and he wiped his hands, glancing up at the sign. "Yeah, looks good." He turned to her with a smile. "Nana would be so proud of you."

Warmth rushed through her. All the years she'd hoped and wished for this day, and it was finally here. Nana would be proud, more than proud actually. "I wish she could have seen this," Remy said, glancing at her storefront. Nana had perfected all her creams and candles over the years. She wanted to help people. And it felt so good that Remy could see that come to life now.

Finally, Remy's life was on the right track.

Movement passed by the window and Remy noticed Kinsley and Peyton putting stuff on the bookcases along the far wall. Boone and Rhett were both coming out of the back room with boxes. For the last week, Remy had been in her kitchen making up batches of Nana's potions and creams. "I actually can't believe this is happening," she said, turning back to Asher.

His eyes went soft. "It's a damn good thing your mother came through for you."

Remy grimaced, glancing away before she realized he would call her out.

And of course, he did.

His finger tucked under her chin, drawing her gaze up to his steady stare. "Don't feel bad for taking your mom's money. She hasn't been there for you your whole life. It's the least she can do. I'm just happy to see she's finally thinking of you and not herself. You deserve this."

*I'm going to hell. Straight to hell!* When Remy bought the store, Asher had arched that eyebrow of curiosity at her, and she'd told a little white—okay, huge—lie that the money came as a gift from her mother, who had given part of *her* inheritance to Remy. All lies. Her mother hadn't gotten a cent from Nana. Her grandmother left everything to Remy, and her mother didn't have a cent to her name. "I only feel partly bad," she said, getting off the subject. "I'm mostly excited."

"As you should be," Asher said, dragging his fingers unnecessarily slowly off her chin. Heat flickered in her southern regions, and his eyes darkened in response. He hooked his finger into her pocket and dragged her forward. "I'm really proud of you."

Dear Lord, she lost brain cells. They just up and died right there and then. His eyes glinted with heat and promise as he dropped his head enough for some hair to dangle down. She cleared her throat. "Thank you. I'm really proud of me too."

The side of his mouth curved sensually. "I'd like to congratulate you."

The air stopped moving around her when he dropped his mouth close to hers. "How do you want to do that?" she rasped, her heart pounding in her ears.

"I can think of a few ideas," he murmured, dropping his mouth right near hers, waiting her out, giving her the chance to back away.

She stayed put.

Then his lips got *really* close as a young voice said, "Do you have a black cat too?"

Asher grumbled something under his breath and then he smiled at the girl with big blue eyes and brown curls, who appeared to be around eleven, standing next to her dad.

Remy cleared her throat, flushed from head to toe, and said to the girl, "Yes, I do. His name is Salem."

The girl beamed.

Her dad wasn't nearly as impressed. "You're selling magic here?"

"Oh, yes, a little bit of magic for sure," Remy explained, and then winked at the little girl, who giggled in return. "Our grand opening is tomorrow. Stop by and I'll show you." Okay, she did have a grip on reality. Magic wasn't real, but she'd seen Nana's spells do magical things for people. She also knew it was all about a good mixture of herbal medicine combined with the power of the mind that made magical things happen.

"Yeah, okay, sure," the man scoffed, then nudged his daughter forward. She gave Remy a wave.

Remy laughed softly and lifted her eyebrows at Asher. "I guess some people will never believe in all this."

"You'll make them," Asher said, shoving his hands into his pockets. "All they have to do is meet you."

His flattery felt so much more than flattery. He meant what he said, and part of her began to question why she'd shut him out for so long. He'd been back in Stoney Creek for five years now. For four of those years she'd fought like hell not to even look at him, knowing when it came to him, those gorgeous green eyes would devastate to her. She barely said a word to him, and avoided him at Whiskey Blues if she was working behind the bar. But then when she met Damon and fell in love, a part of her had wanted Asher to see her happy. To know that his leaving hadn't ruined her. Her smart plan backfired, of course. And even though she cared for Damon, she hadn't loved him like Asher. She realized now that shutting him out had been wrong. He might have been a bad boyfriend, but he was a great friend. Every day since he objected at her wedding, he'd been there, helping her get her feet on solid ground again. Whatever she needed or wanted—including when she jumped him—he gave her. Every step along the way had been on her terms, and that bit of kindness was not something she was used to with men. "I haven't thanked you yet for everything you've done for me. For the long talks, the laughs, and for helping me these last two weeks get the shop ready, thank you." She smiled.

He shifted on his feet. "Don't thank me. I want to be here with you."

The front door opened then, and the gang strode out, laughing about something.

"We're all done in there," said Kinsley, sliding her arm into Remy's and moving her toward the road. "You're all set for the grand opening, just got some little stuff left that's for you to do since you'll inevitably do it better."

"I cannot thank you enough," Remy said, and glanced at Peyton too. "I seriously don't know what I would have done without either of you." They were both business owners. They knew how to open a company and handle all the little things Remy never thought about. Probably things she would have learned if she'd stayed in college.

"I'm so excited about tomorrow," Peyton said, leaning into Boone's embrace as he wrapped an arm around her.

"You're going to kill it tomorrow, Remy," Rhett said, then clicked the key fob of his truck, and the loud beep had Remy moving away from the curb. "I've got a date," he added with a dangerous grin. "I'll be back in the morning to help out where I can."

"Planning a sleepover already?" Boone asked with a laugh.

Rhett got in his truck, then rolled down the window. "Isn't positive thinking good for the soul?"

Everyone laughed as he drove off. Everyone except Kinsley. Remy caught her glancing at her cute high heels. She wore a pretty pink dress and a jean jacket. Kinsley always dressed up when she knew Rhett would be there, and Remy had caught Rhett a few times over the years watching Kinsley. Remy's heart twisted. She guessed there was something that was worse than having a con man for a fiancé, and that was being madly in love with a man who would never love you back. Kinsley had loved Rhett since the tenth grade. Rhett had a reputation, and it wasn't a good one. Boone would never approve, and Remy wasn't sure she would either. Rhett was trouble with a capital *T*, and a world of baggage came with him.

Kinsley finally caught Remy looking at her and put on a fake smile. "I need to get to the bar for my shift," she said.

Remy hurried to her and hugged her tight. "Thanks again for everything. I love you."

"Would you stop thanking me? Jeez." Kinsley hugged her back, then leaned away and grinned. "Love you too, babe." She gave Peyton and Boone a wave, then strode off toward Whiskey Blues two doors down.

"I've got to get into work to finish up some paperwork," Asher said, drawing Remy's attention back to him. He glanced at Boone and they had a silent man-talk.

Boone smiled and then glanced at Remy. "We best be on our way too. We'll be here bright and early to help out all day tomorrow."

Remy hugged Boone first, then when she hugged Peyton, she said, "You've been so awesome through all this. And thanks again for forgiving me for getting paint on that shirt. I'm still not sure I'll ever forgive myself."

Peyton laughed. "Oh, it's fine. It's just a blouse. We'll see you in the morning."

With them on their way, Peyton waved at Boone as she

entered her lingerie shop, and he continued on to the police station. Remy turned back to Asher, but he had already gotten close again. Too close. Dangerously close.

"You've eaten as much food as I have today, which is barely anything," he said, staring at her mouth before meeting her eyes again. "Want to grab dinner later?"

"Ah…." She flipped her hair, her scalp prickling.

He laughed softly. "A 'no' will suffice if you're not interested."

God, sometimes being around cops sucked. They knew body language too damn well. "I just…" Time felt like it slowed down. "I don't trust myself with you."

There, she said it.

"Well, we'll have to change that, won't we?" Then he leaned in and pressed a light kiss to her cheek, like he belonged there.

But her heart promptly reminded her that Asher had a terrible habit of breaking it.

"I'll see you tomorrow, then?"

She nodded. "See ya."

He gave that knee-wobbling smile before striding away, looking like a god in his jeans and leather jacket. She sighed and went into the shop. She glanced around at the bookshelves full of all her nana's creams and bath salts and incense, just everything that Nana had created over the years.

Remy smiled, seeing Nana in all this, and feeling good about everything.

She moved to clean the paintbrushes in the back sink when her front door opened. A good-looking man, who appeared to be in his mid-thirties, entered, dressed in a fine navy-blue tailored suit. His brown eyes held a certain hardness she found unsettling. "I'm sorry, but the grand opening isn't until tomorrow," she said. "Store's closed, I'm afraid."

"I'm not here for the grand opening," he said, shutting the door tightly behind him.

Something about his demeanor screamed *trouble*. He moved slowly, like nothing could get through him. He watched her carefully, almost like he knew her. His gaze scanned the room quickly before returning to her. "You're a witch? You've got magic?"

"I don't personally have magic," she explained, annoyed that this guy was so ballsy not to leave when she asked him to. "But I know a thing or two."

"Interesting." He moved near the bookshelves that held all the small jars of teas. Each one had her logo matching her sign outside on the circular sticker, along with the type of tea blend. "A protection tea, huh?" He lifted up the jar and examined the contents, giving it a grin.

Not a nice grin. A scary grin that made the hairs on the back of her neck rise. "I really think you should leave now." She moved toward the door.

He caught her by the arm, his fingers tightening just enough to let her know he could overpower her easily. "We need to talk."

She jerked her arm away and took a step back. "I don't even know you. Get out. Now!"

"Ah, but I know your fiancé," he said. "Damon Lane."

She felt like ice had been poured over her, all the heat leaving her body. "He's no longer my fiancé. He's been arrested."

"Yeah, I heard that," the man said, finally letting her go and looking her directly in the eye. "Wanted to come see for myself."

"Okay, so you've seen that he's not here," Remy said. "Now you can leave." Things felt like they were moving too fast. He crossed his arms, appearing so much taller than he did a second ago. "I'm not asking again. Leave now and don't come back. Or I'm calling the police."

He gave an easy laugh that shook her limbs when he moved to the door. "There are many things you could do, but trust me, going to the police is not the wisest one." He slammed the door behind him.

Remy stared at the door, not quite able to move. She'd met all types of men working in the bar, and she knew without a doubt that this man was not the type she should mess with. Everything he said repeated in her mind as she quickly cleaned the brushes, then headed out the front door, locking it behind her. The brisk air brushed across her face, waving her hair around her face as she glanced up and down the street, not seeing the man anywhere in sight. Feeling like his creepy eyes still watched her, she scooted forward and entered Peyton's lingerie shop next door.

Uptown Girl was narrow and long and set into one of the historic buildings on Main Street. The walls were painted hot pink, and there was a sales counter out front and white tables set out with the lacy garments, as well as rows of intimate wear hanging on the walls. She found Peyton behind the counter. Though the moment the door closed behind her, another cold breeze sent a shiver down her spine that had nothing to do with the guy. Weight suddenly pressed down on her shoulders and the light in the room seemed to fade. "Oh, damn, we've got to fix this immediately."

Peyton glanced up. "What's wrong?"

"You've got a situation in here." Remy reached into her purse and searched for her black tourmaline stone that she always kept on hand, as well as nearly everything she needed in an emergency. She offered the stone to Peyton when she reached her. "Put this near your register."

"Why?" Peyton asked, unblinking. "And what kind of situation do I have?"

"There's still bad vibes in here." Remy glanced around the shop and shuddered, feeling the hair on the back of her neck now standing straight up. She grabbed her rose water from her purse and began spraying around the front of the lingerie shop, helping protect the space from any lingering darkness that remained. When the sense of dread finally left Remy, easing her chest and allowing her to breathe normally again, she turned back to Peyton to find her wide-eyed. "It's okay, you're not being haunted by the woman who was murdered here. The energy just stays around for a while. We need to cut through it."

Peyton slowly looked around, seemingly ready for a ghost to jump out at her. "If you say so." She finally glanced back and gave a tight smile. "I wasn't expecting a visit. What's up?"

"A guy just came into the store." Remy felt the hair still raised on the back of her neck, and that had nothing to do with the lingering icky energy in the space. "He said he knew Damon."

"Really?"

Remy nodded. "Yeah, and I just got this really creepy vibe off him."

"You should tell the guys," Peyton said.

Remy gave a quick nod. "If he comes back, I will. Who knows, maybe he's just a friend wondering where Damon was?"

"You told him that Damon's in jail?"

"I did, yeah."

"Good. I'm sure you're right. Maybe he just wanted to see for himself that Damon's gone." Remy watched as Peyton moved to the door, then flipped the closed sign. When she turned back, she smiled. "Speaking of Asher, how are things on that front? You both seemed very comfortable together today."

"We are comfortable, but there's nothing more to report," Remy said, moving to the panty table, picking up a black lace thong that she knew for certain Asher would love.

Peyton sidled next to her. "It's yours." She wiggled her eyebrows. "You know, not for any particular detective, just for you."

"Are you sure?" Remy asked.

Peyton nodded. "Most definitely." Then color rose to her cheeks and she glanced up through her thick black lashes. "I hate to kick you out of here, but I need to meet Boone in a bit to chat with our travel agent about the wedding."

"Oh, sure, no probs," Remy said, giving Peyton a quick hug. "Just wanted to stop in to say thanks again for all the help this afternoon." Lies! The thought of going home alone after meeting that guy made her want to crawl out of her skin.

"You really need to stop thanking all of us," Peyton said with a sweet smile. "Everyone wants to help."

Remy smiled to hide the nerves tickling her belly and then moved to the door. "Call me later and tell me how the appointment went."

"Will do," Peyton called as Remy headed out.

Remy didn't look back, scared that if she did, Peyton would see she was rattled. When the cool, crisp autumn air greeted her outside, she took another quick look around. Seeing no one, but still too freaked to go home, she quickly beelined it for Kinsley's bar.

By the time she got inside and plopped her butt on the stool, she was breathless.

Kinsley immediately came over. "Hi, buttercup, miss me already?"

"Always."

Kinsley laughed, then poured Remy a glass of red wine. "So, are we going to talk about Asher nearly kissing you outside today?"

Remy accepted the glass and took a sip. "There's nothing to say," she replied after swallowing.

Kinsley moved around the bar and came to sit on the stool next to Remy. "That's actually what worries me the most. You've slept with Asher, and we've barely talked about that, and you've both got some serious chemistry going on. Neither of you are acting like this is just *friends*. You're acting like flirty teenagers. And all this is on top of everything else you've had going on that you've barely talked about."

Remy exhaled a long breath and felt the tightness in her tummy. "I know it's a lot," she eventually said, looking at Kinsley. Peyton was new to their friendship, and special in her own right, but Kinsley...Kinsley was like Remy's sister. They'd been through all of life together. "But I'm okay."

"Are you?" Kinsley asked, taking her hand. "Asher and you...it's not a casual thing. It's *never* been a casual thing. I just don't want you to get hurt again. I remember when he left. I remember the pain you went through. I'm just really worried that neither of you have your heads clear about all this."

"Well, it's a little murky," Remy admitted, not surprised Kinsley was calling out the hard stuff. "But being with him feels good when I think I should be feeling really bad. That's got to be something, don't you think?"

"Of course," Kinsley said. "But is your heart at risk here?"

"I can't give him my heart again," Remy said firmly. "At this point, I don't think I can give any man my heart. It's just not there to give. But I can have fun, and laugh, and now that I'm not so angry at him anymore, Asher is making me feel all those things."

"He always was good at that." Kinsley gave a soft smile.

Remy considered her next thoughts and then went on. "The sexiness, that was like a blip in time, a moment of weakness, but it's been two weeks and I haven't jumped him again." Though that challenge was becoming harder and harder.

Kinsley laughed.

Remy laughed too. "Right now, all this feels good. If it ever doesn't feel good, this thing between Asher and me stops."

"So, you're not getting back together?"

Remy didn't even have to consider it. She adamantly shook her head. "Us getting back together is not on the table. He's helping me through this shit, and we're finding our way back to friends again. Honestly, thank you for worrying about me. I love you for it." She took Kinsley into a warm hug. "But Asher isn't offering a relationship, and I don't want one. We had a hot night that was spurred from a curse breaker that had way too much booze in it. That's all."

"Okay." Kinsley eventually leaned away and gave a firm nod. "We had the talk. I know you're good. And I love you back." She hugged her tight once more, then jumped off the stool. "And now I need to get back to work. Call me later?"

"You know it," Remy said to a retreating Kinsley, who headed into the back to probably work on the schedule and the books. A job that Remy helped with when she worked there. Which, in truth, would help her succeed in her own business now. She learned everything she knew about business from Kinsley, who actually graduated college with a business degree.

When a group of men entered the bar, talking about where the pretty bartender was, Remy polished off her wine and slid off the stool. Kinsley had obviously found herself some admirers. The dark-haired one was totally Kinsley's type. Remy headed for the door, feeling all loved up and much better than after her chat with Damon's "friend."

# Chapter 9

Back at the station, the promise of caffeine led Asher into the break room. He grabbed a mug from the cabinet and poured himself a coffee. Remy was on his mind. The continuing heat between them ruled his thoughts, as did the fact that she had avoided being alone with him these past couple weeks. He was sure as shit that they were both going to explode if something didn't happen between them soon. He'd done his best to keep things strictly in the friend zone until today, but he remembered her taste, could still hear her sweet moans, and he wanted her again. Badly.

"How's our girl doing?" Boone asked, entering the break room, grabbing himself a coffee.

Apparently, Remy wasn't only on Asher's mind. "She's hanging in there," Asher reported. "The shop is good for her, you know."

Boone nodded, taking a sip of his coffee and leaning back against the countertop. "You're good for her too."

Asher snorted. "I wouldn't go that far." He was part of the

reason she found herself in this mess. He couldn't ever forget that. His guilt ensured he never messed up again and hurt her. "I'll keep an eye on her," was all he said. He turned to head back to his desk to finish looking through Fanning's file, confirming for himself that there was no longer a threat to Remy out there.

"You're the best one to do that," Boone called out.

Asher glanced back, hearing the approval in Boone's voice. Boone thought of Remy as a little sister. Asher had obviously won back Boone's trust where it came to Remy. "Considering what I did to her, and the way her life fell apart, you're being far too easy on me."

Boone gave a slow building smile. "The shiner I left you with in Washington would disagree that I took it easy on you."

Asher snorted a laugh.

"You're doing the right thing here," Boone finally said. "That stands for something. I expected Remy to be far worse off than she is, and she's doing good, not only because of her shop. Just making sure you know that."

Not having an answer to Boone's loaded statement, Asher simply nodded, then turned away and headed back down the hallway. Part of him agreed with Boone, but the other part of him knew two weeks of being good for her was nowhere near long enough to fix the pain he'd brought into her life.

When he drew closer, he found Remy sitting in his office. She looked as pretty as ever, wearing a flowered pattern dress with short brown boots. Asher noted the onion braid in her hand and knew the meaning of that braid. He'd seen her use that braid a few times back in high school. She felt like she needed protection. "Remy," he called as he approached.

She jerked, her gaze connecting with his. And holding. Her eyes were wild with worry.

In two long strides, he was there, reaching for her until she was standing. "What happened?"

"Nothing." She tucked the braid back into her purse and gave a forced smile. "I changed my mind about dinner."

At that, he arched an eyebrow. "You want to have dinner with me?"

"Yeah." She averted her gaze and shrugged slightly. "Sounds nice, right?"

"Sounds incredible," he said, watching her carefully. "You know I want to spend time with you, but I want to know why the change of heart. You turned down dinner with me earlier."

"It's just food, Asher, no big deal," she said, rolling her eyes. "Are you in or are you out?"

He couldn't help himself, he grinned like a fool. "You know I'm definitely *in*." Desperate to get the color back in her ashen face, he closed the distance and tucked his finger under her chin, staring into eyes that desperately tried to avoid him. "Remy, I know you," he said gently. "I see that something has happened that's made you very upset. Talk to me."

"It's nothing." She finally looked at him, fingering her necklace. "I…I just want to spend time with you. I changed my mind, all right? Is that a crime?"

"Not, it's not a crime," he retorted, not letting her cop out. "But it's also not something you do." She listened to her cards and her dreams and never acted spontaneously. Never. Not once in her life. He pointed at her purse. "You made an onion braid, which you only use for protection."

She blinked. Twice. "I can't believe you remember that." Then she lifted her chin and firmed her voice. "Well, I went to the market and got bored." When he continued to stare at her not believing a word she said, she shrugged. "Maybe it's time for a new me."

"No, it isn't." He held his ground. "I happen to like the old you. The one who leaves fate to decide her path."

She held his stare for a long moment before something changed in her expression. Something that pulled him in sharply. Fear glistened in her gaze. "Remy," he murmured, and closed the distance, not caring of the consequences, only knowing he needed to get closer. "Did something go wrong at that store?"

She swallowed deeply, shaking her head. "Someone came by the shop after you left." Asher's back straightened at the tremble in her voice. "I'm sure it's nothing, and I don't want to cause a fuss—"

Fear was a very real thing. So were instincts. Asher never overlooked either. "Do you know the person?" he asked.

"No." She rubbed her hands down the front of her dress. "And he didn't give a name."

"Did he talk to you?"

She nodded.

"What did he want?"

She hesitated. Then she said tightly, "I think to scare me."

Asher inhaled and exhaled sharply, feeling his muscles quiver beneath his flesh. "A friend of Damon?" he guessed.

"I think so, he came by asking for him," she said with a small shrug. "I'm sure he's gone—"

"We still need to check him out." Asher helped her back into the client chair before shutting his door. He got looks from his fellow cops and Hank, the chief of police. Both Boone and Kinsley shared their father's blue eyes. He was slightly shorter than Boone, but definitely held a strong presence and an air of authority, and also thought of Remy as a daughter. Most of his fellow cops knew about Asher and Remy's past. Many of them would ask him questions later, no doubt, as would Hank.

Asher moved behind his desk and told her, "A month ago or so, Boone installed cameras across the street to extend to Peyton's store for security." Kinsley's bar had cameras on both the front and back doors. Some would call them paranoid. He called them smart.

He logged into his computer and then into the security cameras that he helped Boone install. He played through the video from the time he left the store, and he saw the big guy in the fancy suit. He turned the screen. "This him?"

She squinted at the monitor. "Yeah, that's him."

Asher's jaw clenched as he turned the screen back to face him and then fast-forwarded until the guy came back out of the shop and got into a black sports car. He wrote down the plate number on a sticky note, "You don't need to worry about this guy. I'll handle it." He sidled back up to her and offered his hand. "Come on, we've got something to do."

Remy's eyes widened at his outreached hand. "What's that?"

"You asked me to dinner," he reminded her with a grin.

"But—" She rose.

Yeah, he knew a bad excuse when he saw one, but there wasn't a chance in hell he'd let this one slide. "It's just food, Remy," he said, using her words back on her. "No big deal."

She burst out laughing. "Well played, Asher Sullivan, well played." He chuckled and then felt the temperature in the room go up a few degrees as she took a step toward him and went on. "What's the plan, then?"

"You need food before we do anything further. You *still* probably haven't eaten anything and your skin is ghost white."

She touched her cheek. "And then what's the plan?"

He lifted the sticky note. "Finding out who this guy is and what he wants from you."

* * *

A half an hour later, sitting in the passenger seat of Asher's car, Remy turned toward him next to her. "Just so you know, if this is your idea of dinner out, you've become really weird."

He snorted a laugh but didn't comment.

Which seemed to be his motto for the night. He'd spent most of the time after they'd left the police station driving around town. They'd grabbed burgers and fries—Remy's favorites—from the burger stand on the side of Carriage Road. When they finally returned to Main Street, he stopped in front of Stoney Creek's famous and historic B and B while they ate dinner. The Victorian house was the first summer cottage built in 1868 and had remained the most beloved place to stay in town. Remy had gone with the flow so far, but enough was enough. "If you've been expecting me to guess what we're doing, I can tell you it ain't gonna happen."

Asher bit into his burger and gestured out his front windshield. "See that black car over there?"

Remy followed his gaze and found a fancy black sports car sitting right outside the B and B. "Yeah?"

"That's the car of the guy who came into your store today."

She stared at the car, reassessing. "How do you know that?"

"Same make, same license plate," was Asher's muffled reply as he chewed his burger.

The first thing that went through her mind was that the guy was obviously rich. He had to be to own such an expensive ride. The second thing that went through her mind was wildly inappropriate. She lifted her fingers to her mouth, her breath suddenly quickening when she glanced Asher's way. "Are we on a stakeout?" she asked, hearing the slight rasp of her voice.

He swallowed his food and wiggled his eyebrows. "Exciting, isn't it?"

Her nerve endings stirred and tingled. "Maybe a little."

Staring into Asher's eyes, seeing the softness there, her heart melted. She liked that he was including her in all this. The old Asher would never have done so. He'd controlled *everything*. Always did things by the book. Followed all the rules. She liked this new side of him, one where he thought of her as his equal, and didn't make major decisions without her input. With a smile warming her from the inside out, she glanced out her window, lifting her burger off the paper on her lap and then taking a bite. The flavor of the chipotle mayonnaise and grease exploded in her mouth.

Outside her window, the town was busy with tourists enjoying the shopping that Stoney Creek's downtown had to offer. A quick peek out Asher's window showed the Atlantic Ocean was choppy this evening, the fishing boats out on the water rocking above the crushing waves. Burnt-orange and cranberry-red leaves fluttered down from the mature trees that hugged the road. Fall was there, and as it was her favorite season, Remy couldn't have been happier about that. She had a store she loved, and Asher…well, with Asher…things felt good. And that was something.

"What are you hoping we learn from this stakeout?" she asked, turning back to him.

"Just getting a read on this guy and seeing if we can learn why he's in town." Asher tossed the last bit of his burger into his mouth and then wiped his hands on his napkin. He reached for his phone, searching something on the web before putting it to his ear. "Hi, Mrs. Hathaway, this is Detective Asher Sullivan calling. Yes, ma'am, I'm doing fine, thank you. Listen, you've got a man staying there with you. He drives a black sports car…yup, that's the one. I'd ask that you please keep this between us, but can I get his name?" Another pause as Mrs. Hathaway was obviously talking. "No, ma'am, nothing to worry about," Asher said smoothly. "Just keeping an eye on who comes into our town…yes, we know you appreciate that." He winked at Remy. "How about that name, please?" Another pause. "Yup. Great. Got it." He grabbed a pen and notepad from his glovebox, then wrote: *LARS VIOLI*. "Thank you. Yes, take care too." He ended the call, then texted someone before placing his phone back into the center console. "Rhett's looking into Violi for me."

"Great." Remy settled back in her seat and took another bite of her burger, feeling much more rejuvenated with food in her belly. "What do you think he'll find out?"

"Anything and everything that may or may not concern us." Asher took a long drink of his soda and shrugged. "It's very likely that this guy is just here looking around for Damon. Maybe he thinks something has happened to him."

"I told him that Damon's in jail."

At that, Asher hesitated and arched an eyebrow. He finally returned his pop to the cup holder. "That's good, but then it begs the question, why hasn't he left?"

"Hmmm…that is a good question," she replied with a long sigh, not having considered that.

Silence filled the car while Asher dug away at his french fries. When he neared the end, he asked, "When do you think you'll stop doing your best to avoid being alone with me?"

Damn him. Remy suffered an uncontrolled moment of heat and then gave a self-deprecating laugh. "I wasn't…" She paused at his knowing look. "Okay, maybe I've been trying my best to make sure we're always with others. It's just safer that way."

Asher considered that, finishing off chewing the handful of fries he'd eaten, and then he chuckled, shaking his head. "I went four years without you even acknowledging I was back in town." He side-eyed her. "But just because I can endure the distance doesn't mean I like it. I thought we were giving being friends a chance?"

"I'm sorry," she said, shifting against her seat, feeling like a world-class asshole. "It's just my go-to self-defensive move."

"Never used to be," he countered, grabbing a napkin from the bag and wiping his face. Then he turned his head and stared at her intently. "You don't need to run and hide. I'm not going to trap you and demand that you be mine."

Her heart tripped at the way he said *mine*. Her body shivered at the look in his eye.

The side of his mouth curved. "I told you already, I'm here for you. That's all that's going on here. I think we both know that a real relationship isn't in the cards for us. But *friends* with benefits…"

Her muscles went weak and she gave a long exhale. "And you're honestly okay with us just…friends with benefits?"

He grinned. "I'm okay with whatever you feel comfortable with." He leaned across the armrest, bringing his mouth close to hers. Suddenly, she was hyperaware of his every move, every little masculine thing about him. "I just want you, Remy, however I can have you."

God, he was sweet and hot. So damn hot….and those lips, they drew her forward without thought. Heat enveloped her, her nerve endings lighting up like Christmas morning, and right as she began leaning into him, his cell phone rang.

"Never fails." He snorted, reaching for his phone in the console.

Remy grabbed her soda and took three big gulps. She had no

willpower. None. She might consider it pathetic, if she didn't really, *really* want to kiss him again. She wasn't exactly sure what that said about her, but she discovered she didn't care either. So much pain. So much heartbreak. They had their boundaries. They knew the rules. No hearts on the line. Wasn't it time for her to take all the good she could get out of life, including having the best mindboggling sex?

Asher answered on the second ring and put the phone on speaker. "You're on speaker. Remy's here," he said, keeping those smoldering eyes on her. "What did you find out?"

"This guy is bad news," Rhett reported. "He's from Los Angeles and is connected to some organized crime in Whitby Falls. He's got a rap sheet a mile long." Rhett hesitated, then clearly chose his words carefully. "He's got violence in his past that concerns me."

Remy's chest tightened. She was seriously debating running to hide back under her blanket.

Asher's warm, strong hand slid across her thigh. "It's gonna be all right," he said to her.

She opened her eyes, not realizing she'd shut them, and nodded, wanting to believe him. Yet she felt tense, everything moving unbelievably fast.

"Are there any ties to Fanning?" Asher asked.

It suddenly occurred to Remy that unless Asher was talking with her, he didn't call Damon...well, Damon...and she guessed that made sense since it wasn't his name. Still, she couldn't bring herself to call the guy that she'd almost married anything but the name she knew him by.

"No ties that I can see after a quick look," Rhett answered Asher's question. "But it's going to take some time and some phone calls. I need to look into this more."

"Can't thank you enough," Asher said.

"It's not a problem." Rhett gave a long pause, then rare emotion filled his voice. "Are you all right, Remy?"

Rhett wasn't an emotional kind of guy, but every so often, he'd show his heart. No matter what, she could never forget how lucky she was to have the friends she did. "A little freaked out about it all, but I'm okay," she told him.

"Understandable," Rhett said. "Hang in there. We'll get this sorted out soon enough." Static came through the phone line as Rhett was obviously shifting through papers or something. "Asher, how much do you want me to dig here?"

Something changed in Asher's expression then. His gaze became alert. "Dig as deep as you can. No mistakes. No taking chances."

And in all that, she heard what he wasn't saying. *Protect Remy.*

"Listen, gotta go. Call if you learn more," Asher said, hitting end on the call. He turned on his car, his back straightening, looking alert.

"Well, that was rude," Remy stated. "Do you always hang up on people like that?"

Asher's mouth twitched and he gestured out the window. "The man of the hour has arrived."

By the time she looked out the window, Asher was already inching his car onto the road, following behind Lars.

# Chapter 10

Dusk had arrived and Asher drove a safe distance behind Lars to remain undetected. They'd driven along the coastline heading into Whitby Falls, the larger growing city where business was booming. Commercial office buildings lined the Main Street that was such a stunning contrast to the small village in Stoney Creek.

Driving down First Street, Asher remained four cars back, and when Lars pulled into a parking spot in front of a restaurant, Asher pulled into the next spot he saw. He cut the ignition and he ground his teeth when Lars entered the restaurant beneath the Antonio's sign. He'd never eaten at the restaurant himself, but the name registered as familiar.

"What?" Remy asked.

A slight chill ran up his spine. Not wanting to scare her before he understood the full situation, he shook his head at her and then reached for his cell phone in the cup holder. He hit call and the phone rang twice. "Hey, it's Asher. Remy's in the car with me."

"Hey to you both," Boone said. "What's up?"

Asher knew the response he was going to get, and he spotted the widening of Remy's eyes as he said, "That organized crime case you worked last year, where again was their meetup?"

"Antonio's in Whitby Falls," Boone said.

*Shit.* "All right," Asher said beneath his breath, locking down his expression to show no emotion. "Thanks Boone. We gotta go."

A pause. "Should I be concerned here?"

"I'll let you know if there's anything to worry about." Asher ended the call, not wanting to get into this with Remy sitting next to him. When she told him about the guy in her shop, he knew she'd been afraid. He was beginning to understand why. Damon had friends in dark, underground places where people didn't settle fights with fists, they settled them with gunshots. "Come on," he finally said to Remy, grabbing hold of the door handle. "Let's go see who he's with." He opened his door and got out, finding Remy slowly following him, giving him an *are you kidding me* look.

"I don't know what you've been smoking today," she said when he walked around the hood of his car. "But I am *not* going in that restaurant."

"I'm not asking you to." He took her hand, and a deep part of himself warmed when she didn't pull away. She was slowly beginning to trust him again. That was a start, and that meant he was doing right by her.

The restaurant appeared to be a long rectangular space. It had a fancy wood sign with light spilling out of the glass windows. Asher weaved his way through the people on the sidewalk and then stopped near the entrance. He put his back to the front window and brought Remy close to him, liking the way she gasped in surprise.

Her hands pressed against his chest and her heated eyes came to his, her tongue darting out over her lips. All the heat that had been contained for two weeks suddenly spilled out between them. Asher knew why. Remy hadn't let him touch her, always staying at a careful distance. Now there was only the lasting imprint of how he knew her body and how he could make her feel.

Damn. He wanted to take her up on that invitation, and it took everything inside of him not to claim her mouth right then and there. He slid his hand over her back, bringing her just a bit closer against the hardest part of him. Her cheeks flushed, and her eyes held his firmly. "Look in the restaurant and see if you see him."

She blinked, all the heat fading quickly. "Right. We're on assignment."

He chuckled softly, and yet, her sweet body against his made him grow even harder. She moved her head a little, staring into the restaurant, and he became lost in her. She felt perfect there in his arms, close and safe to him. Part of him wished this would be enough for her. That they could spend time together like they had been and keep things light. Life finally felt good again, like things were turning around for the better. The other part of him knew Remy. She loved love. She wanted the ring, the house, and the marriage. Asher knew what all those things did to love. He couldn't follow in his parents' footsteps. He couldn't hurt her. "Do you see him in there?" he asked, getting his head back into the game.

She shook her head. "He's not in the front anywhere, but I can't see the back very well."

"Then let's get a better look." He took her hand again, then led her down the narrow alleyway off to the side of the entrance.

When they reached the back of the building, he noticed a window there. He tugged her into him. She gasped, her hooded eyes connecting with his as her warm breasts pressed against him. Hot and hard, and just as ready, he grasped her hips and lifted her slightly. "How about now?" He heard the huskiness in his own voice.

She gripped the edge of the window. "Oh, wait," she said, a little breathless. "Yeah, I see him. He's sitting at the table in the center of the room."

Asher slowly lowered her down and reached for his cell phone in his pocket. He took a step forward, pressing her tighter against the wall, and he bit back a groan when his cock brushed against her bottom. Cautious and careful, he took five photos quickly and then made sure they were clear. "We need to find out who these other guys are."

She turned to face him, and she became so close he could feel the heat emanating off her. "Yes."

Asher kept her pinned between him and the wall and he opened a text to Boone: When you get a chance, need to know who these guys are sitting around the guy in the white shirt. His name is Lars Violi.

Boone's reply came a second later. Gonna tell me what this is all about?

Tomorrow.

I'll get what you need.

Asher returned his phone to his pocket, and when he looked back up, he met the heat swirling in the depths of Remy's eyes. He pressed his hands on either side of her head against the brick wall, pressing himself into her lithe body. Maybe he should step away, stop this in its tracks, but there was no turning back now, not when she looked at him like she'd been starved of him. Years ago, he'd made all the decisions, and that ruined her. All of this, every single thing now, was on her terms. "We don't have to do this again, if you don't want," he reminded her, gently giving her an out.

"Yeah, well, I want to," she breathed, grabbing hold of his T-shirt beneath his leather jacket.

He dropped his mouth close to hers and placed his leg between hers, teasing her with what he could deliver. "You want me?" he asked, feathering his lips across hers.

"Yes," she rasped, reaching for more.

"Right here, Remy?" he asked, feeding gas to an already lit fire. She always loved adventure, and that adrenaline always turned into hot arousal, and apparently, that hadn't changed.

She lifted her chin to expose her neck. "Please."

Asher nibbled his way over to her neck, reveling in the hitch of her breath. And when she parted her legs, he listened. He reached beneath her dress and licked up from the base of her neck to her ear, feeling her quiver. When he found the edge of her panties, he tucked his fingers inside. "Right here, Remy, this is where you want me?"

"Yes!" She moaned, her head falling back against the brick wall while he openmouthed kissed his way back to the base of her neck.

He groaned when his fingers met her soaking wet sex. She breathed deeply as he stroked her clit, feeling her legs tremble, the desire pouring off her in waves. Desperate to get closer, he threaded his other hand into her hair, pinning her to him, right where he wanted her. Each second he worked her body made her moan a little more, a little louder, until those soft trembles were growing harder.

"Asher," she breathed.

He fisted his hand in her hair, controlling her pleasure. When she gave him a throaty moan for more, he slid his fingers inside her. One first. Then another a moment later. She gripped his T-shirt, pulling him closer, clawing at him for *more*.

Needing to taste her, he brought his mouth to hers, devouring every sweet moan she offered. She could barely kiss him with every stroke of his fingers, and by the time he was thrusting hard and fast, all she did was moan. Her head fell back against the wall and he leaned away to watch her fall apart.

A couple moments later, she did.

Her eyes were pinched shut and she shattered into pleasure, breaking apart around him, a quivering beautiful mess he'd never grow tired of watching.

"Holy shit," she exhaled when her climax released her.

He chuckled, kissing her lips gently as he slowly withdrew his fingers from her quivering muscles.

Asher went to fix her panties when the back door opened, and a teenage kid with a garbage bag came walking out. He took one look at them and yelled, "Hey, get a goddamn room!"

Asher grabbed Remy's hand and took off jogging back to his car. By the time they got back, she was laughing. That laugh, free and inhibited, slayed him. That was *his Remy*.

\* \* \*

They made it back to Remy's loft in good time. Asher had insisted on walking Remy up to her door and then came inside to check the place out while she waited. He'd gone into every room, turning on all the lights and having a look before coming back out. Admittedly, Asher was a beat cop when she'd been with him. Now Asher looked precise, skilled, and lethal. A combination that was doing all sorts of wild things between her thighs. But maybe that was because he'd proven many times now how easily he could make her body explode.

When he began checking the locks on her windows, she asked with a laugh, "What exactly are you looking for?"

"This is for my own peace of mind," he said.

"Do you honestly think someone is coming after me?"

"I don't know anything about this guy, so I can't answer that," Asher said. "It never hurt anyone to be extra cautious." His gaze swept back to her. "You can stay with me tonight."

She leaned against her door, shaking her head. "I'm good." She wasn't being difficult or playing hard to get; she couldn't lean on him any more than she already had. The last thing she wanted was to fall hard and fast...*again*, then be tossed aside...*again* because he had major commitment issues. At some point the cycle had to stop, and that point had come. She controlled when and where and everything in between, and that felt good. Mind-blowingly good, in fact. "I just wish we knew why Lars was here in the first place, you know?"

"He might be here for other business." Asher climbed the stairs for the loft, then vanished, obviously checking the windows upstairs. "But I won't know more until tomorrow when I get into the station and see what the guys found out." He came down the stairs and moved into the living room to begin checking the locks there.

"Do you really think he's got some involvement in organized crime?" Remy asked, seriously hoping that was *not* the case.

Asher shrugged. "Don't know."

"Do you think he's a friend of Damon's?"

"Don't know that either."

Remy exhaled heavily, wishing she had all the answers. "But we know he's not leaving?"

Asher glanced back over his shoulder. "Not tonight, it appears." He opened the door to the balcony, having a look around before coming back inside and locking the door again. "But I still suspect that he's a friend of Damon's and just sniffing around to ensure Damon is where we said he is."

"And that's it?"

"That's it." Asher moved into the kitchen and began checking the windows there. "Tomorrow I'll know more and can hopefully give you some answers." He finished up with the final lock and then stepped back. "All right, you're good."

She smiled. "So, it's safe for me to sleep in my own house?"

He glanced over his shoulder, his eyes suddenly dark with desire. "How do you know I'm not making sure that you can't get out and you're stuck with me?"

Heat flooded through her, causing goose bumps to prickle across her flesh. She'd given up on fighting the intensity burning between them in the alleyway. That touch, that body, once it all got close, she couldn't help herself. All she needed to do was keep her head on straight and make sure her heart wasn't on the table. Besides, her heart was currently too beaten down to even be at risk. She'd always done the right thing. Been the good girl and wanted forever. Now she wasn't thinking of Mr. Forever. She wanted Mr. Right Now, and Asher fit into that category at the moment. "Oh, locking me in, huh? Should I be scared?" she asked, hearing the answering need in her own voice.

Asher's mouth quirked and he approached in his slow easy stride, his gaze taking his fill of her. When he stopped in front of her the air thickened. "Scared..." He tucked a finger under her chin, lifting her mouth. "Never be scared of me, Remy." Then he began to slowly bring those kissable lips closer to his.

She backed away and placed a finger on his lips. "No kisses goodbye."

Asher arched an eyebrow. "I *just* kissed the hell out of you an hour ago."

"But those were sex kisses, not goodbye kisses," she pointed out. There had to be boundaries there or she couldn't do this with Asher, and she *really* wanted to do *this* with Asher. "What we're doing here is casual, remember? No dates. No romantic stuff. Just fun, because all this feels good right now." Because without boundaries, there was too much emotion, and emotion was a dangerous thing when it came to Asher Sullivan. No matter how much growing Asher had done over the years, she couldn't forget what happened. He'd left her completely shattered and never came back, never called, never checked in on her, when her life totally fell apart. "We need to rewrite our story and I need to learn how to trust you again. We sucked at love, so let's keep doing the exact opposite. So, no kisses good-bye, no cuddling, nothing like that."

She didn't want to ever again be the woman he left behind. Now she controlled when and what they did. That had to be a better way than how she'd been living. And somehow, a part of her thought that if she could heal her heart from what Asher did and truly forgive him, maybe she'd move on with her life and make better choices.

"All right," he finally said after a long moment. "I can deal with that."

"Excellent." She strode forward toward the door, feeling like for once she was running her life. Saying it like it was. Demanding what she wanted. Hell, yeah, that felt good. When she met the door, she asked, "Will you call and fill me on whatever you learn?"

"That's up to you," he said. "Do you want me to?"

She didn't even have to think about it. "I want to know everything that's going on and why he's here. Don't protect me, Asher. Keep me involved in this every step of the way." Hell yes, she was totally nailing getting back on her feet.

"I can do that." He uncrossed his arms to grab his keys from his pockets and began walking toward her. "The most important thing right now is that you're safe. If you feel uneasy about anything, you'll tell me, right?"

"Of course." She watched him for a moment, seeing that maybe she wasn't the only one changing. The Asher she knew before wouldn't have let her get anywhere near any of this. He'd want her safe. He'd get the guy out of town in any way possible. It occurred to her now that he had this new confidence about him that she'd never seen before. And it almost felt like he was there to support her instead of taking charge of everything, making all the decisions. And after he made the decision to leave that ultimately broke her heart, this was a nice change.

For the first time ever, she realized that being apart let them both grow into better versions of themselves. She didn't give too much. He didn't take too much either.

His gaze finally lifted to hers again. "I'll see you tomorrow at the grand opening, then?"

She nodded. "You will." When he took a step out the door, her heart suddenly pounded. "Asher?" she called.

He turned back. "You've changed your mind and you want to come back to my house?"

She laughed softly and shook her head. "Thank you. You know, for keeping me safe, for being there for me…for everything."

Something dark and haunted crossed his expression. "I should have always been here for you like this. Sleep tight, Remy."

Unsure how to answer that, she stayed silent, smiled at him, and then locked the door and hurried into her kitchen. Asher had his way of protecting her. She had hers. Remy grabbed Nana's book of spells out of the old antique cabinet and she flipped through the pages until she found what she was looking for: PROTECTION BREW. The ingredients were written in Nana's handwriting. Rue, rosemary, vetivert, and hyssop sprig of mistletoe.

Right as she began adding the ingredients into the big cast-iron pot she always kept on the stove, Salem sauntered in and meowed. "Oh, don't give me that attitude," Remy said, waving the wooden spoon at him. "I'm sorry for waking you up, but we've got a spell to make."

Salem blinked, then meowed again, sitting at her feet.

By the time she was done with the brew, he looked further annoyed. She used a ladle to scoop out the brew into a small bowl, and then Salem began to follow her as she went exactly where Asher had traveled. She anointed every window and door in her loft, finishing up with the four corners to prevent negative energy to enter.

"There," she said, turning back to Salem.

If a cat could have rolled his eyes, she was sure he would have done so. He flicked his tail and sauntered back upstairs to the bedroom.

"You'll be thanking me when no one breaks in," she called to Salem.

He didn't look back.

# Chapter 11

Bright and early the next morning, Asher's eyes felt heavy after he hit the alarm and dragged himself out of bed. He was weighed down with concerns for Remy. He wasn't sure how much sleep he got through all the tossing and turning he did last night, but it definitely wasn't much. He had wanted her with him, wanted her close. Christ, he wanted her in his arms, where he knew no one could touch her. But that was pure testosterone talking, and he refused to take a wrong step, especially since she was finally stepping toward him again.

When he arrived at the station carrying a bag of food and a tray of coffees, he found the place quiet. The receptionist didn't come in until eight o'clock; as for the beat cops, the shift change would have happened at seven in the morning, sending them out onto the road. Any special units or investigators didn't typically start their shift until nine o'clock. The dispatcher was the only one sitting in the back of the station, set up at her desk in the corner, and the only sound that carried through the station was the clicking of her fingers against the keyboard. "Morning, Gianna."

The feisty sixty-year-old lady with the short brown hair and olive-colored skin turned around in her swivel chair. She smiled at the coffee cups. "Please tell me one of those is for me."

"You know I'd never forget you." Asher handed her the coffee with one cream, just how she liked it.

Gianna grinned. "I've taught you well, my boy."

Asher smiled. Gianna had been a close friend of his mother's when she'd been alive. He supposed that after her death, Gianna had stepped in to make sure he always had a birthday card, or congratulate him on an achievement, and she always invited him for Christmas dinner, even though Asher went to Boone's every Christmas. "Busy night?" he asked, noticing the dark circles under her eyes. Night shifts were hard. No way around that.

"A couple domestics and an accident," Gianna said, taking off the lid of her coffee cup. "Nothing serious."

"Glad to hear it," Asher said.

"How's—" The telephone on her desk rang and she smiled softly. "Let's catch up when we can." She gave him a wave and then answered the phone.

Asher turned away, fighting against the tightness in his chest. While he appreciated Gianna, seeing her was hard. Years had gone by since Mom died, but it felt like she'd passed away yesterday. His world never quite looked the same without her there. He missed how she'd light up and hug him whenever she saw him. He missed the smell of her cooking. He missed the way that, no matter what happened, she'd always made him feel like everything was going to be fine.

Until, it wasn't fine at all.

Through the glass windows, he found Rhett and Boone already waiting for him in the command center. Rhett noticed his arrival first. He looked at Asher's hand and then said, deadly serious, "Breakfast burritos. You're either buttering us up or want forgiveness."

Asher snorted a laugh. "Neither. Call it being grateful." When Asher woke up bright and early this morning, he knew he needed more than coffees to get Boone and Rhett into work at seven thirty. "Thanks for coming. I know it's early."

Boone grabbed a burrito out of the bag, then handed the bag to Asher. "I'm guessing this has something to do with Remy."

Asher took his burrito out before handing the bag off to Rhett. "The guy I had you look into for me, Lars Violi, came into Remy's shop and scared her."

Boone froze, halfway to taking a bite of his burrito. "This Violi doesn't have any connection to the phone call you made last night about Antonio's?"

"Yeah, he does," Asher said.

Boone set his burrito down, his brow furrowing. "How did Violi scare Remy?"

"Just came in asking about Damon and where he was, but she was shaken," Asher explained, then took a sip of his coffee. "What did you get from the photograph I sent last night?"

"What photograph?" Rhett asked with a full mouth.

Asher grabbed his phone from his back pocket and brought up the picture. "Remy and I followed Violi when he left the B and B where he's staying." Both men went brows up. Asher snorted and went on. "Kill the lecture you're about to give me. Remy wants to be involved. Until it's not safe for her to be, I'm letting her."

Rhett whistled.

Boone's mouth twitched.

Yeah, Asher had gone totally soft. He already knew that. "The photograph," he repeated, staying on task.

Boone finally reached for his burrito again, and said, "The other two guys in the picture you sent me are big players in some underground crime. Money laundering. Dirty business."

Asher finished off his bite and then dropped the burrito to reach for his napkin. "I don't want this prick anywhere near her. We need to find out the connection here. Anything that can help us ensure we get this guy moving on from here and back to where he came from."

Boone watched Asher a moment, then nodded. "I couldn't agree more. What do we know about Violi?"

"I've dug around," Rhett said, reaching into his backpack and pulling out a file. "I found out some interesting things about him last night." He handed the file to Asher. "He's got a rap sheet a mile long, connections to people you don't want on your bad side, all matched with a terrible attitude."

Asher opened the file and stared down at Violi's cold, dead eyes in his mug shot. Rhett wasn't wrong. Aggravated assault, harassment, the list went on and on. And the more Asher read, the more he wanted this guy far away from Remy. Dammit. He should have demanded she stayed with him last night. He reached for his cell phone, then texted Remy: Rise and shine.

A second later, she texted back: I'm rising but I'm not shining.

Asher smiled. Hope the grand opening at the shop today goes well.

She sent him a kiss emoji. Now he was really smiling as he tucked his phone back into his pocket, and he became aware of the silence around him.

Boone was hiding his laughter with a cough.

Rhett was outright grinning.

"Shut up," Asher told them both and then tapped his finger against the file folder. "We need to find out why this guy is here."

Boone finally stopped smiling and reached for his coffee cup. Before taking a sip, he asked, "How do you want to proceed from here?"

That was precisely the problem. Asher didn't know. "Get some eyes on him. He's staying at the B and B. I want to know when he leaves and what he's doing. There's gotta be a reason he's come to town. If he's partnered with Fanning, the last thing he'd want to do is draw attention to himself after Fanning's arrest."

Boone and Rhett nodded agreement.

Asher ran his hands over his tired eyes. "There's gotta be something we're missing about him. We need to find out what that is, and what the hell he wants."

"You're all in early."

Asher glanced over his shoulder, finding Hank. "I called them in," Asher explained. "We've got a situation."

At that, Hank's head cocked. "Anything to worry about?"

Boone explained, "Remy's got a visitor we don't want her to have."

"Oh," Hank said, moving in to sit at the head of the table. "Tell me everything."

It came as no surprise that Hank would want every single detail. Remy was like a second daughter to him, growing up right alongside Kinsley. Asher recounted what had happened and left out no detail of what had unfolded so far.

When Asher finished, Hank rubbed his jaw and said, "It's odd that Fanning would be connected to anyone in the dark underbelly of Whitby Falls."

Boone agreed with a firm nod, then turned to Asher. "After you sent that picture, I had a look to see if there was any connection between Fanning and that group, but I couldn't find anything."

"And," Rhett added, "Fanning scammed money off women. I couldn't find anything in Violi's record showing a mutual affection for that particular crime."

"Another mystery then," Hank said, rising to push his chair back under the table.

"A mystery we don't want Remy involved in," Asher said, now rubbing at the building tension across his neck. "If it's all right, boss, I'd like to take a few days to sort this out. I'll take some vacation time."

"Nah, it's all right," Hank said, moving toward the door. He stopped in the doorway, then looked back at Asher. "Clean this up for Remy. See that all this shit gets put behind her." To Boone and Rhett, he said, "I've got a new case. Come to my office when you're done here."

Boone nodded at his father, then waited until Hank left the room before tossing the last bit of burrito into his mouth. "You need to watch your step with these guys," he told Asher firmly. "They're well connected and dangerous. If you need us, bring us in on this."

"Yes. Please." Rhett grinned, his gaze all but twinkling. "Please bring us in on this."

Asher chuckled, leaning back in his chair and stretching his arms. "If I have my way, Violi will see Fanning in jail, then he'll leave, and that will be the end of this."

Rhett arched an eyebrow. "And if that doesn't happen?"

"Then I'll tell him to leave," Asher stated.

Boone snorted. "You'll ask him nicely."

Asher grabbed the file to take back to his office to learn as much as he could about Lars Violi. "Now *that* I can't promise."

Boone gave him a level look. "Don't do anything stupid."

"Yeah, like piss off mobsters because you're trying to right a wrong from your past," Rhett offered.

Asher frowned and rose. "When have I ever done anything stupid?"

"When we went joyriding when we were thirteen," Boone said.

Rhett nodded and added, "When you thought building that skateboarding ramp was a good idea and broke your arm."

"Ah, yeah, good one." Boone barked a laugh. "How about when you were sure the lake was frozen enough to handle the snow mobile and lost it in the water."

Asher flipped them the bird and grinned before heading to his office, hearing them laughing behind him, calling out more stupid shit he'd done as a kid. They weren't wrong—he was reckless and foolish as a teenager.

But he wasn't that kid anymore.

* * *

Lemon incense infused the air as Remy rang up another customer. Two hours she'd been open, and the store hadn't slowed down yet. Most of the people Remy recognized, the townsfolk coming out to support her. Customers were standing around the small table that had cookies and a large thermos of hot apple cider, grand opening gifts from the owners of the bakery down the street. All of the shelves were being restocked by Kinsley and Peyton, who'd pitched in to help today. Asher had stopped in and then had to run to Remy's loft to grab more of the healing oil. Sales were off the charts, and at this point, Remy hoped she could keep up with demand.

She stared out at *her* shop, her heart in her throat. So many bad decisions along the way that lead Remy to a place in her life when she thought her dreams would never come true, and now they had. Though she couldn't stop the slight pain in her heart that when she used to dream of this moment as a teenager, she thought she and Asher would be married with a couple of kids. She always knew Asher would have been an amazing father, even if he obviously feared fatherhood because of his own dad. But as she looked around at Kinsley and Peyton, and having Asher back in her life now—just in a different way—she realized how lucky she was. No matter how much life wanted to sink her, she kept treading the water and somehow made it out alive.

*I did it.*

A loud meow caught Remy's attention. She glanced down, finding Salem sitting on the counter looking proud and handsome as always. "I know, it's fun, isn't it?" Remy asked him, not surprised when he meowed back in answer. Which had been his answer when she tried to leave him at home this morning. Maybe she was nervous and he felt that. Or maybe he knew the store was Remy's life now. Salem always squeezed himself into her life from the very first day he showed up at her doorstep as a sick kitten needing help.

The bell above the door chimed when another customer left. Remy gave Salem a final pat, then moved around the counter and sidled up to Peyton and Kinsley near the bookshelves. "I can't believe how busy it's been."

Kinsley tucked her arm through Remy's. Peyton did the same on the other arm and said, "It's because this shop came from a really good place. Your grandmother's love and all her knowledge is wrapped up in this entire store."

Kinsley nodded. "People will gravitate to that."

"Nana would be so proud of this little shop," Remy said,

emotion creeping up in her throat. "All her spells being put to use to actually help people. I'm seriously still pinching myself this has finally happened." Her dream happened. Her life was finally looking up. Life was actually giving her the break she'd always wanted. Gratefulness touched every part of her soul right down to the tips of her toes.

"Remy." Betty-Anne, the dental hygienist who cleaned Remy's teeth every six months, called her over with a wave. "Will this oil really help me with luck?"

Remy nodded. "If you gamble or bet, most definitely."

"Oh, I'm so getting this, then," Betty-Anne said, eyes twinkling. "I can't wait to beat everyone at bingo."

Remy laughed.

"I'll ring you out, Betty-Anne," Peyton said, moving toward the counter.

Another lady stood on her tiptoes, attempting to reach a glass jar on one of the bookshelves. "Oh, be careful there, I can help with that," Kinsley called. "Let me grab a stool."

Remy stood in the center of the shop and exhaled deeply. Life had dealt a couple hard blows over the years. Sure, she had a mom who wasn't around much and a father who never acknowledged her existence, but she had Asher, Kinsley, Peyton, the guys, and Salem. What else did a girl need but that? And now her grandmother's spells could heal, could inspire, and could bring happiness. Maybe the hard road was worth it because it all led her here to *this* moment, where she felt stronger than she had in a long time.

The front door opened again, and time seemed to slow. Her heart rate spiked, nearly exploding from her chest when Lars stepped into her store. All the happiness that had floated through her a minute ago suddenly vanished when she caught his gaze and he gave a smile that held no warmth. He approached her with his back ramrod straight. For one split second, darkness nearly flickered, giving the reminder that nothing in Remy's life could simply be happy, but she shoved that thought aside.

Today was her day. Nothing would ruin that.

"Hi," she said, forcing her voice not to shake. "Welcome to Black Cat's Cauldron's grand opening. Is there anything I can help you find?" She suddenly wondered if he'd seen her and Asher last night following him. "We've got great salves for sore muscles from the gym. Would that be of interest to you?" The guy was all muscle. Scary big muscles.

"Nah, I've got no interest in that." He shoved his hands into the pockets of his black tailored suit. "I'll tell you what does interest me, though: this shop."

Her stomach tightened like a rock when she processed what he'd said. "What about it?"

"I inquired over the property," he said.

She clenched her hands to not let him see her shaking. "Okay, well, it's mine now. So...sorry that you lost the chance to buy it."

A crooked smile tugged on his lips.

The air shifted around her, the iciness of the danger filling the space between them. She glanced around, finding no one near her, though Peyton was staring *hard* at this exchange while she checked Betty-Anne out, then Remy moved closer. "Listen, I told you before, I have nothing to do with Damon. He tried to swindle my inheritance. Now he's in prison. That's all. Like I said, I have nothing to do with him."

Lars dropped his eye level to hers. "That is still left to be seen."

Remy's heart promptly landed in her throat and her insides felt like they were quivering. Before she could even find the words to answer him, another voice said, "We haven't met."

Remy slowly turned, hearing the absolute control in Asher's voice. She realized he must have come through the back door, and she found his expression blank. He slung his arm around her, tugging her back to him, stealing the fear that crept up.

He offered his hand to Lars, like he had no idea who he was. "Detective Asher Sullivan."

As cool and collected as Asher, Lars shook his hand. "Lars Violi." His gaze swept over Asher's protective arm around Remy before settling on Asher again.

"Thank you for coming out today to support the grand opening," Asher said. "Do you need any help finding anything?"

Lars's gaze flicked to Remy. "Nah, I've found everything that I've needed." He smiled at Asher, all teeth and coldness. "Enjoy the rest of your day, Detective." To Remy, he dipped his chin a little. "I've got no doubt I'll see you again."

"I would advise against that," Asher warned.

Lars's gaze cut back to Asher. "I'm sure you would." He left as calmly through the front door as he'd walked in.

"Who was *that*?" Peyton said behind Remy.

"Trouble," Asher said, then ran his hands down Remy's arms as if he knew she was chilled to her bones. "What did he say to you?" he asked gently.

Her mind felt scattered, lost of all things but the honest fear raging through her veins. "He said he had inquired about my shop."

"To buy it, you mean?" Asher asked.

Remy shrugged. "It kind of sounded like that."

"Well, whatever it is, I don't like it," Peyton said. "That guy gave me the total creeps."

"You and me both," Remy agreed. She turned to Asher. "You still can't find out a connection to him and Damon?"

Asher exhaled a long breath before responding. "Not yet." He must have seen her worry, because he tugged her into his embrace, and she went willingly, needing his warmth. "But that doesn't mean we can't find out why he's here and what in the hell he wants." He stared down at her, tucking her hair behind her ear. "He won't get close again. I promise you that."

"Remy," Kinsley called, standing on the other side of the store. "Can we get some help over here?"

"Yes. Yes, of course," Remy said. She stepped out of Asher's arms and asked, "Do you think I should start worrying now?"

Asher hesitated, then offered, "I'm going to get a cruiser to sit outside your place, just to keep an eye on things, until we know what we're facing. All right?"

Of course that only told her that *yes*, she totally had something to worry about. Not a very settling thought.

It took everything inside of her to fully step away, not really wanting to create distance between her and his strength. There was no denying that she'd always felt better in his arms than out of them. And Lars was scary. Really scary.

Her emotions must have showed, since Asher squeezed her hand. "You're going to be okay."

She drew in a long breath and put on a brave face, then turned to face him. "I know. I've got you watching my back, how could anything go wrong?"

The quick flash of surprise and honest warmth in Asher's expression made the chill from Lars quickly vanish. Remy smiled at him, then strode toward Kinsley and the customer waiting, trying so desperately not to allow Lars to ruin the best day of her life.

# Chapter 12

Later that night, Asher pulled his Camaro into the parking spot next to Remy's Honda Civic. He grabbed the brown paper bag holding Thai takeout—Remy's favorite—off the passenger seat and then got out of his car. Next to Remy's car, he found the patrol car resting with the rookie Ian sitting in the driver's seat. Hank had been on board with giving her protective detail after he learned of Violi's second visit to the shop, as Asher knew he would. "Hey," Asher said, sidling up to the window. "Things been quiet?"

"Crickets," Ian said, giving his scruffy beard a scratch. "I've got the next couple hours, then Fitz will be taking over."

"Good job." Asher patted the top of the cruiser. "Keep alert."

"Always." Ian nodded.

Confident that his fellow cops were going to make sure no one got through Remy's door, Asher strode off, spice emanating from the bag he carried. After Violi visited Remy's shop, Asher installed a motion video camera near the counter. If anyone broke into her store, Asher would know about it. Besides, Boone had video cameras watching Kinsley's bar and Peyton's lingerie shop, which extended to Remy's shop. No one was getting anywhere near the front door. That's why Asher put the protective detail in the back. When he reached the metal steps at the back of Remy's shop, he trotted up and knocked on the door of her loft.

It opened a second later to a breathless Remy. "Get in quick."

"What's wrong?" He stormed inside, shutting the door behind him and locking it.

"It's my herbs." She was already hurrying through her living room. She was up the stairs and vanished a moment later.

Asher shook his head and followed her. When he got into her bedroom, he found the balcony door open and he headed outside, finding she'd pulled down another set of metal stairs on the side of the building and was climbing up. Careful not to kill himself on the ladder, he climbed up, holding the bag of food tight in his arm.

When he made it onto the roof, he found Remy kneeling down in the middle of a long rows of raised garden beds. Strings of Edison bulbs ran from one length of the roof garden to the other, casting a warm glow over it. Behind her there was a small greenhouse. A pergola covered in ivy with a wooden swing underneath sat nearby.

"I had no idea you had this up here," Asher said, slowly approaching, not wanting to interrupt whatever she was working on.

She used a small watering can to water the herb. "That's because I don't let anyone come up here and bring all their weird energy near my herbs."

"My energy is all right, then?"

She glanced up and squinted her eyes at him. "A little tense, but nothing negative. You're good."

He was tense because he was worried for *her*. He lifted up the food bag. "I brought Thai."

"My favorite," she said with a smile, keeping her focus on the herbs. "Thank you. I'm actually starving, I haven't had a chance to eat yet." She gave him a quick smile, and then focused back on the herbs. "My devil's claw is dying and I don't really know why." She stroked the leaves. "Come on, baby, you must flower. I need you more than ever." She added a little more water, then sat back on her knees and sighed. "This is really very bad."

Asher frowned. "That the devil's claw doesn't have a flower?"

"Yes, exactly." Remy nodded like everything should make total sense. "They bloom in October, then die. It hasn't flowered yet."

Sometimes he felt terrible for not understanding her lingo. Other times, he figured looking dumb was better than not understanding. "Care to explain the problem more clearly?"

"Devil's claw is used for protection," she explained. "Keeping away evil spirts, confounding enemies, that kind of thing. My plant is dying, and that tells me I'm in grave danger."

On one hand, he wanted to tell her it was just a plant. On the other hand, with Remy, these herbs meant something. Her belief in these things inspired people, and he'd seen the power of the mind do truly incredible things. That's why people believed in Remy, because she believed in this magic so fiercely. Even now, she talked soothing words to the plant, putting so much love into what she did there. Clearly, she spent hours in her garden. All that love got transplanted to others, and *that's* what Asher found so fascinating about her. She wanted to heal, to make people happier, and they trusted her to do that.

"Come on," he said gently. "Let's get some food in your belly. You're hungry. Your plant can wait."

She stroked the leaves of the plant one last time. "Keep strong, little one." She rose and headed for the swing. Asher followed her.

He sat next to her and handed her the container with pad Thai and chopsticks, then took his out too. After he ate a bite, he asked, "Are you happy with how the grand opening went?"

She pulled her legs up to sit cross-legged, chopsticks in one hand, the takeout container in the other. "More than happy. Truly, it was amazing."

"I thought it went really well too. Everyone seemed very excited about what you'd done there."

She gave a sweet smile. "What *we'd* done there. I didn't work alone to get the shop together. You all helped with that."

Asher returned the smile, supposing that was true. He glanced out at the garden, inhaling the rich aromas infusing the air. "Mom would have loved this garden." His mother had been an avid gardener. Something she'd done with Remy the entire time they were dating. They'd always be out there together at his mother's house, laughing, loving every second of it.

"I dream of her sometimes."

Asher's gaze cut to her. "Of my mother?"

Remy nodded. "Ever since you came home. Maybe that's my subconscious doing that."

"Or maybe it's something more?" he pressed.

She shrugged and took a big bite of her food, obviously not intending on answering.

He followed her lead and ate for a while, but then curiosity got the better of him. "What does my mom say to you in the dreams?"

Remy finished chewing and wiped her face with a napkin. "It's always the same dream. I'm sitting in the hospital with you. You've got your head bowed and you're crying." Probably much like he had been when his mother passed away. "But she suddenly sits up and looks right at me. And she says, *'Don't let him run.'*"

Asher glanced away and stared at his boots pressed against the cement, the only thing keeping him grounded at the moment. His chest was so damn tight he could barely get air in. He forced his voice to work. "That's it?"

"That's it," Remy said, turning her attention back to her meal.

Asher ate three more bites, then suddenly he wondered if maybe it was Remy's subconscious, worried about what might happen again because it happened before. He couldn't let that slide anymore. "Next time, if you see Mom, tell her that I'm not running, all right? Not anymore."

Remy glanced up, wide-eyed. "Okay," she finally said. "I'll do that."

"Thank you." He took another bite of his chicken, savoring the spicy kick on his tongue.

They finished their meal in silence, and only when he stopped chewing did he realize there was music coming from the greenhouse. A slow rock song that he recalled that he'd danced with Remy at prom. With his mother on his mind, and that fact that he had run from himself and Remy for a very long time, he set his empty container down, rose, and offered her his hand. "Dance with me?"

"Seriously?" she asked with a laugh.

"Seriously. Friends can dance, you know." In truth, he expected her to shoot him down. She'd set boundaries, but she glanced at his outreached hand and rose. He tugged her into him, gathering her in his arms. For a minute she was stiff, keeping a distance, but then suddenly she stepped closer, her entire body going soft.

Her head pressed against his chest, and he rested his cheek on the top of her head. Right there, that's where he wanted her. Safe. Happy. "I should have done this with you more often."

"Danced with me?" she asked, keeping her head in place.

"Danced with you," he said, pressing his lips to the top of her head.

\* \* \*

Dancing with Asher on her rooftop garden stayed with her, even an hour and a half later as they arrived at Rhett's house after a call saying the gang was getting together for an impromptu campfire. Asher had never treated her as tenderly as he had as they'd danced. She couldn't help thinking about how much he had changed in the last ten years. Every minute she spent with him, he kept surprising her.

Remy exited Asher's Camaro and followed him down the driveway. Rhett had bought the property from his father when his parents moved to Pennsylvania for work. The house itself wasn't much to look at. A tiny bungalow with only two bedrooms, small kitchen, and living room, but Rhett's mother had made the house warm and cozy, and Rhett hadn't changed the place much since they'd moved. The beauty of this home was its location. Right on the Atlantic Ocean, the house itself sat up on the top of the cliff, while stairs had been built on the side leading down to the cove, with a sandy beach hugging the water.

Remy carefully followed Asher down the steep steps that had lanterns lighting them up, having nearly killed herself while drunk on these stairs many times. Rhett's parties back in high school were legendary. His parents were definitely the coolest of the bunch, and didn't mind the kids partying at their place on the weekends.

Halfway down the stairs, Remy spotted Peyton sitting between Boone's legs near the bright campfire. Kinsley sat next to them, with Rhett sitting on a tree stump across from her.

"You made it," Kinsley said, and jumped up. She hurried over as quickly as she could in the sand and threw her arms around Remy. "How's the plant doing?"

Remy sighed. "Not any better. Got any beer?" Today felt long and exhausting, and a cold beer sounded right up her alley.

"I got 'em here," Boone called, and opened the cooler next to him, taking out two beers.

Asher accepted a bottle, then took his seat next to Rhett. When Remy took her beer, Kinsley snatched her hand, pulling her down next to her to sit on a hollowed-out log. She smiled at Peyton. "Hi."

"Hey." Peyton wiggled her eyebrows. "Kinsley was just telling me that this was what you all did for fun growing up?"

"Hells yeah, it was," Kinsley said. "It's not like we had Merlots club back in the day. You had to make your own fun. We had some killer parties here."

"The only bar we did have was a complete shithole," Rhett said.

Kinsley smiled at him. "Which, of course, now that is not the case."

Rhett inclined his head in agreement, then took a swig of his beer.

The wind suddenly flew by, chilling the air as the water sloshed against the rocky cove on the right. Asher got up and grabbed a blanket from the pile next to Rhett, then draped it over Remy's shoulders. Her heart skipped a little at that. Such a small gesture, but one he'd done so many times before now. He'd always been the guy who seemed observant of what she needed or didn't. Those were the little reasons she fell in love with him. "Thanks." She smiled.

He nodded, then returned to his spot next to Rhett.

She wrapped the blanket around her tight, the crackling fire sending embers high into the sky. Across from her, Asher watched the fire, the golden hue flickering on his face. How different he looked now from the boy who left her. So grown up. So strong. Her heart swelled at all the good memories they had at Rhett's beach parties throughout the years. Her whole teenage years had him in them. For a really long time, she forgot those. It felt good to remember them again.

"I will never forget the last party you had when we were kids," Kinsley said to Rhett, breaking into Remy's thoughts. Kinsley set her gaze on Remy, her smile beaming. "Remember when you kneed Gavin Hoist in the nuts, then attacked him like a rabid kitten?"

"I remember," Asher said with a laugh. "I'm the one that had to peel her off him."

"Gavin deserved his nuts pulverized," Remy announced proudly. "He'd grabbed my boob. He's lucky he didn't get worse."

"You seriously did that?" Peyton asked with absolute shock in her wide eyes. "I never would have thought you were capable. You're just so bubbly and bright."

"Until someone does something they shouldn't," Asher said with a smile. "Then the claws come out."

"Hey, first of all, he's lucky I didn't create a voodoo doll to teach him a lesson." Laughter filled the space around her. To Asher, she said, "And I also remember you knocking out Jake Wilson."

"That's different," Asher grumbled.

"Do explain why that's different?" Kinsley asked.

"He was actually a threat," Asher said firmly.

Rhett nodded, then gestured at Remy. "No shit. We all saw how you looked at him."

"Okay, yes, he was gorgeous," said Remy with a roll of her eyes. "But you're all stupid. Back then, I only saw Asher."

Silence hit the group so hard that every single second that passed felt more awkward than the last. But soon Remy caught Asher's gaze on her. His face was an unreadable mask. She quickly looked into the fire, watching the vibrant colors and losing herself in the crackling heat.

Blessedly, and like she always did, Kinsley jumped to her feet to come to Remy's rescue. "I'm skinny-dipping, who's coming with?"

"The water is freezing," Boone pointed out.

"So what, live a little, would you?" she countered, and then kicked off her shoes. "Rhett's got towels. We'll go inside if we need to warm up. Who's coming?"

"Yeah, I'm in." Rhett began to rise. Boone glared. He slowly sat down. "Actually, on second thought, I enjoy my life too much."

Peyton slapped Boone's arm. "Stop scowling. It'll be fun." She rose. "I'll join you."

"And no one else," Boone said, giving Rhett another firm look.

Rhett chuckled and then chugged back his beer as the girls took off running toward the water.

Remy rose too, but not for the same reasons. "I'll be back in a few," she said to the guys.

Asher's brows drew together. "All right?"

"Yup, all good." She smiled, though even she knew it probably looked a little tight. It occurred to her then that there wasn't just one reason she was feeling emotional. Maybe it was *everything*. From Damon, to her shop, to Asher…it was all just so much. She left the others behind at the campfire, hearing Kinsley and Peyton scream as they ran into the water, and she purposely didn't look Asher's way. She couldn't quite take any more of those raw eyes of his matched with all the fond memories they had shared in this spot. Away from the campfire, the stars were even brighter, the moonlight shining against the calm, dark water. She exhaled deeply, letting go of all the weight she'd been holding lately. A big boulder to her right where she'd sit and read sometimes when Asher threw a football with Rhett back in the day caught her eye. She climbed up on top like she had so many times, only this time she felt so different. She *was* different.

"You always did love this spot."

Remy exhaled again before turning her head, finding Asher standing a foot away with his hands stuffed into his pockets. "It's a good spot."

"Mind if I join you?"

She shook her head, not sure what she wanted.

He climbed up and sat down next to her. Silence filled the space between them for so long she thought he didn't plan on saying anything, but then he surprised her. "Do you ever wonder what would have happened if my mom hadn't died?"

The question was so loaded, all she could do was stare at him for a while. "I know what would have happened. We would have gotten married, had some kids, and I'd have my shop, most likely."

"But do you think we would have been happy?"

She shrugged. "An impossible question."

"Probably is." He looked out to the water.

She followed his gaze, thinking over her life. "Actually," she said, changing her mind. "I think we would have been as happy as we could have been then." She turned her head, finding those intense eyes on her again. "But…if I'm honest…I think whatever happiness we find now will be better because we had to work for it. I'm definitely stronger than I was back then."

He considered what she said, then nodded. "Pain and loneliness definitely put things into perspective. It shows you what you want and what you're missing."

"Yeah, it does."

Comfortable minutes went by as the water sloshed against the rocks.

"Remy."

She turned her head.

"I'm sorry. Really sorry."

Pain dripped off his voice. Everything felt different now. The anger that once was there was gone, and without it, she saw Asher's pain too. She reached out for his hand and tangled her fingers with his. "I know you are. And I'm sorry that your life crumbled so badly that the only thing you could do was run from everyone you cared about." She knew now that couldn't have been easy. "But can I ask you something?"

"Always."

"Why did you leave the FBI and come back?"

He sighed and stared out at the water. "Nothing made sense there. For the first four years, I felt robotic almost. Just doing the shit I needed to do to get through my days. But then something happened."

"What?"

"I saw your mom in a show."

She felt her eyes widen with the shock blasting through her. "You did?"

He nodded. "Yeah, she was in town playing this gig at this total dive."

Remy had never heard anything about this. "She never told me she saw you."

"Because she didn't," he said. "She didn't know I was there, I stayed at the back."

More silence. Remy tried to piece together what he was saying but fell short. "Okay, so, you saw my mom and that made you want to come home?"

He finally turned toward her, the moonlight casting a shadow on his cheekbone. "I realized I'd become her, the very thing I once hated."

Remy blinked. Twice.

Something changed in the air, becoming warmer and thicker, when he placed both of his hands over one of hers. He played with her fingers and went on. "I had always hated your mother for what she'd done to you. How she treated you."

"You never told me that."

"Because it wasn't my place to," he said after a moment. "Telling you that would have hurt you." He hesitated, his voice filling with pain Remy understood. "But as I stood at the back of that bar, I saw that I'd hurt you worse than she had. She never made you promises. I did."

Remy swallowed. Hard.

"After that night, nothing felt right in Washington," he eventually said into the silence. Remy tried to find words to give back to him, but they didn't come. He went on when she kept quiet. "I regret not being here when Nana passed away. It kills me that she knew how much I hurt you before she died, and she didn't get to see me try to fix it."

Remy swallowed again, forcing her heart back into her chest.

"She didn't know the real reason you left," she managed. "I was stubborn. I downplayed it all and pretended I wasn't hurt. She thought the break-up was mutual."

He glanced down at their held hands. "She didn't know I'd hurt you?"

"No, she didn't know." Tears filled Remy's eyes at the deep pain etched into Asher's features. She'd always only considered her pain. She'd never considered Asher's, not truly.

He finally looked her way. "I still should have been there when she passed away."

Instead of finding the impossible words to let him rid his guilt, Remy hugged his arm and dropped her head on his shoulder. She shut her eyes, feeling the tension in the air fade away when he dropped his lips onto the top of her head. And she didn't make a peep about her no kissing rule.

# Chapter 13

The next morning, Remy arrived to work still feeling emotional from last night. With Salem tucked under her arm, she was still pinching herself that this was her life now. The thickness in her throat about spending Damon's money was slowly fading. Life had kicked her enough, and finally, she began believing that happiness was possible again. Slowly, even with Asher, she felt like last night was a big step forward, and yet clouded things too. She didn't want to get emotionally involved—and she knew Asher had his hang-ups about relationships too—but she couldn't help but see things for what they were. Asher was in deep pain. Pain he didn't deserve.

He'd grown up surrounded by abuse. His mother killed herself. His father, the coward, ran away. When they were together, Remy didn't think about Asher's home life very much because he'd always been put together and solid. But maybe he had to be? Maybe all of it had been a front, and when he left it was because he simply couldn't be strong anymore.

Most of all, maybe he left because he thought he'd hurt her

if he stayed. Her heart twisted at the thought. Had he punished himself to protect her from the darkness in his life? It most definitely was the wrong thing to do, but for the first time, she began to understand what drove Asher to leave.

Remy didn't have it all figured out, but she felt like the pieces of her past were slowly coming together.

With Asher firmly on her mind, she spent the morning attending to new customers and helping a middle-aged lady with eczema pick out cream that would help her irritated skin. Nana's cream with colloidal oatmeal, evening primrose oil, witch hazel, and sunflower oil were sure to clear things up. Remy had seen that cream work wonders on every type of skin condition out there. Cinnamon incense infused the air throughout the shop. Remy figured an extra punch of protection and personal power wouldn't hurt, especially if Lars came back into the store today.

The rest of the morning was steady, the tourists flooding in to check out the new store. And just before eleven o'clock, during a lull in business, Remy grabbed her tablet off the counter beside a sleeping Salem and dialed her mother on FaceTime.

Mom answered on the fifth ring. "Remy." Joni Brennan gave a warm smile that lit up her green eyes, the same light color as Remy's. But that's where their likeness stopped. Her mother had a body that, at forty-five years old, looked better than Remy's. She had the boobs, the curves in all the right places, and knew how to dress to extenuate everything she had. Her mom was also a natural redhead with gorgeous long curls and freckles dusting her nose, where Remy took after the father she never met, being a blonde, and she only got freckles in the summer with her tan. "I'm so happy you called," Mom added. "I meant to call on the grand opening, but you know…life." She shrugged.

Yeah, Remy had heard every single excuse in the book. She used to have a hard time accepting her mother's way of life. She tended to take the sting of rejection personally, but in her twenties, she finally realized Mom was just Mom, forever a selfish wild child. "I wasn't sure if you'd be awake yet," Remy said.

"The band got the night off last night," Mom said, taking a seat on a black leather couch and holding her phone up, showing her face, with a dingy-looking hotel room behind her. "Show's tonight."

"Where are you now?"

"I don't even know anymore," Mom said with a laugh, glancing back behind her. "Ah, Atlanta." She peered into the phone again. "Now enough about me. Show me the shop. Let me see what you've done."

"Okay...I hope you like it." Remy flipped her tablet around and scanned the area before slowly walking around the shop, showing her mother every nook and cranny. "We've got the creams here, then the bath salts and candles."

"Very nice." Mom's voice came from the speaker. "I just love it, Remy."

"It's all really come together." Remy did a final sweep, then turned the tablet back onto herself. "The whole gang pitched in to help me get up and running. I'm so proud of what we've done."

"As you should be," her mother said, pride twinkling in her eyes. "I'm so proud of you. Nana would have been proud too. It's so nice of Kinsley to lend you the money for the down payment."

Remy swallowed back the remorse for lying to her mother about how she'd financed the shop. "Thanks, Mom." She smiled, imaging Nana standing in this store, just bursting with excitement that her gifts could actually help people too. And really that's all that mattered, because Nana gave Remy this life.

The front door suddenly chimed open, then Kinsley and Peyton entered. "The girls are here, Mom, I gotta go," Remy said, glancing back at her tablet.

"Hi, girls!" Mom called.

Remy angled the tablet to face them, and Peyton waved. "Hi, Joni."

"Send us tickets for the next show that's close," Kinsley called. "We love those festivals you do."

"You know I'm good for it," Mom replied.

Remy turned the iPad back to herself. "Have a good show tonight."

Mom smiled. "Always do, babe. Love ya."

"Love you too. Bye." Remy ended the FaceTime chat and then looked up to see the girls smiling at her.

"Your mom would be so cool if she were…well, a better mom to you," said Peyton, moving toward the table with the creams.

Salem woke up, yawned, then promptly fell asleep again. "Honestly, I'd rather a boring mother who's home, than one who's cool and always gone." Nana had been simple but she'd been the most important person in Remy's life, and she missed her terribly.

Peyton's eyes saddened.

Remy waved her off. "Don't feel bad for me. I had an amazing life with my nana. My mom always felt more like…I don't know…a sister, I guess. She's not really nurturing or anything like how my grandma was."

Kinsley hopped onto the counter next to Salem. He peeked open an eye but stayed put. "I wish you could have met Nana," she said to Peyton. "She was a really special lady."

Warm memories filled Remy. Nana had taken Kinsley under her wing too, since Kinsley's mom had taken off to California to start a life with a new family when Kinsley was young. Remy supposed that's what happened when anyone lived in a small town. Sometimes people just needed out.

"All right," Kinsley said. "Now that we've got you alone, tell us about the guy who came into your shop yesterday."

Remy grabbed a box off the floor and set it on the table. "The scary-looking guy that made Asher all broody?"

"Yeah." Kinsley nodded. "*That* guy."

"To be honest, I don't really know exactly who he is," Remy explained, taking out some purification bath salts she'd made last week. So far the healing bath salts were a best seller, but Remy found the purification baths much more relaxing. "He came into the shop the other day asking about Damon. Kind of freaked me out."

Peyton reached for another tester cream. "I see why. He had that totally creepy vibe going on."

"Totally creepy," Remy agreed. Which was exactly why Remy had pulled out her biggest protection spells ever and drenched the store in all of Nana's knowledge. The space felt so full of light every time Remy walked in. All she could do was smile. "After he came into the shop the first time, I told Asher about him and we followed the guy the other night."

Kinsley blinked. "You. Followed. Him?"

Remy nodded. "Into Whitby Falls." She placed two of the small thin bottles of bath salts on the bookshelf, then turned back to the girls, who started at her intently. "Asher's concerned. The guy met up with some other guys that Boone arrested last year—something to do with organized crime."

"That sounds bad," Peyton commented.

Remy shrugged. "Well, it's certainly not great, especially because I have no idea why he's sticking around here."

Kinsley examined Remy, her eyes narrowed thoughtfully. "If Asher's on it, then I've got no doubt he'll get this guy out of town soon enough." She jumped off the counter and moved a little closer. "And speaking of Asher, you two looked *very* cozy on that rock last night."

Remy shrugged. "Things are good, and I'm letting it be whatever it is."

Peyton moved on to the tester candle and took a deep sniff. "Are you two going to get back together?"

"God, no!" Remy exclaimed before reining it back in and sighing heavily. "I just like spending time with Asher again. And with all that's happened…"

"Having amazing orgasms is just a good thing." Kinsley grinned.

Remy bit her lip.

"Ha!" Kinsley said, pointing at Remy with a smile. "I knew it. You two are totally getting all hot and heavy!"

Heat swept through Remy's cheeks. She quickly turned away and organized some jars on the bookshelf. "Don't get all worked up about it. We're just…like I said, whatever, and we're trying to figure out how to be friends again without all the painful memories."

Kinsley moved even closer. "Well, 'whatever' looks good on you. If you're happy, I'm happy." She threw her arms around Remy.

Remy hugged her back, getting a good whiff of Kinsley's honey and oats shampoo. Which Remy recommended she used because most days Kinsley was high-strung. It seemed to relax her some. Though she told Kinsley the shampoo was for dry skin. "You know," Remy said, leaning away, "as crazy as it all is, I actually feel happy. I always thought I needed a plan, but where did that get me? I'm just doing what feels good and not putting too much thought into that."

"I don't think that's crazy one bit." Peyton hugged her next, squeezing tight. "You deserve to be happy, Remy."

"Thanks." Remy smiled as Peyton leaned away.

"I've got to scram to get ready for tonight," Kinsley said, moving toward the door. "The bar's going to be jampacked." When she opened the door, she turned back to Remy. "Drinks after work?"

"I'm in." Remy grinned.

"Me too," Peyton said.

"Girls' night," Kinsley yelled with a hand in the air as she left the shop with a laughing Peyton following behind her.

Remy chuckled, loving the hell out of those girls. She put her mind back on stocking her shelves.

By the time the end of the workday came, Remy felt ready for her couch and her slippers, but she'd promised Kinsley and Peyton she'd be at the bar tonight. She locked the front door and flipped the closed sign before scooping up Salem on her way out the back door. After giving Salem dinner, and freshening up her makeup a little, she headed back down the stairs, then headed through the alleyway toward Kinsley's bar, when something—or more importantly, *someone*—caught her attention. Across the street from the shop, sitting on the bench along the sidewalk, was Lars, his gaze set on hers, that scary crooked smile on his face.

"Hi, Remy!" Hannah, who worked at the post office, said, causing Remy's attention to jerk to her. "Cute shop. I heard the grand opening was a huge success and that your heal-all cream is amazing."

Remy forced a smile. "Thanks. I'm glad people are loving the cream."

Hannah smiled and lifted the big box in her hands. "Gotta run, but I'll be back soon to grab that cream." She hurried off, then headed into the hardware store a couple stores down.

Remy turned, half expecting Lars to have vanished. He didn't. He sat in the same place, one arm draped over the back of the bench, his ankle crossed over his knee. Most people might think he was there relaxing, taking in the day. Remy knew better. Those cold, dead eyes were narrowed on her.

She contemplated turning away and going into Kinsley's bar, but then something came over her. She looked both ways before crossing the street. "Why are you following me?" she demanded when she reached Lars.

He cocked his head. "Who says I'm following you?"

"Well, something is up," she said with a huff, putting her hands on her hips. "Listen, I don't know what you want with Damon, but I have zero contact with him. I confronted him because he was an asshole who tried to scam me, and then saw him once more for closure, but I haven't seen him since. If you want answers from him, you're going to have to go and talk to him."

"That might be a little hard," Lars said.

Remy crossed her arms, trying desperately to portray annoyed, not scared. "And why is that?"

"He's dead."

A sudden coldness struck her core and she took a step back, nearly falling off the curb. Her mind shattered, desperate to stay strong, but everything spun away from her. One part of her heart broke, instantly reminding her that she was not nearly as healed as she'd led herself to believe. *Dead?* Sure, maybe she'd never loved him like she'd loved Asher, but she had decided to make a life with him. She cared for him. "He's dead?" she breathed.

Lars nodded. "Found in the jail's hallway about an hour ago."

Remy stared at him, incredulous, trying to understand. The ground was rocking beneath her. "Did he kill himself?"

Lars smiled. Honest to God smiled. "Nah, he'd never get off that easy. Looks like a stabbing."

Remy hugged herself tighter. If Damon was killed, Remy had no doubt that Asher would know that before anyone else. Either Asher was protecting her for another hit of pain, or Lars knew about the death because he'd ordered it. Remy glanced around, suddenly very aware of how alone she was with this hardened criminal, even though people strode Main Street around her. When she turned back, he hadn't taken his cold gaze off her. "How do you even know that information?" she asked.

"I've got friends of friends in the Whitby Falls jail. Word gets around quick."

"Okay," she said, not believing that for one second. She took a deep breath, picking her heart up off the ground, and put on a brave face. "I'm not sure if you're expecting a reaction here from me. Right now, my feelings are at level *fucked up*. I don't know how to feel about Damon's death or even what to say."

Lars cocked his head and watched her intently for a long moment, then he finally gestured next to him. "Take a seat."

"No, thanks," she said adamantly.

He hesitated, and without moving, but seeming way larger and way scarier, he stated, "That wasn't a choice." Again, he gestured next to him.

Wanting to keep this talk friendly, she slowly moved, sitting as far away as she could.

At that, he grinned. "I won't bite unless you ask me to."

"What do you want, or are just here to play games?" she said firmly, forcing her voice out without a tremble.

He snorted a laugh, then glanced ahead at her shop. "Damon was married to my baby sister, Christine."

Her thoughts froze until she managed, "You're Damon's brother-in-law?"

"*Was* Damon's brother-in-law—or Andrew's brother-in-law, I should say, since that's how we knew him," Lars corrected. "He left my sister two years ago, and it's taken me that long to find him."

Remy drew another deep breath and blew it out slowly, trying to get a grasp on this new development. "I'm sorry that he did that to her." And she was sorry. So damn sorry. Even more sorry that she was wrapped up in all this. "But if you know that Damon is gone, why are you sitting outside my shop?"

"Ah," Lars said, projecting a sense of calm and ease. "I'm curious about his life here." His gaze darkened. "About you."

A sudden sense to flee washed over her. She rose, not liking the scary intensity in his gaze. "Believe me, I'm not that interesting."

Lars smirked. "Somehow I doubt that. I think you've got lots of secrets to tell."

Her heartbeat raced, nearly exploding at his dark smile. Last time, she ran, scared shitless. Not this time. "I want you to stop following me," she told him firmly. "Stay away from me."

His grin only darkened further. "I find it cute that you think you make the rules here."

"I do make the rules," she said, proud her voice didn't quiver. "And I have no qualms about getting a restraining order against you."

He barked a laugh now, stretching his arm out against the back of the bench. A laugh that made her jerk and her blood run cold. "Go get that restraining order, sweetheart. I dare you."

She wanted to hit him with an epic comeback. That's not what happened. Her feet were moving her across the street, as far away as she could get from his lifeless eyes.

# Chapter 14

The day had passed by slowly as Asher sat behind his desk, glancing down at the evidence of a recent burglary at the pharmacy. No matter how much he tried to focus his thoughts, his mind kept drifting back to Remy and their talk last night. He finally felt like he was getting things right. He wasn't moving too fast with her, but he wouldn't stop moving forward until she trusted him again, fully and completely. For the first time in years, there was a bright spot in the darkness, and that happiness was having Remy back in his life. He glanced up at the photograph on the wall of the night they'd gone camping. He'd taken her virginity under the stars, and somehow fallen even deeper in love with her.

A lump began forming in the back of his throat and he cleared it quickly away. He missed hearing his mother's advice. She'd know exactly what he needed to do to fix everything and get his life back on track. When he'd left Remy for Washington, he knew she wanted to get married, but the idea of marriage freaked him out, and that hadn't changed. He saw what commitment did to people, how that vow of sticking it out through thick and thin destroyed lives when people gave themselves completely to someone else. Remy had loved Asher blindly, not realizing the danger he could be to her. After his mother died, Asher couldn't function normally, let alone find a way to make sure he didn't become his father. A man who took and took from a woman until she had nothing left to give. It occurred to him now that he could do the friends with benefits thing as long as Remy wanted, but he would eventually have to let her go. Not falling for her again was challenging, but he only needed to look back into his memories of his mother lying in the hospital bed to remind him why he wanted more for Remy than he could give.

"Asher."

He jerked toward the voice coming from his door, realizing that hadn't been the first time his name had been called. Boone and Rhett burst out laughing as they filed into his office.

"Got a certain woman on your mind?" Rhett asked, dropping down onto a chair.

Asher nearly answered but then felt the tension coming off Boone as he took the seat next to Rhett. "What's up?"

"There's been a development," Boone said, handing Asher a thumb drive.

Asher plugged it into his computer, then opened the file. The moment the video popped up on his screen, he realized the development hadn't been a good one. "Shit." He leaned in toward his computer monitor, watching Damon being stabbed with a homemade shank in the jail's hallway surrounded by a dozen or so men in orange jumpsuits. "Did this happen today?" he asked.

Boone nodded. "Yeah, earlier this afternoon, but we just got a hold of the video now."

Asher kept watching the video, seeing the exact moment that Damon took his final breath, his jumpsuit completely covered in blood. The man attacking him eventually jumped up and a moment later, the guards stormed in. Asher sat back in his chair causing it to squeak beneath him and crossed his arms. "What do we know of the killer?"

"Not much, except that the killer's wife received a large cash gift in her bank account a few days ago from an offshore account," Rhett reported.

Asher didn't like the sound of this. "A hired hit?"

"Looks like it," Boone agreed with a nod.

"Damn," Asher grumbled.

"Speaking of that hired hit," Rhett said. "I did a little more digging on Violi and am beginning to get an idea of why he's here." He hesitated, then said slowly, "Violi's sister was one of Fanning's victim."

"You're fucking kidding me?" Asher asked, incredulous.

"Shocked the hell out of me too," Rhett said, lifting a file folder in his hand.

Asher took all this in. The Damon he knew was a fool, but to have this level of stupidity seemed unbelievable. "Fanning actually scammed the sister of a known dangerous criminal?"

"I'm guessing he didn't know who he was dealing with," Boone said with a shrug. "When he met Violi and discovered who he was messing with, he ran."

"A possibility," Asher agreed with a slow nod. "But then why not just pay back the money? Fanning's got millions in his account."

"A good question only Fanning could answer," Boone said, dryly.

Too bad they couldn't ask him. Asher hated Fanning, but

he hadn't wished Fanning dead. Remy filled his thoughts. He wondered how she'd react to this news. He considered next steps and how to even proceed now. "Violi has the connections to secure a hit like this?"

"If he's hanging around the King criminal family who meet up at Antonio's, without a doubt," Boone confirmed.

Still, where did that leave them? Nowhere. What they knew and what they could prove were two different things.

Asher pondered what he'd heard. Back in the nineties, the King family had been big players in racketeering and money laundering. When the head of that family, Stefano, got taken down and put into jail, most of the organized crime in Whitby Falls ended. Until Stefano's son, Joaquin, got old enough to take over. He was a smarter criminal than his father, and a rich one at that.

Obviously, following Asher's line of thinking, Boone added, "We can look, but if King's men are involved, we will find absolutely nothing tying Violi to Fanning's death. It'll look like a fight between inmates."

"Who's working the case?" Asher pressed on.

"Detective Smithson in Whitby Falls is looking into the large deposit into the suspect's wife's account," Boone reported. "But even that will be neat and tidy, and they'll have a reason to explain it all." Frustration tightened the corners of Boone's eyes. "Joaquin King and his men are a step ahead of the game, always."

And they all knew why. Whitby Falls had a few dirty cops in their ranks. They always seemed to avoid the clean cops attempting to take them down, and internal investigations had yet to weed them out.

Asher's back stiffened at the thought of Remy being anywhere near anyone connected to Joaquin King. "Which wife was Violi's sister?"

"The most recent one," Rhett said, opening the file folder and handing Asher a photograph.

Asher studied the picture. The woman looked nothing like Remy, a complete opposite with dark features and dark hair. Asher dropped the photo onto his desk, then rubbed at the tension along his neck. "That explains why Fanning only managed to get a few hundred thousand from her. He got a lot more from the other wives."

Rhett inclined his head. "That's where my thoughts went too. Fanning must have realized that scamming more money from her would've sent him to the grave. He took what he had and booked it."

Asher inhaled sharply and exhaled slowly, running a hand over his face. "I want this cleaned up for Remy, and yet, somehow we only seem to get more in the thick of it as things go by."

"With Fanning gone now," Boone said, causing Asher to lower his hands, "this guy has gotta be on his way soon."

"Let's hope for that," Asher said.

Rhett rose from his chair and moved to the doorway. "Besides, Fanning's death happened in Whitby Falls's jurisdiction. It ain't our problem. The way I see it, Remy got her justice too. Violi will be gone, and we can put this matter to bed."

"Is anything ever that easy?" Asher asked with a snort.

"This time, let's hope so," Rhett said before leaving the office.

Boone rose from his seat and said, "Thought you should know that Kinsley called a bit ago. Remy's at the bar and she looks upset but won't talk about it." He made it to the door, then turned back. "Let me know if something's up."

Asher nodded. "Does she know about Fanning?"

Boone shook his head. "No one knows but us."

Asher watched Boone leave his office and then he cleaned up his files and his desk. He grabbed his leather jacket on the back of the door on his way out. The station was bustling, a couple cops walking a handcuffed inebriated woman into the back of the station. Two officers were typing up reports, and the receptionist was busy on the phones. Asher was only thinking about Remy when he made it outside, sliding into his jacket as the cool autumn air brushed over him. He walked the few blocks, the leaves blowing down the street, and he entered Kinsley's bar a moment later.

On the black shiny stage, a woman with a gravelly voice sang her heart out while playing the piano. He found Remy sitting at the bar, her shoulders curled, with Kinsley standing on the other side of the bar, her chin in her hand, saying something to Remy.

When Asher got closer, Kinsley saw him coming and straightened. Her mouth moved again, then she turned away and headed toward the end of the bar. She must have told Remy he was coming, because she looked his way when he slid onto the stool. He took one look into her face and frowned. "You know about Damon."

She nodded. "Lars told me."

Asher's back straightened. "You spoke to him?"

"When I closed up the shop, Lars was sitting on a bench outside and told me." She glanced away and sipped her vodka and lime. A drink that was her go-to stressed-out drink. "Obviously, he had some part in that."

Asher's gut twisted at Lars being anywhere near Remy. He nodded, then gestured at Kinsley to bring him the same drink as Remy. "We're assuming the same thing."

She swallowed her drink, then glanced sideways at him. "I guess you know then that Damon was married to Lars's sister?"

"Just learned that myself," Asher said with a nod, when Kinsley placed the drink in front of him. Obviously aware of the tension, she hurried off again. He took a long sip of the drink, relishing the bite of the vodka. "While I wish he would stay away, we've got our answer now for why he was here."

"Yeah, I guess we do," she said, staring into her glass.

Asher took in her empty stare, her flat, monotone voice, realizing she wasn't scared about Lars at all. "It's okay to be sad about Damon's death," he told her gently.

"I don't know what I am right now," she said after a long moment.

"Sad but confused about being sad because he tried to steal your inheritance?" Asher offered.

She shrugged, still staring down into her drink. "Something like that, I guess."

"You cared about Damon. Were with him for a year. You almost married him," Asher said, tucking his finger under her chin to capture her gaze. He wished he could steal the sadness from her eyes. "That doesn't go away in a day, no matter what he did to you. All this is confusing shit. But your feelings, what you felt with him, those are true and honest, and it's okay to mourn the fact that the guy you cared about died today. You've got a big heart, Remy, feel what you need to feel."

Her chin quivered and tears welled in her eyes.

Fuck Damon. Fuck Lars. Asher didn't need to see more than that. He gathered Remy in his arms, pulling her in close, and let her cry against his chest, satisfied with knowing that tonight, nothing else could hurt her.

* * *

Another vodka and lime later, the bar was packed full. The opening act, which had been an up-and-coming blues singer, had wrapped up an hour ago, and the headline act was now belting out some dirty jazz that had the crowd on their feet. Most people were up on the dance floor. Boone and Peyton were up there, but Rhett, Asher, and Remy stayed back at the bar with Kinsley. Not that they saw much of her; she was busy tending the bar. And Rhett was busy hitting on the brunette next to Remy, which only made Kinsley stay far away. Remy hoped one day that Rhett noticed Kinsley in the way that Kinsley noticed Rhett. Even if nothing came of the relationship, because Rhett was such good buddies with Boone, at least Kinsley would be *seen*.

Remy glanced next to her at Asher, his gaze on the band on stage. She hadn't lied to him earlier; she still didn't know how she felt about Damon's death. She was sad, yes, but confused by that sadness too. She supposed that maybe this would give her closure. She didn't have to wonder where Damon was and if he was still in jail. But there was this little part of her that felt broken by his death. No matter what he'd done to her, he didn't deserve that fate; no one did.

The crowd cheered and clapped at the end of the song, then quieted when the singer took to the microphone again. Remy looked Asher's way again and found him looking at her. He stared for a long moment before the side of his mouth curved. She supposed if anything, Damon's brutal death was a reminder of how short life was. Here one minute. Gone the next. Asher had been there lately in a way she never thought he'd be there for her again. And more and more, she was seeing his pain past hers...theirs to deal with together. She felt the pull to him like she always did, drawn to be closer, forgetting everyone else in the room. His blue T-shirt stretched against his chest and dark blue jeans fit his thick thighs to perfection, his hair falling free of the gel he must have put in this morning, and he looked lethal and sexy all at once. It occurred to her that she got where she was now by doing exactly what she wanted. And right now, lost in the building heat in his eyes, she wanted Asher.

She strode forward until she pressed herself against the strength of him. He dropped his chin and caressed her cheek before tucking her hair behind her ear. His mouth came to her ear then. "You want to get out of here?" he asked.

She nodded. "With you."

His gaze flared with wicked promise as he cupped her face and then his mouth met hers, and there was no crowd, no music, just them. He kept the kiss sweet and pure until he tilted her head…then there was nothing gentle about it. He held her face tight in his grip, deepening the kiss until he left her breathless. She gripped his T-shirt, wanting more, and he chuckled and moved his mouth back to her ear. "Yeah, come on, let's go." He took her hand and led her toward the front door.

Remy had no doubt Rhett saw them together, maybe even Kinsley did too, but really, it didn't matter anymore. She wanted to feel beautiful, sexy, and alive. Life was just so fucking short.

When they made it outside and headed down the alleyway to the back of the building, Remy noted the cruiser was gone. Asher had obviously taken over protective detail for the night, knowing he'd be in the bar with Remy. She pulled on Asher's hand. Maybe it was the drinks giving her liquid courage, but after all he'd done for her, she couldn't put it off any longer. "I never did properly thank you."

He arched an eyebrow. "Thanked me for what?"

She stepped closer, pressing her hands on his chest, feeling the steady race of his heart. "For protecting me from Damon."

Asher dropped his mouth close to hers. "That is not something I ever need to be thanked for, Remy."

She cupped his face, relishing in the hard lines of his body against hers. "Actually, I think you do. You didn't need to keep an eye out for me, and you did that. You always have protected me, even when I didn't see it. So, thank you, Asher."

He brought his mouth even closer. She felt his breath on her lips. "I've told you before, and I'll say it again: I protect you, Remy. That's what I do." Then he kissed her, and that was really all she needed. She felt the wildly out of control emotion in every swipe of his lips across hers. She threw her arms around his neck and kissed him back.

When his kiss turned hot and wicked, leaving her mouth to move to her neck, she slid her hands into his hair, desperate to get closer. He grasped her hips and turned her around until she was placed in the shadows at the back of the building. His mouth returned to hers and he kissed her harder, a low growl ruminating from his chest speaking to the feminine side of her. She felt safe and beautiful when Asher touched her and took control of the pleasure.

His kisses skimmed her jawline, then moved to her neck, and she slid her hand between them until she stroked his erection outside of his jeans. He groaned in her ear, making goose bumps rise along her arms. She played right there, using her fingers to trace his thick cock until she rubbed the tip. Asher finally brought his mouth back to hers. This time, he didn't kiss her; he devoured her. She nearly let him until she wanted something more. She broke the kiss and switched the positions. His back was now against the wall. "Can the cameras see us in this corner?" she asked.

His eyes were dark, full of desire. "No."

"Good." She grinned and reached for his jeans. She freed his hardened cock, stroked him twice, and then squatted in front of him and took him into her mouth.

"Fuck, Remy," he growled.

She glanced up, finding his head tipped back. Feeling powerful and sexy, she sucked on the tip knowing how much he liked that, and he dropped his head, looking at her. Her stomach clenched with the heat burning between them. Letting him watch her, she slowly licked from the base to the tip, loving his slight tremble. He tangled his fingers tangled in her hair, and she knew what that meant too. He wanted *more*.

She took him deeper into her mouth, sucking her lips around him and stroking her hand in front of her mouth, until she heard his soft, low moan. She was already backing away, fully aware that that sexy, deep masculine sound indicated he wanted *her*. In seconds, his pants were back on, and she was in his arms, and he was carrying her up her steps. He put her down only for her to get her door unlocked and open, then he tugged her inside and slammed the door shut with his foot. He braced her face while he kissed her, until he began ripping at her clothes. Her shirt…gone. Her pants…gone. Those panties Peyton gave her…gone. He never stopped kissing her. Not when he unclothed her, or himself, or even when he sheathed himself in a condom.

He only broke away when he pressed her back against the door and hooked her leg onto his arm. "I need nothing like I need you." He pressed himself against her and entered her in one swift stroke right to hilt, making her gasp and sending her on her tiptoes. "I want nothing like I want you."

She moaned against the way he stretched her so perfectly. "You have me."

He thrust forward hard, sliding his hands across her face. "Do I?"

"Yes." She rocked her hips against his cock, needing more. "Asher, yes, don't stop!"

Something primal and fierce came into his eyes then. He held her face, stared at her intently, and pumped his hips hard. This didn't feel like lovemaking, this felt like possessive need, and she gripped him with the same desperation, feeling all those things too.

With every hard thrust sending pleasure skyrocketing through her body, she clung to him, not wanting to let go. In that honest truth, her pleasure rose until there was nothing but satisfaction flying through her. And with a final roar, he thrust forward, bucking and jerking against her, following her right over the edge.

Many minutes later, when she could move and breathe easily again, she lifted her head from his shoulder and opened her eyes, her loft hazy in front of her. She blinked, still in Asher's arms, his sweaty body against hers. His chest heaving and falling against hers. She blinked again, then slowly the view came clear. "Asher," she said, breathless.

"Mmm," was his response as he slowly withdrew.

"We have a problem." He looked up at that and she gestured behind him at her loft that had been totally ransacked.

He glanced over his shoulder, seeing what she saw. Someone had broken in.

Everything happened so fast. One second, she stood there naked against him, the next he had thrown a blanket at her. He threw on his jeans, his muscles flexing and bulging, especially the vein in his neck. "Do not move from that spot." Then he grabbed his cell phone while slowly moving farther into the apartment. "Get Rhett and come to Remy's," he obviously said to Boone. "We've got trouble."

# Chapter 15

Fun and games ended in a millisecond as Asher searched the living room to ensure Remy was safe standing at the doorway. He already knew Remy was a distraction. He just didn't know how much of a distraction she really was, and apparently, when her sweet body was against him, he didn't see shit. Boone and Rhett had descended on Remy's loft once Asher sidled back up to Remy, who now had the blanket wrapped around her tightly. Boone and Rhett had cleared the rest of the property from top to bottom, ensuring every hiding spot possible had been searched.

Only when they returned did Asher gather Remy's clothes so she could get dressed again. "Here, the entourage will be arriving soon," he told her gently. "Better get some clothes on."

She gave him a quick nod, and with white knuckles and an ashen face, she scooped up Salem off the windowsill. She hugged the cat and fled to the bathroom without a look at either Boone or Rhett.

Asher had a bad taste in his mouth as he stared at the closed door. He'd been aware of Violi, had kept a very close eye on him, but now this needed to stop. Remy needed to feel safe, and Asher was going to get it for her.

Asher moved back to the front door and grabbed his T-shirt from the ground.

"Let me get this straight," Rhett said, hands shoved in his pockets, leaning against Remy's couch. "You were too busy screwing to notice her place had been broken into and ransacked?"

Asher pulled the T-shirt over his head. "I meant to leave out that part when I told you what happened."

"Classic." Rhett burst out laughing.

Boone chuckled along and then examined the windows in the living room, careful not to touch anything. "I checked the security videos." Which either Asher or Boone could do from their cell phones. Technology was a godsend most days. "The video caught someone going through the back door, then coming back out, wearing all black. Can't see his face."

"This has gotta be Violi," Asher said, voicing his earlier thoughts.

Rhett moved to the window next to him and glanced out. "I see why your mind would go there, but what would Violi want in Remy's loft?"

"That's what we need to find out." A sudden knock on the door had Asher biting back the curse words sitting on his tongue. He turned and opened the door, finding that the crime scene investigators had arrived. "Miss nothing," he told them. "Extra attention to detail here."

"Sure," Tony, one of the tech guys said, entering Remy's apartment.

Asher's vision tunneled on her living room, and his jaw muscles flexed with the adrenaline pulsing through him. Asher wanted to clean up her place and get it back to normal for her, but the scene needed processing. He shut the door behind the crime techs and his gaze returned to the bathroom door. She should have been out by now. He knocked on the door. "Remy?"

A pause. "I just need a minute more." Her voice cracked.

He gritted his teeth, picturing the tears streaming down her face. "Take your time," he called. Then he turned around and growled, "I want to wring that motherfucker's neck."

"Which will get you nowhere fast," Boone said.

"Except for feeling better," Asher mumbled, obviously loud enough for Rhett to hear and chuckle.

Another knock came at the front door before it opened and the chief entered. He gave Boone a long look and a nod at Rhett before turning to Asher. "Is Remy all right?" he asked.

"Rattled, but okay." Asher glanced toward Tony as he began fingerprinting her coffee table. Asher didn't even want to consider what might have happened if she'd been there tonight.

"All right, that's good," Hank said. He scanned her loft, assessing the damage, then sighed. "Where is she?"

"Bathroom," Asher replied.

Hank nodded, then frowned at the mess. "Any idea what someone would be looking for?"

"No idea." Tension rippled across Asher's shoulders. He moved to the wall and leaned against it, folding his arms. "Fanning's dead. Why is Violi still here, breaking into Remy's place?"

Hank rubbed his chin. "Is it possible this has nothing to do with Violi and this is simply a break-in?"

"It's possible," Boone said, "but also highly unlikely. Violi has been in contact with Remy a few times. That's too coincidental for my liking."

For Asher's too.

Hank nodded again and then shoved his hands into his pockets, tapping his boot against the hardwood floors. "Let's say we go with the Violi theory. There's gotta be something there that you're missing. Breaking in here had to serve a purpose. What is it?"

"Scaring her," Rhett said.

"Yes, but *why*?" Hank pressed. "Why would Violi go to these lengths to scare her? What could it possibly get him?"

Asher began pacing in front of the coffee table, where there was a clear path, unable to stand still any longer. His fists clenched tight, the desire to protect Remy surging through him. "That's the very thing I keep asking myself over and over again." He ran a hand through his hair. "Why is this bastard sticking around and tormenting her?"

"Because Fanning was married to his sister?" Rhett offered.

"Which has nothing to do with Remy," Asher stated.

Boone frowned.

When no one had the answer, heaviness filled the room.

Until Hank broke the silence. "Keep at it. You'll get the answer. You boys always do." He moved to the bathroom door and knocked. "Remy? Can I come in for a minute?"

The door slowly opened and Hank vanished inside. Asher started at the door, his chest rising and falling with his heavy breaths. "Someone was in this goddamn apartment. Touched her things. She could have been here."

A firm hand came on Asher's shoulder. "And we'll find out who and why," Boone said.

Not soon enough.

The bathroom door opened again. Hank came out with wet marks on his shirt. Remy's tears. Asher closed his eyes and breathed deeply. He wanted Violi to feel those tears, every single one of them. The taste for vengeance slid through Asher's veins, and his ears pounded.

Hank's steady voice opened Asher's eyes. "I'm aware this is a hard situation for you because it's personal." He cupped his shoulder, squeezing tight. "But you need to keep your emotions out of this one. Figure the case out, get it solved, and that's the best way to protect Remy." He leaned in and his gaze firmed. "I don't want you anywhere near Lars Violi. If you want to question him, Boone takes the lead there. Am I understood, Sullivan?"

Asher instinctively wanted to rebel against the order. "Yes, sir."

"Good." Hank dropped his hand and his gaze swept over Rhett and Boone. "Update me once the crime techs have finished and if anything develops there."

"Will do," Boone said.

When the front door shut behind Hank, Rhett said, "Violi is still at the B and B. We've had eyes on him the entire time, and other than him sitting outside Remy's shop and her approaching him, he hasn't taken a step out of line."

"Until he had someone break into Remy's loft," Asher grumbled, running a hand over his face. He studied Tony, who was still fingerprinting the scene. Asher could break the order of his superior and frighten Violi the way he'd frightened Remy, but that wasn't doing right by her. Not in the way she needed him. "I'm taking Remy back to my place until we've got prints or something we can move on."

Rhett's gaze swept the mess with a frown before he glanced Asher's way. "I'll keep close tabs on Violi, but I doubt we'll get anything from that."

"You've got eyes on him," Asher said. "That's good enough for me right now."

Boone agreed with a nod. "I'll keeping digging and see if anything comes up in Violi's past. Chief's right—there's gotta be something here we're missing."

Done with thinking of anyone but Remy, Asher moved toward the bathroom door. "If you get anything, call."

He heard the guys leave through the front door, and the chatter of Tony and the other crime tech behind him, when he knocked on the bathroom door. "Remy."

"Come in."

He opened the door and found her sitting on the floor with her back against the wall. Asher contained the blistering rage boiling beneath his skin. Remy had been through so much. Too much. Asher lived by the law. He was ruled by the black and white, never living in the gray area. But Remy's damp, overly bright eyes, and the way she flinched at the noises outside the bathroom, made Asher want to make Violi pay. "I have an idea," he said.

"What's that?" Her voice shook.

His gut churned at the emptiness in her eyes. "How about we go to my house, get you into the bath, burn that smelly protection stuff, eat some chocolate, and build a fort you can hide in."

Sudden warmth spread across her face with her small smile. A smile that eased the weight in his chest. Asher offered his hand, and as soon as her cool fingers twined with his, he could breathe easier.

He pulled her into him, and she came willingly. "I'm sorry this happened," he said, pressing his lips to the top of her head.

She sniffed, trembling against him. "It's just really scary."

"I know. It is scary." He leaned away, tucked a finger under chin, capturing those eyes holding a soul he'd do anything to protect. "But you're not alone." He cupped her face, then brought his mouth close to hers, and before he claimed the kiss, he said, "I'm here and I'm not going anywhere."

* * *

The drive back to Asher's place had felt like an hour, even though it was only ten minutes. Remy couldn't quite wrap her head around what happened. Not that someone broke into her house. And certainly not that she was potentially now in danger. And she was still trying to come to terms with Damon's murder. But all those worries and concerns seemed to drift away when she lay back in the hot bath, the rose oil–scented steam rising up in the small bathroom. She brought all of her grief for Damon into this small space with her, feeling every little bit of it, when she lit the white votive candle on the small pedestal sink. She'd let that flame burn all night, and when it went out, Damon would find peace and cross over. Where he'd go from there, she didn't know, but that wasn't for her to decide. What she did know was that her grief and sadness over Damon would drain away with the bath water.

She couldn't take these feelings with her, not with what he'd tried to take from her.

The flowered wallpaper was the same as it had always been. Remy had been surprised when they arrived at the house to find that Asher hadn't changed much of it except some of the furniture. She wondered if maybe that was because this was Asher's childhood home. To change anything would be like letting his mother go.

The flame flickered light across Remy's bare knees poking out of the water. This house felt like a second home. Remy spent most of her days growing up in this house. Maybe it even felt like *home* now, considering Remy had sold Nana's place after she'd passed away. Remy couldn't be there without Nana in it. That's why she'd moved into the loft, but the loft never felt like home. It always felt temporary.

She shut her eyes, letting the hot water relax her tense muscles. She said a little prayer for Damon, hoping he crossed over with ease and peace that did not happen in his death. After that, a thousand things rushed through her mind. So many who and what and where, but in the end, she had no answers for anything. Though she did have one thing—suspicions, and there was only one person she wanted to talk to about that: Kinsley. She felt bad excluding Peyton, but Peyton had Boone, and Remy didn't want to mess up their relationship by forcing Peyton to keep secrets from her fiancé. She knew Kinsley could keep secrets from her brother. They had been doing it for years.

The ringing of her cell phone snapped Remy's eyes open. She quickly grabbed the towel off the floor and dried her hands, then reached for her cell and smiled at the screen. "I was *just* thinking about you," she said into the phone.

Kinsley laughed softly. "Our soul-sister bond at its finest." Then her voice went tender. "Boone told me what happened. Are you okay?"

"Yeah, I'm all right," she said with a long sigh, moving her toes in the warm water. "I'm at Asher's now. It's just scary, you know, and so freaking creepy that someone was in my house looking through my stuff."

"Totally freaky," Kinsley agreed. "Boone said that he thought Lars might behind all this. What do you think?"

Remy shrugged, even if Kinsley couldn't see it, and the water rippled beneath her. "It's gotta be Lars. Who else would it be? He's the only criminal that's hanging around me lately."

"I mean, I get that, but why would he ransack your house?"

And that's where Remy's suspicions came in. "You know, after we found my place all messed up, I went into the bathroom and had a mini breakdown in there."

"Understandable," Kinsley commented.

"Yeah, I suppose so." Remy took in a deep breath. "But the more I sat in there by myself, the more I kept wondering...do you think it's possible that Lars knows about the money and that's what he's looking for?"

"No," Kinsley said in an instant. Then she paused. "I mean, why would you think he'd know about the money?"

"I don't know. It just popped into my head." Remy stared up at the candlelight flickering on the ceiling. "It's just that, every time I see Lars, he keeps saying that he was interested in me and my shop. I thought it was all about Damon at first, but then after someone broke in and seemed to be looking for something, I can't help but think, what if it was the money?"

Kinsley paused even longer this time. "I guess that wouldn't be totally impossible, but Lars's sister will be paid back the money Damon stole from her. Remember, he had tons of money in the bank account. Besides, Boone also told me that the lawyers were already working through all the finances."

Good and all, but... "Maybe this isn't about money so much as it is about principle. Damon took something from Lars's sister. He wants revenge for that."

"Well, I'd say killing him is enough revenge, don't you think?"

Remy's throat tightened but she pushed past it, placing her wet hand across her forehead. "Ugh. You're right. Just something about all this feels...connected or something, I don't know."

"I think you need to look at it like this," Kinsley said. "How would Lars even know that Damon had the money in your house?"

Another thing that came to Remy's mind in the bathroom. "What if Damon told him," Remy pointed out. "When I went and saw Damon in jail, he had asked me for a favor, remember? That's why I went looking in the first place. What if the favor was that he needed me to get the money to Lars because he knew if he didn't, his life was in danger?"

Kinsley huffed. "Now just wait a second, missy. Don't even start that, Remy Brennan. Damon's murder is not even remotely close to being your fault. Even if what you say is true, and Lars wants the money, it still wouldn't be your fault." She hesitated, then her voice softened. "I think you're way off base here. Maybe the break-in has nothing to do with Damon or Lars at all."

"Maybe," Remy said, more or less to end the conversation, swishing her legs in the water. Her instincts told her everything felt connected somehow…she just didn't know how exactly.

The bathroom door slowly opened, spilling light from the hallway into the bathroom as Asher strode in carrying a beer and a wineglass. "Listen, Kins, Asher's here. Can I call you later?"

"Of course," Kinsley said. "Don't worry about anything. Everything is going to work out, Remy. It always does."

*Does it?* She had finally felt like everything was back on track, yet life always seemed to put a major road block in her way of happiness. "Yeah, I know. Thanks for checking in. Love you."

"Love you back. Bye."

The phone line went dead as Asher handed her the glass of wine. She offered her phone before accepting the glass.

He arched an eyebrow. "Everything okay?" he asked.

Everything wasn't okay at all, but how could she possibly

tell him the mess she'd gotten herself into or anything about her suspicions? "Now that I have wine, it's better." She forced a smile.

"It's been a day," he said. "Mind if join you?"

"Not at all." She leaned her head back against the tub and wiggled her eyebrows. "Trying to improve my day?" she asked, hearing the rising heat in her own voice.

"Always." He grinned, reaching for his T-shirt and pulling it over his head in that fast way men do. His jeans and boxer briefs followed, then Asher stood in all his masculine beauty with hard *everything*. The candlelight made his skin glow, putting shadows in all the grooves of his muscles. Her gaze fell lower, and her mouth watered at how much he wanted her.

"Ignore that," he said, lifting her focus to his amused eyes. "You're naked. I can't help it."

She licked her lips. "What if I don't want to ignore it?"

His eyes darkened and his voice deepened. "All the better, then. Scoot forward."

She slid forward in the tub and turned around while he got in, holding his beer in his hand.

The water rose to the edge of the tub, the overflow drain kicked in, sucking the water away as Asher submerged himself. He wrapped an arm around her and then tugged her onto his lap, causing her glass to shake.

"Oh, look, I spilled my wine all over your chest," she said, her knees settling on either side of him in the tub. "Maybe I should lick it up?"

He grinned, holding her tight enough against him so her sex pressed against his hardened length. "I'm not stopping you."

She leaned down a little and licked the trail of wine, feeling him jerk beneath her. "Yummy," she said, looking back into his eyes. She swirled her hips and discovered how good she felt rocking her hips against him just like *that*.

He groaned. "Toss back the rest of it so I can do something else with that mouth."

She did exactly that and then placed the wineglass down and rocked her hips again. "Remember when we used to do this?" she asked, rubbing herself slowly against him, sliding her hands across the width of his shoulders. "When you were too good to have me, and this was all you'd let me do to you."

His beer bottle soon rested next to her glass, and his jaw muscles worked as he reached for her breasts. "Yes, I vividly remember." He tweaked her nipples. "Especially how much you liked this."

She tossed her head back against the sudden need flooding her. Hot and wet, she slid her hands into his hair and then sealed her mouth across his, never stopping the thrusting of her hips, back and forth, rubbing herself against him, taking pleasure, giving pleasure.

His hands left her breasts, sliding down her back until he squeezed her butt and held on tight, helping her gain move-ment. "I've never forgotten how you used to fuck me like this, and how this made you fall apart." He bit her neck.

She shivered and gasped. "No matter how much I begged you to take me," she said, breathless, speeding up now, falling into the speed they set together. "You would never let me." She lifted her hips until she found the top of him, reveling in the masculine sound that rumbled from his chest. "But I'm not that innocent girl anymore." She took the tip of him inside her, knowing what she wanted. "I'm safe, protected, and clean. I want you, Asher."

"You've got me," he growled, then thrust her down on him in one swift stroke.

She arched against the intense pleasure and then lost herself in how they fit together. She'd never had unprotected sex with anyone but Asher, and the memory of him exploded into every molecule. She rocked her hips, the water sloshing around them to land on the bathroom floor. His deep grunts echoed her sensual screams, driving her higher and higher. She gripped the edge of the tub while his fingers dug into her hips, helping her move faster, harder, until she screamed, breaking wide open, and he crashed over the edge with her.

# Chapter 16

The next morning, Asher woke to Remy still sleeping next to him. He'd left her there, wishing she could sleep until this hell was behind her. If she was in his bed, she was safe. But he knew Remy wasn't the woman he'd left behind. She'd want to face this head-on, but he'd rather her stay safe instead. But back in the day, he'd made decisions that got them into a mess. He'd never decide anything for her again.

While he showered to get the rose oil scent from their bath off his skin, a plan formed, one that he doubted the chief would approve of, but one that was necessary for Asher to put Violi behind them. Nothing else mattered but that.

When he came out of the bathroom, he found Remy gone from the bed, Salem now sleeping on her pillow. He hurried into a pair of jeans and a black T-shirt and then headed downstairs. "Remy," he called, moving quickly down the hallway into the small kitchen, but then the spike in his heart rate instantly slowed when he caught sight of Remy outside in his mother's garden. He opened the back door and leaned against the doorframe.

Remy wore jeans and one of Asher's sweaters that was over-sized on her. He remembered she used to love wearing his leather coat, and he loved seeing her in it. His mind drifted, returning to a moment in the past where his view had been nearly identical.

*Sweaty and starving, Asher entered the house and dropped his duffel bag on the floor after an intense workout at the local college. Everything hurt. From the tips of his fingers the whole way down to his toes ached, muscles he didn't even know he had were strained, but once he graduated college he had his sights set on the police academy.*

*"Mom?" he called, moving through the hallway. He heard music coming from outside and followed the noise. When he reached the back door, he found his mother in her garden. But that's not all he found.*

*Remy stood behind her, watering the flowerbeds with the hose. Her jeans were rolled up to her knees, her white T-shirt covered in dirt, tied up, exposing her belly. Damn. He was having trouble keeping his hands off her lately. Before he got hard in front of his mom, he focused on the flowers.*

*A song from the eighties played on the radio. Remy sang, danc-ing around the garden like she always did, which made her breasts bounce and ass jiggle. Shit.*

*"Asher."*

*He jerked his gaze at his mother and then smiled. "Having fun?" he asked.*

*"Always," Mom said, her green eyes sparkling and her brown hair up in a ponytail. Dad wasn't anywhere in sight, which explained the peace on Mom's face. Asher told her to leave him. They'd be okay once Asher got out of college, but Mom never listened, always saying Asher just didn't understand his father. He*

*loved her in ways Asher couldn't comprehend. She gave Asher a
kiss on his cheek when he reached her. "Remy is just so good with
all the herbs and things."*

*"It's all my nana," Remy said with a smile. "What I know, I
learned from her." She came over, stood on her tiptoes, and gave
him a quick kiss. "Ew. You stink."*

*"I missed you too." He grinned.*

*"You do smell, sweetie," Mom said. "Go shower and then I'll
make us some dinner."*

*Remy winked at him and turned back to shake her ass again.
He swore she did that on purpose just to tease him. Her eighteenth
birthday was only three weeks away, and it couldn't have come
any sooner. She wanted him. He wanted her. Damn his mother
for making him promise to be "good" until she was officially
an adult.*

*Now sweaty, starving, and hard, he turned away to go deal with
the latter and the sweatiness in the shower when suddenly Remy
said, "Actually, I think a shower here is better."*

*He turned just in time to get sprayed in face with the jet of
water. His mother's laughter echoed in the air, followed by Remy's
squeal as he charged forward, stole the hose, scooped her up, and
soaked them both.*

"You're awake."

Asher blinked, thrust back into the garden where his mother
no longer stood. Those memories used to haunt him. The happiness he had with his mother was one of the reasons he left Stoney
Creek. She'd been everywhere, and that hurt more than Asher
could bear. "Good morning," he said, grabbing his sweater and
tugging her closer to him. "Getting your hands dirty already?"

She frowned up at him. "What happened to your mom's
garden?"

"I happened," Asher said with a laugh. "No green thumb, remember?"

"Well, it's such a shame," Remy said with sad eyes. "We're going to have to fix this and get it back in tiptop shape."

She went to walk by him, and he grabbed her again, picked her up in his arms. He loved the surprised gasp she gave, as much as he loved that she didn't stop him from kissing her. He kept the kiss soft and sweet and backed away before she could remember her kissing rules. "Did you sleep well?" he asked, placing her back onto her feet.

She nodded. "Like a log until Salem jumped on my head."

Asher laughed and tugged on the sweater. "I like this on you."

"I know." She grinned up at him with heat and promise. "That's why I put it on." She turned and headed into the house.

He followed, then locked the door behind him. "Listen, I'm going to drop you off at your shop. I've got somewhere I need to be, but I texted Kinsley and she's going to come and hang with you for the day. Plus, we've still got a cruiser at your place." When he turned around, he found her frowning at him. "What?"

She studied him a moment with her hands on her hips. "What you are you up to?"

"Nothing."

Her brows raised.

"Nothing that needs to concern you," he appeased.

Her eyes narrowed. "You're not going to get all protective and do something stupid with Lars are you?"

The old him would have, but just as Remy wasn't that innocent girl anymore, Asher wasn't that hot-headed kid either. He shook his head. "The chief has given me a direct order to stay away from Lars."

"All right," she eventually said, obviously believing him. "I'll be ready in a jiffy."

"Great." He smiled, moving back into the kitchen to make them both coffee.

While he couldn't talk with Lars today, he did have a plan, and that plan was set into motion after he dropped Remy off at her shop and waited for Kinsley to arrive. After that, with Rhett sitting in the passenger seat, Asher made the three-hour drive to Portland. He'd purposely left Boone behind, since Boone wouldn't approve of this visit. Rhett was always up for a little trouble, and Asher couldn't sit around and do nothing. He needed answers and he'd get them.

The GPS finally indicated to turn off the I-295, and a handful of turns later, they were driving into the suburbs and pulled into a gorgeous home with manicured lawns and a black BMW sitting in the driveway. Asher pulled in beside the car, then cut the engine. "Now we know why Fanning targeted Violi's sister," he said, opening the car's door.

Rhett whistled and began getting out. "That car alone costs more than our yearly salaries combined."

Asher followed him out and then sidled up to him. They strode toward the limestone bungalow and Asher knocked on the dark oak wooden front door with a wrought iron lion's head doorknocker.

The door opened a moment later to a slender woman in her mid-forties. Violi's sister looked identical to the photograph he'd seen. Dark eyes, dark hair, and full lips and pink cheeks. "Christine?" Asher asked.

She opened the door a little wider. "I take it you're the detectives from Stoney Creek?"

When Asher called Christine to see if she'd talk face-to-face with them, he wasn't sure how to take her willingness. Now he suspected she had nothing to hide. "We are. I'm detective Asher Sullivan." He gestured at Rhett. "This is my partner, Detective Rhett West." They exchanged a handshake before Asher continued. "I'm very grateful that you agreed to speak to us."

"Of course." She moved out of the doorway and let them enter. "Please come in, but I'm not sure what else I can tell you about Andrew."

Andrew aka Damon aka Kyle. "We just have some questions of our own about what happened with Andrew," Asher said, removing his shoes and following behind her into her sitting room. The furniture was pristine, everything too new, too nice. Asher almost didn't want to sit down.

Rhett actually didn't take a seat. He moved to the window and stood there, folding his arms across his chest.

That's why Rhett didn't deal with victims. His broodiness made people uncomfortable. Boone was usually the brains when it came to a case. Rhett had great attention to detail with evidence. Asher had a way with victims, and always had. People trusted him. He had an innate instinct when to push and when to pull back. Everyone talked with Asher and gave up information they might not even have known they were withholding. That was a skill that had caught the FBI recruiter's attention in the police academy, and that's what led to the job offer.

Asher wanted Christine to be comfortable and to start talking. He sat across from her, extending his arm along the back of the couch, projecting ease. "I am so very sorry to hear what happened to you with Andrew. We've had a similar case in Stoney Creek against him. What happened to you shouldn't happen to anymore."

She glanced away and gave a little shrug. "Yeah, well, as much as I hate him, I was sorry to hear of his passing."

Asher stared blankly at this woman. She was the polar opposite of what he expected to find today, and also the exact opposite of her brother. He took that in and gave Rhett a quick look before he focused back on Christine. "We actually haven't come to talk about your ex-husband per se, but to discuss your brother, Lars Violi."

"My brother?" she asked, wide-eyed. "Why?"

Asher leaned forward, staring at her intently. "I need to understand your brother's involvement with your ex-husband."

Her face suddenly lost all of its color. "We should not be talking about this." She rose, fidgeting her hands. "You should go. I know nothing about any of this."

Which, of course, told Asher she knew *something*. He'd let the Whitby Falls PD know that she might be someone to interview in regard to Fanning's death, but Asher's focus was on Remy and her safety. "A very good friend of mine almost married Andrew recently," he explained gently, not moving from his spot. "Instead of healing now, she's dealing with your brother coming around and asking questions. We suspect he is behind a recent break-in at her home. That's why we're here."

Christine watched Asher a moment, her eyes sad, and she returned to her seat. "There's been another victim?"

Asher nodded. "And just like you, she doesn't deserve what happened to her. Your brother wants something from her. I need to understand what that is so I can help her."

Christine twirled her finger in her hair, looking everywhere but at him. "I'm not sure why you think I can help you. I've only seen my brother twice in the past four years."

"Is there are reason for that?" Rhett asked.

She gave Rhett a quick look, then glanced away. "My choice. I…I don't like who my brother surrounds himself with. He understands and respects that."

Asher had seen cops and FBI agents alike interrogate criminals and interview families of criminals. He'd seen them go up against people and fail. And he'd learned from their failures. "Christine, look at me," he said softly. She jerked her head up, blinking rapidly. "I see that you're afraid of your brother, and I understand why. Lars will never know that we've come to talk to you. But I need you to understand that a woman I care a great deal about—a woman whose life has been shattered—now has your brother breathing down her neck. Think of what that would be like for her."

Her bottom lip trembled, and her head bowed. "I won't be able to stop him. I can't help you."

Asher softened his voice further to comfort her. "I know you can't stop him. I wouldn't ask you to, but you can tell me what you know about your ex-husband and what Lars could want from him."

Christine hesitated for a long moment and wrung her flighty hands together. "I went to Lars when I had suspicions about Andrew." She finally looked at Asher, tears in her eyes. "By the time Lars had confirmation that Andrew was stealing my money, he'd already run." Her voice broke. "I didn't know, you know…what would happen to Andrew."

"That's not why I'm here, Christine," he told her. "Please, think, what could Lars want from Andrew?"

Christine's eyes darted from Asher to Rhett and then back to Asher again. "I honestly don't know." She paused, her gaze flicking up to the ceiling.

"Anything will help, Christine," Asher pressed.

She looked back at Asher straight in the eye. "There is one thing you should know about my brother. He's honor-bound to protect his family. If he feels anyone has threatened or hurt them, he won't stop until he gets revenge."

Asher read between the lines. "So, in his mind, you think he feels that my friend has done something to hurt your family?"

She shrugged. "That's the only thing I can think of that would keep him hanging around."

"That's ridiculous," Rhett said with a snort. "There's gotta be something more."

Christine challenged him with a fierce stare. "I'm telling you, I know my brother. If he is pursuing her for any reason, and doesn't seem to back off, it's because she's done something that Lars feels has hurt me."

Asher glanced at Rhett, who frowned.

"This woman," Christine said, drawing Asher's attention back to her. "Are you sure she's as innocent as you believe?"

"Beyond a doubt," Asher stated clearly.

Christine hesitated enough to draw in a deep breath. "Well then, all I can think of is that maybe she's done something that's made Lars believe she's not Andrew's victim, but is his partner."

# Chapter 17

A few minutes after five o'clock, Remy stepped out into the cold, cloudy fall afternoon and locked the shop's front door as Kinsley said behind her, "I'm not supposed to leave you."

"You've got a bar to run and they need you for a minute," Remy said, turning around. Kinsley's employees called, reporting missing booze from the storage room. "I just want to grab some plants and take them over to Asher's, then I'll be right back. I'm fine. Meet me back here in fifteen minutes."

Kinsley firmed her stance and crossed her arms. "No."

Remy rolled her eyes, hating the fuss, but loving them all for it too. "Okay, how about I get the cop at the back to follow me to Asher's place. Sound good?"

Kinsley considered that and nodded. "That'll do. Better to be safe than sorry." She leaned in and kissed Remy's cheek. "Once you're back, come to the bar, and then we'll go hang at my place."

"Sounds like a plan." She walked side by side next to Kinsley until she reached the alleyway. "See ya later."

Kinsley waved and then headed into the bar.

Remy walked the dozen or so steps until she spotted the cruiser sitting in the same spot it had been since Asher put protective detail on her loft. "Hi, Fritz," she said to the cute, dark-haired twentysomething cop. He had gorgeous blue eyes, and probably was a killer with the ladies. "I'd like to pick up some plants and take them to Asher's. I feel absolutely ridiculous asking this—"

"It's not a problem," he said firmly. "I'll follow you there and back."

She smiled. "Perfect. Thank you." She rushed to her car and got in quickly, driving her car to the front, with Fritz closely following her. She parked in front of the hardware store and hurried inside.

Huxley Hardware had been around for as long as Remy could remember, and probably had been there before that. The rectangular-shaped shop had an odd smell of something between dust, mold, and musk, but Remy smiled at the memories of when Nana brought her here as a child. Remy had always been sure that Mr. Huxley and Nana had a thing going on, but she never could confirm that.

"Hey, Remy," Clifford Huxley, the grandson of Mr. Huxley, called when the front door chimed behind her.

Clifford stood behind the counter with the old register. He was two years younger than Remy, and cute, with his black-rimmed glasses and stylish haircut. They'd gotten to know each other well, especially after Nana passed away and Remy came in to buy the herbs she needed. "Hey!" She smiled in return. "How're things?"

"Good around here," Clifford said. "I hear the grand opening was a huge success. Congrats on the shop." He hesitated, then glanced up through his thick lashes. "Sorry about all the rest."

Word traveled at light speed in this town. "Thanks." Clifford had always been a good guy. Genuine and kind.

Obviously sensing she didn't want to stay on the topic of Damon and the break-in, he moved around the counter. "What can I help you with?"

For a little blip, she had a moment. One where thinking about Damon and his death didn't fill her with unruly emotion. The water cleansing obviously did the trick. But she knew that moving on from Damon had a lot to do with Asher too. Just another thing that made her smile. She never thought the guy who broke her heart into a million pieces would help her re-build her life now. Life was such a peculiar thing. "I know it's late in the season, but what have you got in terms of something I can plant?"

Clifford gestured toward the back of the shop. "We don't have much left, but honestly we'll give you a good deal on whatever we've got."

"Perfect," Remy said, and followed him through the rows of screws and tools. When she'd seen Maggie's flowerbeds this morning, her heart broke. Not only because Maggie had loved her garden, but that Asher had let the flowers and plants die. Seeing the gardens must have been too much of a reminder of his mother. When she was out there today, she knew that she needed to return the favor. He helped her rebuild. She needed to do the same for him, and that started with bringing the good memories of Maggie back.

As she entered the back area that led to a small greenhouse, she smiled, realizing the past didn't seem so hard anymore. She and Asher wouldn't ever go back to that time before he left her, where she believed love was all rainbows and sunshine, but maybe they'd found something new. Something that was more mature, real, and honest. Something that said no matter what happened, they'd always come back to each other, one way or another. And that their friendship mattered. He'd been there for her, picking her up when she was at her lowest of lows. Now she wanted to do the same for him. And he was at a low; she saw that now.

"What do you think?" Clifford asked when they entered the practically empty greenhouse.

Remy took one look at the twenty or so pitiful plants desperate for a chance at life. "They're perfect. How much for all of them?"

Clifford gave her a look like she'd lost her mind and examined the twenty plants with a scrunched nose. "Gimme twenty bucks and we'll call it even."

"Great," Remy said, then glanced at the plants, reassessing. "How much to help me get this stuff in my car?"

"Ah, that I'll do for free." Clifford smiled.

It took ten minutes to load all the plants into the trunk and back seat of her car, and then Remy was careful on the drive over to Asher's place so she didn't send any of the plants flying, with Fritz following closely behind. As it was, the plants were going to need some TLC before winter hit. Some would probably die, but at least she'd get those flowerbeds looking better than they did now. Remy hoped it gave Asher a little peace.

She turned up the radio, singing along to the song, still wondering where he'd gone today. Usually whenever the guys got quiet about what they were doing, it involved a case. She just hoped it wasn't hers.

When she finally pulled into Asher's driveway, the clock read 5:22 on her dashboard. She hurried out, planning on dropping the plants off and coming back with Kinsley later to plant them.

Fritz pulled in behind her, cutting his ignition too. She gave him a wave, which he returned, and then she moved around to the trunk to start unloading, when someone called her name.

She turned at the exact moment that two gunshots rang out and bulging arms wrapped around her and yanked her into a car. She screamed, but it was soon muffled by a hand over her mouth. She bit down hard, tasting the metallic tang of blood on her tongue.

"Fuck," the man grunted.

He released her and she was flung onto the leather seat next to him as the SUV sped off. It took a moment to get her bearings, but she watched Fitz running after them with his gun drawn through the back window, his car tires blown out. Relief that he hadn't been shot overwhelmed her, but then she realized the danger she'd been put in. She jerked her head forward and noticed that the man next to her, who was wrapping a handkerchief around his hand, wasn't a stranger. Neither was the man sitting in the passenger seat.

Lars sat casually, that crooked smile on his face.

Next to him was one of the men who had been at the restaurant, keeping his attention on the road ahead. And the man she bit was the other guy from the restaurant.

"Scream and we'll have trouble," Lars said. "Be quiet and we won't."

She held back that scream he mentioned, and her stomach hardened like a rock as she glanced around trying to get a grip on reality. "Stop this car. Now!"

"Not going to happen," Lars drawled. "You need to pay for what you've done."

Remy glanced outside, trying to see where they were taking her, but they were already out in the vast wilderness of Maine.

*Asher*... "I haven't done anything," she nearly yelled back at him. How many times did she have to say it?

"Bullshit," Lars growled, his lip curling. "I know that you barely had any money to your name. I know you bought your shop instead of renting it. I know that you're not as innocent as you say you are."

The world stopped turning. No, she wasn't totally innocent, but she also wasn't as guilty as Damon. Remy noticed then that the driver had an earpiece, indicating he might be security of some kind. Her heart hammered, nearly exploding, and her gaze fell to the guy next to her. She contemplated unlocking the door and jumping out. Sure, she'd most definitely get injured, but at least she wasn't a sitting duck waiting for the very worst thing to happen to her. The road was busy enough that someone would see her and help.

She slowly lifted her hand to reach for the lock, when the guy next to her said, "Bad idea." He slid his tailored blazer aside, revealing a gun. She squeezed her trembling fingers together. "Where are you taking me?" she managed.

Lars glanced over his shoulder. "To—"

"Whitby Falls to have a chat," the guy next to her interjected. "And then we'll return you home after."

Lars scowled. "I never—"

The man ignored Lars and said, "You're difficult to get close to because of the detective. Measures needed to be taken to ensure we've got time alone with you, but you have my word that you're safe and you'll be returned home afterward."

It occurred to her that she shouldn't trust anyone, but the guy had surprisingly trusting hazel eyes. Both he and the driver were easy on the eyes, in fact. They looked strong, military maybe. Maybe that's what made them good killers. They looked like men who protected the country. "Who exactly am I meeting?" she asked to understand her situation.

"Joaquin King."

The name registered immediately, and Remy felt the blood drain from her face. She'd read the newspaper articles and seen the reports. Joaquin King wasn't just a criminal; he was the head of the King crime family.

*Fuck.*

* * *

Asher's knuckles were white against the steering wheel as the engine purred beneath him. He'd driven to Portland in three hours. He made it back home in two and a half hours. The call from Boone repeated in his mind every second on the drive back to Stoney Creek. *"Remy's car was found at your house with the door left open. She's missing. Fitz was with her. They shot out his tires."*

How could Asher have let this happen? He shouldn't have left her. He should have been more careful, been smarter, knowing who she was dealing with. He should have realized something more was going on. *Fuck.* His fingers tightened against the steering wheel.

Once again, he was back to wishing he'd done more for Remy. And once again, he'd failed her.

"Stop berating yourself," Rhett said, sitting easy in the passenger seat, obviously reading Asher's mind. "There's no way you could've anticipated this."

"I should have anticipated everything," Asher shot back, wishing he had a cruiser to hit the sirens and fly through town.

He slowed the car when he came up behind an old Chevy and then he hit the gas and passed the car. "All the signs were there that things were escalating."

"Escalating from what?" Rhett snorted. "You're connecting things in your mind that aren't there. Beyond making assumptions, the break-in wasn't linked to Lars. He hasn't made a step out of place that would suggest he'd abduct her."

Asher shifted into a higher gear, speeding his car up on the open roads. He took the back way, which was longer in most cases, but there weren't traffic lights or congestion. "Lars better not lay a finger on her. I'll fucking kill him."

"And I'll help you," Rhett stated dryly.

Another few agonizing minutes clicked by, and soon, Asher turned onto his street, his tires squealing. He caught the cruisers blocking off the intersection near his place, then screeched to a stop next to one of the them and jumped out, running to where Boone stood near Remy's car. "Anything?" he asked, hearing the desperation in his own voice.

Boone shook his head, arms crossed over his chest. "Nothing. The chief is back at the station monitoring things from there if anything comes in. We've put out an APB on the SUV. Fitz got the license plate as Remy got yanked in."

"Did he fire at the vehicle?" Rhett asked.

"He didn't trust his shot," Boone said gently. "He didn't want to hurt her."

Asher needed to talk with Fitz once he got Remy back. He understood the type of guilt Fitz likely suffered, and Fitz was just a rookie, only finishing the police academy six months ago. Which was exactly why the chief could spare him and Ian to keep an eye on Remy. "I had no idea she was coming over." His fists clenched against the fear Remy must have faced when she got dragged into the SUV. He moved closer to Remy's car, glanced in the back, and saw plants on the floor and in the back seat.

Damn. She came to fix his mother's garden. Her sweetness had put her in danger, and Asher felt the guilt of that sit hard in his gut. If his inability to face his mother's garden got Remy hurt or worse…He shook his head, not letting his mind go there. "What else do you know?" he asked.

Boone's forehead wrinkled and he lifted one shoulder. "Only what I've told you. Fitz said he saw the SUV drive up, they shot out his tires, then grabbed her. I'm afraid that's all I've got." He cupped Asher's shoulder. "Now tell me what I don't know."

Asher dropped his head and exhaled slowly, trying to find the sane part of his brain. The one that didn't want to tear the town apart looking for Remy. "We went and spoke with Lars's sister, Christine Violi. She has had no contact with her brother. It's pretty clear that she's not comfortable with the fact that he's involved with Joaquin King."

"Smart woman," Boone said, folding his arms.

Asher agreed with a nod. "Although they're not close, she did indicate that the only reason Lars would be interested in Remy is because she'd done something that hurt his family."

Boone lifted an eyebrow. "Any idea what that is?"

"Not a clue," Asher said, beginning to pace the sidewalk. He kept feeling like he was one step behind this. Not a favorable position.

"If you ask me," Rhett said, examining the skid marks that the SUV obviously left when it sped out, "there's something we don't know." He placed one foot on the curb. "Remy's got herself involved in *something*. Nothing about any of this makes sense. We know Lars met with King, and somehow that connection relates to Remy."

Asher pondered. "It's gotta be Fanning. That is the only connection here."

"I'm not arguing with you," Boone said with a knowing look. "But the only one who can help us understand that connection is Lars, and right now, he's gone."

"What happened to the tail we had on him?" Asher asked.

"He lost them," Boone reported. "That call came in twenty minutes before Fitz radioed in."

Asher moved to Remy's car, leaned against it, and folded his arms. Pounding behind his eyes clouded his vision as he stared down at the very spot that someone wrapped their arms around her and yanked her into danger. "This doesn't fucking make sense." He rubbed his hands on his face, feeling the tension roll through him. "What in the hell does Violi want with her enough to abduct her?"

Rhett kicked at the curb. "You found nothing connecting Lars with the two King guys he met at that restaurant in Whitby Falls?"

Boone shook his head. "They're two retired Navy SEALS who are now working for King, but beyond that, I couldn't find a single link between them."

"Perhaps Lars has hired them?" Asher offered.

"It's possible," Boone said.

"Yeah, it's possible," Rhett countered. "But what would Lars need protection from? Again, there's a piece missing from all this."

A sudden squeal of tires had Asher glancing down the road. For a heartbeat, Asher held his breath, hoping to hell it was Remy. Disappointment settled in a second later when he saw Kinsley driving her Jeep with Peyton in the passenger seat. They parked behind one of the cruisers and then came running to them.

"Did you find her?" Kinsley asked, her face ashen.

Boone shook his head. "Not yet."

Kinsley dropped her head into her hands, her shoulders shaking with her cries. "I should have gone with her to the hardware store. I've done this."

"You haven't done anything," Boone said, taking his sister into a hug. "No one is responsible for this but Lars."

Peyton's eyes watered. "What does this guy want with her?" she asked.

"Exactly what I want to fucking find out," Asher growled, thrusting his hands through his hair. "I don't even fucking know where to look for her." The world spun a little and Asher squatted, leaning against her car. A thousand things flashed through his mind; terrible things of what Lars was doing to Remy. Having seen people at their very worst, it was impossible not to let his mind wander to dark places. "I can't lose her."

He wasn't sure if he said that aloud or in his head, until Boone said, "You won't lose her. We've got every station from here to Portland looking for that SUV. Someone will see it."

What if that call came in too late?

The world rocked beneath him, nothing seeming stable, everything crumbling around him. "I can't lose her," he repeated, the thought sending him falling into a dark pit he knew he'd never climb out of.

Kinsley suddenly squatted next to him and placed a warm, comforting arm around his shoulder. "What can we do to help?"

Asher shut his eyes. He was always the strong one. The comforting one for victims. He knew what to say to make everyone feel better. That's what he did. That was his job. He felt lost now, spiraling out of control, with no answers for anyone.

Rhett broke the silence. "Looks like Remy went to the hardware store and got some plants for the backyard." He opened the trunk. "Kinsley, why don't you and Peyton see to getting that done for her? It's one thing she won't have to worry about when she comes home."

A tear slid down Kinsley's cheek, but she wiped it away quickly, then threw her arms around Asher. He couldn't even hug her back. He couldn't move, couldn't breathe. He needed Remy. Right there. Safe. The guilt began to drown him. Kinsley eventually let him go and moved to the trunk, where Rhett waited.

Peyton gave Boone a final kiss and then grabbed a plant. When she walked by Asher, she said, "Boone's right. You guys never fail." Her gaze strengthened. "*Never*, Asher."

Asher nodded and rose, leaning against the car to steady himself. Peyton wasn't wrong—they never failed at any case. He, Boone, and Rhett were an unbreakable team, one that caught the worst kinds of criminals, who didn't stop until the good guys came out on top.

"Remy is smart and quick," Rhett said, sidling up to him. "She'll keep herself safe until we get there."

"I know she will," Asher said, his gut burning. "But she shouldn't fucking have to." All he wanted to do was fix things for her, and everything seemed to be disintegrating.

But that didn't mean he'd stop trying.

He'd never stop protecting her.

His feet were moving him in the direction of his car before he could even decide where they should take him. After he got in and the engine purred, the passenger-side door opened. Rhett slid into the back and Boone took the front seat.

"Where to?" Boone asked, buckling up his seat belt.

Asher put the car in first gear. "The station."

"For?" Rhett asked from back seat.

"For Boone to grab his files on King," Asher explained, hitting the gas. "I can't sit around and wait. We've seen Lars with the security team working for King. You've got a list of all their known meeting places?"

"Yeah," Boone said.

Asher shifted into gear. "Then we'll hit every single one until we find Remy."

# Chapter 18

The SUV pulled into a long curving driveway hugged by a forest, and sweat beaded against the back of Remy's shirt. She contemplated running when she exited the vehicle but she caught sight of the weapon again and went willingly toward the front door. Asher and the guys would find her. That she trusted wholeheartedly. She simply needed to stay safe until then, and to do that, she needed to be smart.

Flanked by two men, she was led into a large log home set back in the woods, with Lars trailing behind them. She hastily took in her surroundings. From the expensive-looking furniture to every little design element, the cottage screamed money. They moved through the open-concept living room and into a library that held a big cherrywood desk and wingback leather chair. But it was the man sitting at that chair who quickly drew her focus.

Joaquin King. Son of the King crime boss, Stefano King, who had been sent to prison back in the nineties and died there. Remy knew all about him from Hank and Boone casually talking about him, and from the news. From what she recalled from their talks, Joaquin had picked up where his father left off, but he was a different kind of criminal than his father. Where his father had been brutal and cutthroat, Joaquin was smart and ruthless. He'd created an empire where business walked the line between dirty and clean, and he'd played the game so well that he'd never been arrested. Not once.

Joaquin's dark blue eyes regarded her intently as she entered the room. His presence was as threatening as it was imposing. His black suit jacket was resting on the back of a leather chair, and the sleeves of his white dress shirt were rolled up on his strong forearms. His face was all hard lines and his five-o'clock shadow only seemed to heighten his dark broodiness. "Remy Brennan," he finally said in a low, throaty voice. "Please, come sit."

She swallowed her nerves and sat in the client chair in front of the desk.

"Do you know who I am?" Joaquin asked, forearms casually leaning on the armrests of his chair.

She nodded. "I do."

"Good, that keeps things easy," he said with a smile that never reached his eyes. For a moment, his gaze flicked over her shoulder before returning to her. "Lars has indicated that you and Andrew Phillips have been in business together, but I wanted to hear that from you."

"I have no idea who Andrew Phillips is," she admitted.

Joaquin gestured with a flick of his chin. "How can she not know who Andrew is?"

Lars sidled up next to Remy's chair, hands laced behind his back. "She knows him as Damon Lane."

Joaquin's hard gaze returned to Remy. "Is that true?"

Remy noted a certain calmness about Joaquin that was utterly terrifying. Remy got the real sense that one wrong move on her part and she wouldn't see tomorrow. "Yes, I know Damon Lane. I almost married him a few weeks ago, but luckily, I found out that he was conning me out of my inheritance."

"Fucking lies," Lars spat, a vein in his head nearly popping.

Joaquin coolly arched an eyebrow at her. "Is that a lie?"

Remy finally breathed, letting the tension go from her chest and shook her head. "I've told Lars on multiple occasions now that I have nothing to do with Damon, or Andrew, or Kyle, or whoever he is. I was the victim in all this, and I'm not sure why he keeps thinking that I have some part in it. He's wrong."

Joaquin frowned at Lars. "I'm beginning to think that you've got a problem here."

Remy took a quick look at Lars and saw the slight tremble of his hand. It dawned on her then that Lars wasn't the bad guy there. He was a man caught in something he needed a way out of, and Remy was his way out.

Lars drew in a deep breath and set his hard gaze on Remy. "She's a fucking liar. She bought a shop recently, without any money in her bank account, and with cash. She thinks she can outsmart us, but she's in this with Andrew. I promise you that."

Joaquin leaned back in his chair and his eyes narrowed thoughtfully on Remy. Everything in the room seemed to freeze under his careful regard. Her heart pounded in her ears when he suddenly rose and moved to the window, staring out with his hands in his pockets. "I'm going to explain the situation to you, Ms. Brennan," Joaquin said, not looking back at her. "I am a businessman. Unlike my father, I like things to stay on the right side of the law if possible. Mr. Violi's sister had agreed to invest two hundred thousand into a company of mine. The deal had come through, Mr. Violi, isn't that right?" He glanced over his shoulder at Lars, and the fierceness in his expression sent her heart into her throat.

Lars glanced at his feet. "Yes, sir."

"I take my investments very seriously, Ms. Brennan," Joaquin continued, turning around, staring solely at her now. "And when the investment came due, we learned from Lars of the situation with Andrew…" He paused and his mouth twitched. "Excuse me, Damon Lane, running off with the money." Joaquin returned to his seat. "I instructed Lars to not only find Mr. Lane, but to find the money that had been stolen from me."

A sudden coldness struck Remy to the core. Sure, all along she'd had her suspicions that Damon's money had something to do with all this, but now she understood *why* Damon's money had something to do with all this. It wasn't Damon's money at all. Nor was it Lars's money. That money belonged to Joaquin King, and that's very likely the reason Damon died.

"When Mr. Violi found Damon Lane," Joaquin continued, "he agreed to return the money that he stole from me, and in doing so, we could put this matter to bed."

"Too late for that," Lars spat, "she fucking spent it."

Joaquin's fierce gaze cut to Lars, and he took a step back.

Remy became very aware that the two security guards moved a little closer in their direction. "This is where we are at, Ms. Brennan," Joaquin said, coming to lean forward on his desk, his strong forearms flexing. "I need the truth from you. Have you spent the money that Damon Lane was supposed to return to me?"

There were times to lie and times to be honest. The darkness in Joaquin's eyes told Remy the latter was the *only* option. "I thought the money was Damon's. I found it in my house."

"You didn't think to turn it in to the police?" Joaquin asked.

"Yes, of course, I did," Remy explained. "But—"

"You fucking spent it," Lars injected.

Joaquin's nostrils flared. "If you interrupt our conversation again, Mr. Violi, we will have a problem."

Lars shut his trap and moved back to the door.

Joaquin's expression softened a smidgen when he glanced at Remy. "Go on."

She drew in a deep breath and then said, "I'd been hurt by Damon, and when I found the money, I felt like…"

"You were owed the debt," Joaquin finished for her.

She shrugged. "Something like that."

He sat back in his chair and watched her for a long moment, tapping his thumb against the desk. "I believe what you're telling me."

"Thank you," she said. "It's the truth."

He acknowledged that with a nod, then added, "But regardless of the fact that I believe you, this has created a situation for you, Ms. Brennan."

She shut her mouth now, sensing a shift in him, a hardness that had her knowing the best thing to do was stay silent.

"That money," he added firmly, "is my money. I do not take kindly to people who spend money that is mine. Do you understand?"

Oh, yeah, she *fully* understood. She'd seen the news articles detailing the murders of men and women who got in the way of business deals that all came back to King. She also remembered Boone's frustration when he worked a case involving Joaquin. His men were wicked smart and had yet to leave a single trace of evidence, and those who worked for King were loyal to the bone. "Yes, I understand." She needed to get that money back to him, and she needed to do that yesterday.

Right then, the door opened, and another well-dressed, well-muscled man entered. He didn't even acknowledge her and moved to Joaquin and said something in his ear. Joaquin rose. "You've got three days to return my money, Ms. Brennan." Everything about Joaquin screamed deadly, but most of all the cold iciness in his eyes was what kept her pinned to her seat. "You seem like a smart woman," he added, slipping into his blazer. "Do not disappoint me. I'll be in touch."

His men followed him out, along with Lars, who glared at her on his way out the door.

Right as that door closed, another door flew open and Asher charged into the room, his weapon aimed out in front of him. Everything that had been wrong a second ago was suddenly all better with those green eyes on her. There was a flurry of chaos as Boone and Rhett followed him inside, quickly scanning the room, weapons drawn.

Asher's gaze stayed trained on Remy. He lowered his gun and rushed forward, taking her in his arms, giving her a good look over. "Are you all right?" he asked.

She nodded, her adrenaline making her shake all over. "Yes, I'm all right."

Rhett kept his weapon aimed down the hallway. Boone entered the room farther and glanced out the window. "Are you alone?"

"Now, yes." She gestured at the other door. "They went out that way."

Tires against gravel cut through the air and Boone turned away from the window. "They're gone."

Asher took Remy's hand and tugged her in front of him and behind Boone. "Let's get you out of here."

"I've never been happier to hear those words in all my life," she breathed.

All together, they backed up out of the room and then Rhett carefully led them down the hallway. They hurried into Asher's car, Remy and Asher in the back, and Boone in the passenger seat. Rhett jumped in the driver's seat and with a squeal of his tires, he sped away.

Silence thickened the air in the car as Asher yanked her to him, holding her tight. He kissed the top of her head and said, "Jesus Christ, Remy. I have never been so fucking scared." He leaned away and looked over her again, scanning her from head to toe. "Are you okay?"

She nodded. "They didn't hurt me, they just wanted to talk."

Emotion flared in his eyes. He cupped her face and pressed his lips against hers. His kiss was fierce and everything she needed to ease the chill in her bones. She'd landed herself in quite the mess, and she considered how to explain all this. Just spending Damon's money was bad. *This?*

A total clusterfuck.

When Asher broke away, he said, "You must have been so scared. I'm sorry I wasn't there. I should have fucking been there." He pressed his forehead against hers.

She leaned into his strength and warmth. "I knew you'd come."

He moved away then, brushing his hand across her cheek. "Always, Remy. I'll always come for you." Then he sealed his mouth against hers again for a long, sweet moment. He gathered her in his arms even closer and held her tight like nothing would ever touch her again.

They drove for a good twenty minutes, and only when she stopped shaking did she break the silence. "How did you find me?" she asked, realizing she was gripping his T-shirt. She released her hands.

Asher's arms only tightened. "We were looking at known King-associated places, but Fitz got the license plate number. A trucker saw the SUV and called it in. We were only ten minutes away and came." A pause, then his voice tightened. "Was it Lars in that SUV?"

Remy nodded against his warm chest. "He was there, yes."

Asher slid out of his coat, then wrapped it around her like a blanket as Boone turned around in the passenger seat and said, "You need to talk to us, Remy, explain what happened there. What did Lars want?"

Remy knew the reaction she was going to get, but there was no denying that she was way in over her head. She looked at Asher, and he cupped her face as she said, "It wasn't Lars who wanted to talk to me."

Surprised flickered across his face. "Then who was it?"

"Joaquin King."

Rhett slammed on the brakes and pulled the car off the road. He turned back to her. "Joaquin King was there?"

She nodded, inching her way closer to Asher to get his warmth, and her eyelids suddenly felt heavy. "He was the one who wanted to talk to me."

Rhett frowned. "Damn, Remy, what the hell have you gotten yourself involved in?"

Asher tucked a firm finger tucked under her chin. His gaze was firm but tender. "You're not alone in this. Explain what happened so we can help you."

Remy could run and hope that she could hide from this, but she could feel the concern running through the air like electricity. She feared all the good steps she and Asher had taken forward would be erased when she told them the truth. That's what made this all so hard. She'd brought her friends into a dangerous situation, a situation none of them deserved. She let her droopy eyes shut with tears behind her eyelids. "Take me home and I'll tell you everything."

# Chapter 19

*"I found two hundred thousand dollars in my house. I thought the money belonged to Damon, so I used it to buy my shop. Apparently, the money belongs to Joaquin King, and he wants it back."*

Asher stared at Remy. She was sitting across from him on his couch while his ass was parked on his coffee table. He'd repeated what she told them a dozen times, and yet, the words and danger they presented couldn't sink in. She sat cross-legged with her gaze glued on Salem purring in her lap. Asher slowly turned his head, taking in Boone's frown and Rhett's wide eyes, telling him that his hope that he'd heard things wrong was just that…*a hope*. And that Remy had indeed landed herself directly in trouble she shouldn't be anywhere near.

"Damn." Rhett finally broke the silence, standing near the window, arms folded over his chest. "Didn't your cards or whatever smelly shit you burn tell you this was a horrible idea?"

She shrugged. "Spiritually, I actually got the go-ahead."

Thick tension filled the room as Boone took the seat on the couch next to Remy. "I'm trying to understand how this all came about," he said softly. "Doing something like *this*… it's very unlike you, Remy. What were you thinking?"

She kissed Salem, who purred and rubbed his head into her chin. "I was only thinking that I was angry at Damon. I found the money and thought I deserved something for all the shit he'd put me through. His money gave me the shop and made my dreams come true. I thought he owed me that." Her voice trembled as she petted Salem, her full attention on the cat.

Asher stared blankly, still trying to accept that she'd used dirty money to buy herself a shop. She'd never taken a step out of place. What in the fuck had Asher done to her?

Boone gave Asher's foot a kick. He blinked into focus as Boone asked her, "You weren't afraid Damon would come back for the money?"

She gave a little shrug. "I told Damon that I'd found the money and turned it in to the police."

Asher's teeth ground together. He and Boone had driven Remy and Kinsley to see Damon once more in Whitby Falls. They'd told Asher that Remy wanted closure, considering how she'd left Damon before. "You lied to me?" Asher asked, hearing the controlled rage in his voice.

Still not looking up, she nodded. Salem purred louder.

From his spot near the window, Rhett said, "I take it that Damon believed you?"

She glanced up then, and nodded at Rhett. "Yeah, I was convincing."

Asher inhaled deeply and worked at the tension along his neck. Boone's gaze lifted to Asher's, and Boone didn't say a word. Neither did the frowning Rhett. They'd been wrong all along. Fanning wasn't murdered because he'd scammed Violi's sister. He'd been murdered because he owed King money. Money that he'd obviously withdrew to pay back the debt to save his life, but didn't have the chance to repay because Asher had arrested him.

Now that debt fell onto Remy's shoulders.

Adrenaline rushed through Asher's body, tightening his quivering muscles. He couldn't stand her avoidance any longer and tucked a finger under her chin, demanding her gaze. "Do you have any idea—"

The door slammed open. Asher, along with Boone and Rhett, lurched to his feet, with his weapon aimed at the front door.

Kinsley froze, eyes wide and glossy. She raised her hands in surrender. "Holy shit," she breathed.

"Goddamn it, Kinsley," Boone chastised, putting away his weapon. "Do you want to die?"

"Not particularly." She blinked, the color slowing returning to her face. "But when Peyton told me that you guys knew everything, I knew you were probably interrogating Remy, and this is not her fault."

Peyton entered the house and sighed. "Sorry, there was no stopping her." She shut the door and glanced at Remy sitting on the couch. The way she avoided Boone's gaze told Asher that they were all in on this.

Something Boone obviously caught too. "Please tell me you both did not know about this."

"We knew," Peyton said to the floor.

Boone ran off a string of curses that would make a sailor proud. "What in the hell were you all thinking?"

"My thoughts exactly," Asher growled. Unable to sit down any longer, he moved away from the coffee table and began pacing in front of his television. "This was bad enough when only Remy was involved." He set his hard gaze on each one of the women. "But all of you were in on this insane plan?"

"I wouldn't say it was a plan," Kinsley said, moving to Remy and taking a seat next to her. "I'd say it was more of a situation that fell into Remy's lap and we kind of rolled with it."

"Not the time to be a smart-ass, Kinsley," Boone bit off.

"I'm not being a smart-ass," Kinsley said with a glare. "It's the truth. We didn't plan for all this, but fate led us here."

Asher felt the elevation of his pulse as he moved to the window, staring out into the dark night. He breathed deeply, trying to control the simmering rage boiling beneath his skin. His father always lashed out in rage. Asher promised he'd never be like him. He shut his eyes a moment, getting control of the beast inside. When he felt calm enough, he went on. "Whether it was a plan or not, how could you all be so fucking stupid?"

"Actually, it wasn't stupid at all," Kinsley said with a snippy voice, turning Asher around to face her glare. "We were careful, making sure that Damon didn't ever come back for the money. From the way I saw it, all of Damon's other victims were going to be paid back. You told me that, Boone," she said to her brother, and then glared again at Asher. "They were all going to be okay, but what was Remy going to be? Heartbroken, forever, with nothing?"

"Kinsley, you will do well not to defend this," Boone warned, voice tight. "What you've all done is wrong."

"Oh, yeah—why?" Kinsley shot back, her arms folded across her chest. She always could go up against them. A force to be reckoned with, for sure.

Only Asher didn't appreciate that now. "Why is it wrong? Are you fucking kidding me?" He felt his nostrils flare, sensed his control slipping. "It's wrong because now you've got the attention of Joaquin King. A criminal known to *kill* people who owe him money. What do you think he'll do to Remy? Take her apology? That will *never* happen. This money that Damon owed King got Damon killed because he couldn't pay up. That's what is hanging over Remy now. That is what spending that money has done. Her life is now in danger, and the fault lies with each one of you for not stopping this fucking plan."

Asher blinked out of the rage. His hands fisted at his sides. But he knew deep down, this was all his fault. He'd done this to Remy. He'd set her life on this path.

Peyton's head hung, her shoulders shaking. Boone moved to her, tugging her into his arms, obviously not nearly as angry as Asher. But Peyton wasn't the target of King's attention. Remy was.

"Stop it," Remy cried, finally looking at Asher, tears streaming down her face. "I'm sorry, okay? I should have stopped this. I should have known better. I just…" Her voice broke. "I just wanted to be happy."

Asher's gut clenched at the fear, regret, and everything in between he saw in her expression. The blame fell on his shoulders, and yet, his blood was red-hot, his anger simmering, and his control nowhere to be found.

"You have no reason to feel bad, so put those tears away," Kinsley said firmly to Remy, and then scowled at Asher. "How could we have known who the money belonged to? I mean, come on, you know that anything in that bag would have gone to the Treasury Department. It would have sat there for years and then been destroyed. The money was *in* Remy's house. That's *her* property. She didn't commit a crime."

"She didn't commit a crime?" Asher sucked in a deep breath and then spoke in a very controlled voice. "She could be charged with larceny or theft. Fine, you found the money, you should have contacted an attorney for advice on how to proceed going forward if you didn't want to go to the cops."

"Oh, please, that's a stupid idea," Kinsley said with a snort. "Then the money would have been destroyed and Remy wouldn't have gotten any of it. At the time, with what we knew, this made sense."

Boone scoffed. "You do remember that you're the chief of police's daughter, right?"

"I know exactly who I am, thank you very much," Kinsley said, glaring at her older brother. "So I don't live by the letter of the law that you all do, but it was the right thing to do in that circumstance. I don't feel bad about it one bit. We weren't hurting anyone. All the victims were getting their money back. Remy was taking a tiny cut to see her dreams come true. You all know she deserved that, so you can all cool your jets."

Heavy silence descended, making the air feel thick and impossible to inhale. Until Rhett said, "She's not wrong."

Asher slowly turned his head toward his friend and stared, incredulous. "You cannot be fucking serious."

Rhett examined Kinsley for a long moment and then shrugged at Asher. "Does this fall in the cracks between the law? For sure. But I can't think of a single district attorney in any county who would bring up charges against Remy for this. The money was in *her* loft. It's her property."

"That is not the fucking point," Asher spat, feeling his skin prickle with heat. His gut burned. His fists clenched. *The danger...the blame...* Heat rushed rapidly through his veins. "The money is dirty. Remy should be nowhere near that, and now King knows her fucking name. He's seen her face. There is nothing I can do to change that. Do you have any idea of how bad that is for her? How much danger she is in? King had Damon killed. He's going to come after her too."

Boone suddenly moved, catching Asher's attention. He

gestured at Remy and shook his head. Her head was buried in her hands and she sobbed uncontrollably.

Fucking great. Now he was terrifying her.

He drew in a long, deep breath, regretting everything he'd just unleashed. He'd seen this view before. Many times. Only in place of Remy was his mother who'd been on the receiving end of his father's wrath. With a final look at her hard cries, he turned away and left the house before he made everything worse.

*Again.*

\* \* \*

Once Remy opened the floodgates, she couldn't stop, apparently needing to cry more than she thought she did. She had no idea how long had passed while Kinsley and Peyton held her tight, letting her get out the fear and sadness…and whatever else was lingering in Remy's heart. By the time she didn't have any tears left, Rhett had moved into the kitchen, and Peyton and Boone had gone upstairs to talk. When they came back down, Boone and Rhett, looking utterly miserable, grabbed some beers from the fridge and headed out to the porch. Kinsley grabbed three more beers, then returned to her spot on the couch, offering each Peyton and Remy one.

"Thanks for coming to my rescue," Remy said, cracking the beer open and dropping the cap onto the coffee table. "You didn't have to do that, but I appreciate it." She took the biggest gulp of beer of her life.

"God, don't thank us," Peyton said. "We were so scared for you. Boone has told me all about Joaquin King. That guy sounds scary."

"You don't have to tell me that," Remy said. "Here I thought Lars was bad news, but Joaquin was scarier...calmer...cooler...I don't know, just not a guy I want to ever know." Remy placed the chilled bottle against her sore eyes. "I still can't believe any of this. It's all so fucked up, and I've landed myself right in the middle of it."

"This isn't all on you," Kinsley said, then shrugged. "The truth is, you wouldn't have spent the money without my pushing you, so I'm as much at fault in all this as you." She drew in a deep breath before continuing. "Besides, I came here the second Peyton told me about what happened because you're way too nice. You never would have said what needed to be said. You did nothing wrong. Damon did the bad thing here—and that fact can't be forgotten. We couldn't have known it would come down to *this*. Now we just have to find a way out of it, is all. And once the guys calm down, they will see that too."

"Yeah, finding a solution is the problem, though, isn't it?" Remy's throat felt raw and sore like a hundred knives had gone through it. "If I had listened to Damon when he asked me for a favor and paid off his debt, maybe he wouldn't be dead."

Kinsley's whole demeanor softened. "You're not responsible. You didn't owe Damon *any* favors. And if you had, you would have placed yourself squarely in King's vision anyway. Who's to say he wouldn't have actually thought you had been working with Damon, which might have only firmed up Lars's suspicions."

From her spot at the window, staring out at the guys on the porch, Peyton said, "Kinsley's right. Damon's death is not your fault. He brought the trouble onto himself."

Remy's heart reached for Peyton. Both her friends were trying to make her feel better, and they'd outed themselves coming to her defense. "Is Boone mad at you?"

"Mad?" Peyton turned away from the window and then

she sank into Asher's leather recliner. "I think he's more disappointed. I'm sure he never thought I'd keep something like this from him. But, of course, he understands why I did. I was protecting you. He gets that."

"I'm sorry," Remy choked out, grabbing the blanket off the back of the couch to wrap around her, yanking it over her head. "I've made a mess out of everything. Now Boone's unhappy with you. Asher's furious. And everyone is danger."

"Oh, stop it," Kinsley said, pulling away the blanket until it settled on Remy's shoulders. "You had no idea that the money belonged to Joaquin King. None of us did. If we had, we obviously never would have spent it." She threw her arm around Remy, and Remy rested her head on her shoulder as Kinsley went on. "The guys are worried. That's all this is. They're not really mad." She paused, then she laughed softly. "I take that back. Asher's mad, but I can't really figure out why he's mad since this totally wasn't on purpose, so I'm thinking he doesn't even know why he's mad."

"Actually, I know why he's mad," Remy said. "I told him I got the money for my shop from my mother."

Kinsley winced. "Okay, yeah, lying is bad. But I'm sorry, you've thought enough about men and how to keep them happy. How about *you* in all this? Asher will either get over this or he won't. But I still say a thousand times over, you deserved your shop, Remy. That money was fate giving you a little help when you most needed it."

"Which is kind of beside the point now," Remy stated. "I'm going to have to sell the store to get the money back."

Peyton's shoulders curled. "As much as I hate that idea, I think that's probably the best thing. You need to give this guy the money and get him to go away quickly and neatly."

"You don't have to tell me that." Remy recalled the coldness in Joaquin's gaze, the firmness that still shook her right down to her bones. "He was really, *really* scary."

Peyton's expression softened. She came over to the couch and sat on the coffee table where Asher had been. She took Remy's hand. "Everyone loves you, most of all Asher. No one is going to let anything happen to you. Boone, Rhett, even Hank, they're all going to help you figure out this situation." She drew in a long, deep breath, firmed up her expression, and then added, "No matter what, the truth remains, you were only trying to find a little happiness in a very dark moment. Kinsley's right—you didn't know that was Joaquin's money. You're a very good, kind person who is always making all of us feel better with your cool witchy stuff and positivity. No one is perfect, and you've kind of been perfect ever since I met you. So, you made one mistake…it happens."

"A mistake?" Remy snorted. "Isn't that putting it a tad lightly?"

Peyton laughed softly, squeezing Remy's hands tight. "Okay, it's like a huge mistake that's landed you in a lot of danger, but that's like one little blip in a whole life of good deeds. When Kinsley told you to take that money, it was done out of love, for you, because you deserve good things and life has been a total asshole to you. Yet since I've known you, that never seemed to get you down. You always get up and try again. You're the first one to go light a candle and say positive word to make everyone feel better."

Tears blurred Remy's vision again. "Are you trying to make me sob again?"

"No, of course not." Peyton pulled Remy into a warm hug. "I just want you to understand all this clearly. Yes, the guys are mad, but it's because they love you. This situation with Joaquin King is scary." She leaned away, held on to Remy's arms, and said fiercely, "But don't think for a second that you deserved anything that happened to you. This is all going to work out, one way or the other. Do you know how I know that?"

Remy took her hand away to clear her tears. "How?"

"Because good things happen to good people." She smiled. "And you're good people, Remy."

Remy's heart turned to mush. "I love you both. Thank you for being here."

Arms suddenly surrounded her in a group hug. After they both leaned back, Kinsley said, "All right, so now we've got to come up a plan to get you out of this mess."

"First, I'm going to sell my shop and get the money back," Remy said. "And second, considering we put me into this mess, I don't think we're the ones to get me out of it."

Kinsley jumped up, hands on her hips, a huge frown on her face. "Now you listen to me, Remy Brennan, we are not the *just sit here and do nothing* women. You haven't gone through all the shit you've gone through to hide away when faced with trouble. Sure, this has taken on a new unexpected 'holy shit' twist, but *we* can deal with this. Do you hear me?"

Remy nodded. "Yeah, I hear you just fine. I also don't have two hundred thousand dollars just lying around to pay Joaquin off."

Kinsley arched a single eyebrow, giving a sly smile. "Don't you?"

"No—" Remy paused at Peyton's wide eyes and open mouth. Then she got her answer. *My inheritance.* "Kinsley," Remy said in all seriousness. "I actually think your ideas might be the very thing that do me in."

Kinsley barked a laugh. "Never. My ideas are brilliant, and as soon as everyone realizes that, life will be a lot better."

\* \* \*

Out on his porch, Asher sat on the stairs staring out into the dark night. All he'd wanted was to protect Remy. To save her from the con man who wanted to take her for all she was worth. To somehow in all this make her life better again. And yet, he'd done what he always did, fucked things up. Instead of being the supportive friend she needed, he'd let his temper get the best of him. He took control of her life, arresting Damon, and now she was worse off than if she'd married Damon and lost all her money. At least she would have been safe.

All Asher had done was interfere in her life and make it worse. Ten-fold.

Boone and Rhett joined him outside ten minutes ago. Rhett offered him a beer, and Asher silently accepted. He cracked the beer open and chugged half of it back. No one spoke for a while, and Asher was glad for it, reeling in his wild emotions. No matter how hard he tried, his father was a part of him. He'd learned to control his anger years ago, but tonight it had spilled out and made Remy cry. Shame nearly suffocated him, and yet that weakness only fueled the rage burning in his gut.

When he finally sighed and glanced up, acknowledging the men around him, Boone trotted down the steps first, while Rhett followed, placing a foot on the last step. Both men appeared as torn up as Asher felt. "Is Remy okay?" Asher asked.

Rhett nodded. "Better now." He took a sip of his beer, then said, "This situation is a fucking mess."

Again, just like ten years ago, everyone else comforted her when it should have been him. Fucking pathetic. Asher glanced down at his boots, wanting to fade into the background until he found a solution. He didn't like any of it. Not Lars. And certainly not the rest of it. "Joaquin has her on his radar."

"Is that what angers you most?" Boone asked.

"All of it makes me furious," Asher said through clenched teeth. "I'm angry that all of this fucking shit has happened to her. That Fanning did this. That he is still fucking hurting her."

"And look at that, now you're hurting her too," Rhett stated. Asher let the dig roll off him knowing he deserved it. Rhett went on. "Losing your shit with Remy isn't going to make this any better."

"I've got to agree with Rhett on this one," Boone interjected, leaning a shoulder against the side of the house. "As much as Kinsley can drive me insane, they could never have anticipated this."

Asher restrained the fury sitting on his tongue and then drank back more beer, trying desperately to get control of himself. "And for that, I hear you, but it doesn't change the fact that Remy now owes money to a man I wouldn't want her a hundred feet near."

Boone nodded. "It's a problem that we need to find a solution to."

Asher agreed. "I want King nowhere near Remy. I want him to forget her name. And if we get involved, he'll always remember that she was the one who brought heat to him."

Rhett dropped his chin, tapping his foot against the wooden stair. "I'm always one for a hard game against a bad guy, but I agree: We need to make King go away as smoothly as possible for Remy's sake."

"And how about Lars?" Boone asked.

"Lars is the reason Remy's in all this in the first place," Asher said, hearing the venom in his own voice. "I blame Lars as much as I blame Fanning"—and most of all, himself—"for getting Remy wrapped up in all this shit. He needs to pay for what he's done to her."

"All right," Boone said, brow furrowed in thought. "We need a way for Remy to get the money to pay King to make him go away. But we also need to have enough evidence to get Lars into custody, and also keep Remy safe."

"Not impossible," Rhett said.

Asher rubbed at his throbbing temple. "How untouchable is King?"

Boone snorted a laugh. "Five counties all working together to take him down and we haven't even got a hint of evidence against him. The men who work for King are loyal." Boone hesitated and then shook his head, shoving his hands into his pockets. "To be perfectly honest, I'm not entirely convinced he's dirty."

"You're kidding?" Rhett asked.

"The investigation a year ago came up with nothing," Boone reported. "From what it appeared, King's a businessman who is riding the fear his father created. If he's dirty, he's far smarter and deadlier than his father. Nothing comes back to him. Ever. He's so clean that the team in Whitby Falls believed that the media had it all wrong, and that he's strictly a businessman giving back to the city."

"What do you believe?" Asher asked.

"Two things," Boone said. "One, he's clever and knows how to play the game. Two, he's not someone you want on your bad side. To go up against King, we'd have to be prepared. And I mean, at least a year of a hard, long investigation. We don't have the time to put this together. And we don't want Remy to be the reason that King gets a new investigation on him."

"No, we don't," Asher agreed.

Silence drifted in as a cat screamed off in the distance. There wasn't a breeze in the cool air, nothing bringing or taking scents, no movement at all, like the world had now stopped giving Asher time to fix this. "The cottage we found her at," Asher said, turning back to the men. "Any word on the owners?"

"Rented from Airbnb," Rhett reported. "False name. Paid for with a stolen credit card."

Boone snorted. "Like I said, smart and clean." He took a sip of his beer.

Asher pondered what all this meant. "So, the only evidence we have showing that Remy was abducted by Lars is her word?" At the nods in return, Asher cursed, shaking his head. "The DA is going to want more than that."

"Yeah, she will," Boone said with a nod.

Rhett tapped his boot against the stairs again, his tell of deep thinking. "Has Whitby Falls said anything about Fanning's murder?" he asked Boone.

"Gang related, or at least that's what the suspect said. He's not changing his story."

At that, Rhett cocked his head. "And you said that this killer's wife ended up with money in her account. How do they explain that?"

Boone gave a knowing look. "A charity from overseas helping out single mothers."

"Unbelievable," Asher said, and took another long sip of his beer, washing back his frustrations. Criminals were often smart. Too smart. Though the more he thought about it, the more he realized that's where they had the advantage. "From what you gathered on King, if Remy came up with the money, would you trust that he'd back off?" he asked Boone.

Boone paused to consider. He eventually said, "I can't say for certain, but I can bet you that money is on his books somewhere. It's clean. An investment. He wants payment."

That was a relief. "There's just one thing about all this that doesn't add up," Asher said, glancing between the men. "King is a multi-millionaire. Why does he care so desperately to get two hundred grand? It's incredibly risky, going after Remy with her ties to us, all for what he must view as pocket change."

Rhett slowly nodded. "The thought has crossed my mind too."

"It's something we shouldn't ignore," Boone said. "We need to expect the unexpected with King. He's thinking ahead, I assure you of that."

Which meant they needed to think one step ahead of King. "All right, for now our only focus is keeping Remy safe, are we in agreement about that?"

Rhett nodded.

"Of course," Boone said.

"I want Lars in jail," Asher said hurriedly. "I want him to understand what happens when he frightens one of ours."

"I'm not disagreeing with you," Rhett said.

"Ideas?" Boone asked.

Asher gazed at the bright half-moon before addressing Boone again. "If what you say is true about King, then he's not our target here. We leave King to the Whitby Falls organized crime department already dealing with him. We don't want to make him an enemy unless it's necessary, not with Remy involved."

"I'm with you on that," Boone agreed. "Which means, she needs to give back the money."

Asher nodded. "That's the *only* option here. We also can't hide this. We'll need to go to the district attorney and tell her about what Remy has done."

"The DA isn't going to do shit with Remy," Rhett said, then held up his hand. "But, to play it safe, I agree, it's best to have full disclosure."

"It keeps this clean, which my father will appreciate," Boone said to Rhett, then added to Asher, "Now all we need to figure out is how to settle Remy's score with King and make this all go away."

"I have a solution to that." At the arched brows surrounding him, Asher explained the thought that came to him the second he stepped outside. "Her inheritance."

Boone frowned.

Rhett blinked in confusion. "Doesn't she have to be married to get access to that…" He slowly whistled. "Damn, brother, I hope you know what you're doing."

Asher snorted a dry laugh. "That bad of an idea, huh?"

"The worst idea ever," Rhett stated.

Boone agreed with a nod. "Terrible."

Asher glanced between the two men he considered to be his brothers. "It's also the only idea we've got."

# Chapter 20

Later into the night, Asher had only given Remy a quick look before silently waiting for everyone to leave his house. Remy knew Asher, but she couldn't tell if he was angry anymore. Obviously over the years he'd learned how to shut off his emotions. A skill he'd probably mastered in the FBI. That was a new thing for Asher, making her see how many new things there was to him now. He wasn't that young kid who had stolen her heart, then crushed it; he was a man now. One who kept bailing her out of every situation she landed herself in, and yet, she could still see that their time apart made them better. Both of them. Stronger, for sure. "I'm sorry," she said, the moment he shut the door and locked it behind all their friends.

"No, I'm sorry I got so angry," Asher said softly, and turned back to her, hitting her with his emotion-packed eyes.

"It's okay," she said, suddenly aware of the guilt in his eyes. "You reacted and rightfully so. I have made a mess of everything."

Something close to frustration crossed his expression before he closed the distance between them in a single breath. "No, Remy, this is all on me, not you."

She stared up into the warmth of his eyes and leaned into his touch when he cupped her face. "How is this your fault, Asher? I spent Damon's money."

"Because had I not left you, none of this would have happened." He held her face, not letting her look anywhere but at him. "I shattered you when I left you standing there in the rain. I did that to you. All this shit that happened after that moment in your life, it's my fault, not yours. That's why I'm so fucking angry about all this." He hesitated. "I never should have yelled, and I'm sorry that I made you cry."

She couldn't even believe her ears. "Okay, somewhere things have gotten wonky. First of all, you left me because you needed time and space to get yourself right again. You had just lost your mother. You were going through a lot, I get that now. I made my choices. That's what led me here. And second of all, you are not your father, Asher. You didn't make me cry because you got angry. I cried because I did something bad."

He glanced away before his haunted gaze held her captive. "You're letting me off the hook far too easily."

Her heart broke at the pain in his voice. As much as she hadn't deserved how her life fell apart, neither did he. She closed whatever distance was left, needing his touch. "I understand that you changed after your mother's death. I don't hold that against you." She hesitated, then shrugged. "Maybe I did for a while, but I see now that the things you had once promised me before were promises that were impossible for you to keep."

"You should hold it against me," he said, his jaw muscles working. "Everything that has happened to you since I left happened because I'd been a fucking coward. I was so damn scared to lose anyone else. I was in such a dark place I couldn't see anyone but myself. I ran because I thought I was protecting you from me, but that was the easiest way out. All of this, every single fucking thing comes back to my leaving you that night and you looking for love in all the wrong places. That's on me, Remy. That will always be on me."

"Asher, you didn't do this."

He shook his head. "What's done is done and there's nothing I can do to change any of it. All I care about now is keeping you safe and making sure you are happy again. That's our only focus going forward. We need to pay back King."

"I can sell the shop." She offered the first plan before going into the second, way more complicated plan.

"I considered that idea," he said with a shake of his head. "But selling will take time. King is not the type of businessman you keep waiting." He paused to examine her, obviously deciding to level with the truth. "Look at what happened to Damon. We're not going to play around here. Do you understand me?"

She nodded.

"Tomorrow morning, I'm going to meet with the district attorney and explain the situation."

Her heart promptly landed in her throat. "I know you have to do what's right. I'll plead guilty, of course."

His mouth twitched and his eyes flickered with quick amusement. "I'm not going to let you be prosecuted, Remy. Like Rhett said, it's doubtful the prosecutor would bring up charges. For one, Damon is dead. For two, the money was on your property, and there are many other ways we can wiggle out of this. But she's going to want something, and we will give her Lars."

"Okay, I'm not sure how you will do that," Remy said, but

she didn't question him either. This was his show. "What do you need me to do?"

"Marry me."

She blinked. "Pardon?"

"I know it's a crazy idea," Asher said, as steady as ever. "It's not something I would suggest, considering our history, but I think it's a solution that gets you out of contact with King fastest, and *that* is all I'm thinking about right now. We need King to go away. This can be a business arrangement between us, nothing more than that."

Her mind reeled for many more seconds until she finally accepted that he'd just said what he said. "Actually, I don't think it's a crazy idea at all," she countered. "Because of my plan to marry Damon, the documents are all drawn up, the money is there as soon as I provide a marriage certificate."

Asher inclined his head. "I suspected as much."

Her heart suddenly began to pound in her ears and her palms grew clammy as the realization dawned on her. *We are getting married!* The floor began to creep up on her; all the rational thoughts about this idea suddenly didn't seem so rational anymore.

Asher's head suddenly cocked, his eyes searching hers, then everything about him softened. "I need you to be honest with me, Remy. More honest than you have ever been in your life. Can you do that?"

"Yes." No more secrets.

His thumbs brushed across her cheeks. "Can your heart handle this?"

Said heart skipped a beat. "It would be so easy for me to say yes that I can handle this, but I'd be lying. Of course, it will be...emotional, but I think as long as we create rules to keep it more like a business transaction, then I'll be fine." The words sounded right but felt all wrong. She'd dreamed of marrying Asher. She wanted it with every fiber of her being. But as she looked into Asher's eyes, she didn't see desire for her to be his wife, she only saw his need to right what he considered wrongs. He would, as always, protect her. And she knew from the guilt that cloaked him that he wouldn't trust himself to not hurt her again. They had too much history, and they both had too much baggage for this to ever be a real marriage. She needed to remind herself of that. She couldn't think about a man before herself anymore.

She'd love Asher, always, but she'd love him deeply as friend, where her heart remained safe. She'd be grateful to him, but emotion had no place here. Not now. Not with so much, including her life, on the line. She swallowed back the emotion filling her throat. Asher needed this as much as she did. He needed to help her keep her shop, see her dreams come true, to ease the guilt he endured.

Hell, they both needed this.

Asher studied her a moment and then took her hand and led her to the couch. "Name your rules."

"No vows." That would be too hard.

"Agreed," he said. "What else?"

"Just a 'yes' in response to any question asked," she said. "Let's keep it clinical and on point. Like we're signing a commitment on a loan."

"Good. Anything more?"

"Let's get some plastic rings or something and throw them out after." She swore his jaw clenched, but the reaction was gone so fast she wondered if she'd imagined it. "I think that'll keep this like a business transaction and nothing more." But even as she said the words, her heart recoiled.

Tomorrow would be hard, but what choice did she have?

Whatever emotion crossed her face caused Asher's ironclad expression to slip, and emotion seeped into his eyes. "Whatever you need from me, that's what you'll get."

But not his heart, never his heart. He'd always think she deserved better than him. Truth was, she did. She deserved a man who was all in, all the time. She would always want Asher, but it seemed he could never fully want her.

She kept silent, and he glanced at his fingers tangling with hers, then addressed her again. "Soon, all this shit will be behind you. You'll have your shop, and then you can move on and finally be happy."

She stared at him intently, feeling a slight pang in her heart. For the five years that Asher was home, she'd wanted an apology, an explanation...*anything.* Now that she knew the truth about what made him leave that night, she realized that what she wanted most was the old him. Without the guilt, without the pain, without his duty of fixing the past. She wanted the Asher who loved *her* and couldn't imagine his life without her.

This wasn't that.

She couldn't forget that.

"Tomorrow this will be all behind us," she said, suddenly realizing tonight was all they had left. He'd been there for her, helped her through this time in her life, but that's where this ended. Because nothing had changed. Asher couldn't see past his guilt, past his pain. She needed a man who let her in. She shifted a little closer, suddenly feeling the slight unsteadiness that this was her last night with Asher. "But we still have tonight."

His frown quirked into a smile. "Yeah, we sure as hell do." His lips met hers in a kiss that stole the air right out of her lungs.

She climbed onto his lap and then he rose with her in his arms. He broke the kiss to travel up the stairs to his bedroom and he gently laid her out on the mattress. His mouth sealed across hers again, and in this moment of time, there was nothing but the desperation for time to stop. Tomorrow would happen. Everything would change after that, Remy felt it in her bones. Since the day he objected at the wedding, Asher had been helping her heal. She'd been forgiving him. But this was where something would have to change, and she could feel in his kiss that Asher knew it too. Because time couldn't be erased, and they weren't the same people they were when they'd loved each other so fiercely. Too much had happened. Too much had gone wrong. They'd changed too much.

And tomorrow she would be Mrs. Sullivan. But it would be a lie.

His gaze bore into hers as he pushed her shirt up and over her head, then flicked her bra open, pulling the straps down her arms. He kissed her stomach while he unbuttoned her jeans, then those and her panties were gone soon after. She struggled to reach for his shirt, so he helped her and removed it quickly. While he nibbled her neck, she opened the button on his jeans. He pulled them and his boxer briefs down, exposing his thick cock.

She wrapped her arms around his neck, pulling him closer, needing him *now*. Once more. She wanted the intimacy that Asher gave to her. He was her first kiss and her first touch, and she needed him desperately to be that guy one more time before she forced herself not to care about him tomorrow morning. A task that seemed impossible.

She cupped his face as he hovered above her, and spoke the truth deep in her heart. What needed to happen for her to survive the wedding. "This can't happen again after tomorrow."

Asher didn't even hesitate. "It was always meant to end." He slid deep inside her, and she welcomed him easily. He kept his body close on hers, and she wrapped her legs around his strong thighs. He leaned up on his arms while he slowly thrust his hips, bringing pleasure with each movement. He didn't kiss her feverishly, tease her, or get her fired up. He stared at her, right in the eye, looking at her like he used to. With all the love in the world. Like he couldn't exist without her. And with the understanding that she couldn't exist without him. And yet, she knew that was a lie.

They could exist without each other. They had for ten years. And she'd have to again tomorrow. Though, as they began to move together, she realized that, while their old love was gone, he'd cared about her enough now to see her happy. Tomorrow she'd be free from everything dark in her life, but would Asher?

Wanting him to find peace too, and in the warmth of his embrace, she said, "It's no one's fault."

Asher froze, buried deep inside her. "What's no one's fault?"

"What happened to us," she said, hoping he truly heard her. "It's not our fault that we fell in love when we were so young. It's not your fault that you have a terrible father. It's not my fault that I don't know my dad, or know why my mom chooses herself over me. And it's not your fault that your mother killed herself. All this pain we've endured and faced, it just happened. None of it was anyone's fault, we just did the best we could." She felt him soften inside her, and she slid her hands up into his hair. "I keep thinking I want to go back to that time in our lives where nothing could have touched us. Where we were bigger than anything and everything and we thought our love was untouchable."

He dropped his mouth close to hers. "But it wasn't untouchable?"

She shook her head, a tear sliding down her face. "No, it wasn't, but that wasn't your fault or mine. Maybe it's time we both forgive ourselves."

Emotion seeped into his eyes and into his voice. "*You* never need to be forgiven." He ground against her, causing her to squirm beneath the pleasure on her clit. She moaned once, then felt him harden again just that easy. His intense gaze bore deeply into hers. "And if you think otherwise, I'll need to do my best to remind you of that." His thrust hard twice, curling her toes. "Do you hear me, Remy?"

"Yes," she gasped, lifting her pelvis, meaning to respond.

But with something that sounded close to a growl, he pinned her hips to the mattress and then there was no more talking. He kissed her with all the passion she knew existed in Asher and maybe even some she wasn't expecting. She lay beneath him, sliding her hands along his flexing back, until she cupped the curve of his buttocks. Meeting him thrust for thrust, moan for groan, she gripped him tight, needing him deeper.

His mouth brushed against her ear as he wrapped an arm around the back of her neck. Then, there was only the way the fit together. There was only pleasure and desire and overflowing lust that spilled out between them.

Until they were only two sweaty bodies tangled together, panting their satisfaction.

He eventually gathered her into his arms, spooning her from behind. She stared out the window seeing the half-moon in the dark sky, her emotions feeling depleted now. "Asher."

"Yeah," he murmured against her neck.

"Whatever sins you think you committed when you left me...whatever pain you caused back then...it *is* all forgiven now. You need to stop punishing yourself. Please tell me you will?"

His only response was to kiss her neck and wrap her tightly in his arms.

# Chapter 21

The next morning, Asher brought Remy home and she dressed in the exact opposite of what she thought she'd wear when she married Asher. Instead of the long, white flowy gown she'd imagined for years, she wore ripped jeans and a black blouse, reminding herself that nothing about this morning was real. Now if only she could convince her heart of that.

Asher had already gone to talk to the district attorney and got everything arranged for the ceremony this morning. She didn't ask much about it all, thinking she had enough on her plate without worrying if she was going to be charged with theft or larceny.

The morning so far had been strange—sunny for an hour, then raining, and now sunny again. Almost like the day knew everything was backward. In her bedroom, and needing something stronger than herself at the moment, Remy moved to her dresser and opened the top drawer, taking out her tarot cards. She opened the box, found the Strength card in the deck, and then placed it down on the dresser. She grabbed a white votive candle and a polished piece of bloodstone. After lighting the candle, she placed the bloodstone on the center of the Strength card. She shut her eyes, envisioning herself absorbing the courageous light of the flame and the strength of the card. Only when she felt strong and ready did she place the bloodstone in her pocket to carry with her. She ran the deck over the flame to cleanse it, then tucked away her tarot cards before blowing out the candle.

When she reached the living room, she tried not to look at the messy state of her loft, but now, knowing the break-in had been someone looking for the money, whether that be one of Joaquin's men or Lars, Remy felt fine being back in her place. She just wanted this to be over. Done. Put to bed.

Everything seemed more up in the air than ever. Something changed last night. First of all, she didn't want to hide away anymore. A strength she hadn't known before had risen somewhere inside her, pushing her to be the reason this matter got solved, not letting someone else deal with it. Maybe that was the positive she could take away in all this. She truly came out of all this stronger. Hell, she and Asher seemed to both come out of this better than when he'd left her, and for that she'd always be grateful, even if it took a whole lot of pain to get there.

The other thing that happened was that she crossed the boundary she told herself not to cross. The emotional one.

When her foot made the floorboard squeak, Asher turned away from the window he'd been staring out of, and the intensity in his gaze nearly undid her. He was just so cold. Any part of her heart that thought that maybe this would affect him like it was affecting her flew out the window. He was there to get her out of this mess, and that was that. He took her at her word last night. This would be a business deal.

A big part of her heart twisted. She admitted to herself that she wanted his love. But she wasn't that woman who needed love above all else anymore. She had to come first, and now she accepted that Asher would always be an incredible protector. That was his role in her life. She could live with that. But her mind accepting that was one thing; her heart needed more time.

Asher's gaze did a thorough once-over before he glanced into her eyes. She expected him to comment on her attire, but instead, he only showed steadiness. "Ready to go?" he asked.

She nodded, exhaling a long, deep breath. "Ready." Regardless that this didn't feel like a transaction at all, and that the butterflies indicated being Asher's wife was an exciting idea, she couldn't back out now. Not for herself. She couldn't back out for the situation that she'd now placed everyone in.

A situation that no one could have seen coming.

If she didn't come up with the money, she'd be in danger, but if she was in danger, Asher would protect her. And by protecting her, he'd place himself in front of that danger, which in turn, would bring in Boone and Rhett. She couldn't let that happen. She made this mess. She had to clean it up.

Asher suddenly closed the distance and placed both hands on her shoulders, bringing his eye level down to hers. "You don't need to do this. We can back out right now and come up with a new plan."

Her emotions must have showed on her face. "Yes, I do," she retorted, lifting her chin. "I spent Joaquin's money. I need to pay him back." She paused, seeing the slight hesitation on his face. "Are you changing your mind about it all?"

"No," he bit off, a muscle in his jaw flexing. "I've got this."

"It's just for a few months, so no one can contest the inheritance," she said. "Though I don't know who would contest it.

Maybe my mother. Anyway, after that, we can get divorced…or an annulment, if we tell the judge we didn't consummate the marriage…or maybe a divorce is better just to keep things easier." She froze at the twitch of his mouth. "Damn, I'm rambling, aren't I?"

"Just a little." He grabbed the hem of her shirt and then tugged her into him, surprising her by wrapping his arms tightly around her. "It's going to be all right, Remy. We can do this."

She leaned into him. "I know."

He placed a kiss on her forehead, then offered his hand. "Ready to go get ourselves hitched?"

She laughed softly. "Definitely."

Two hours of butterflies, sweat coating her skin, and barely being able to sit still later, Remy held the marriage license in her hand. They'd gone to the town office and now stood in front of Judge Mulroney's desk at the courthouse. Dark paneling filled the room, along with bookshelves full of law books. Nana had known the judge's mother, and Remy vaguely remembered hearing about the judge every so often, though Remy had been a kid then and the judge at that time was a wild teenager. Now with her curly brown hair, light makeup, and black pantsuit, the judge couldn't look more straitlaced.

"What kind of ceremony are we looking for today?" the judge asked, sitting behind her desk.

"Simple," Remy blurted out, and she quickly smiled at her hasty response.

The judge nodded and made a note before asking, "How about vows? Personal or already prepared?"

"No vows," Asher explained.

Remy looked his way, finding his lips pinched tight. There was a very big part of her that wanted to stop this. She could see his jaw working, a tell that he was stressed. And yet, if she stopped this, where would that leave them? Only in danger. "Can't we just say 'yes' or 'I will' or something like that?" she asked, glancing back at the judge.

"Of course, nice and simple, nothing wrong with that," the judge said with a soft nod, then rose. "I think we're all set here. Give me a moment to make sure we've got the paperwork all together and ready to go before we begin." She left the office through the side door.

"You can breathe again," Asher said tightly.

Remy blew out the breath she'd been holding, the room spinning around her a little. She stretched out her fingers, not having realized she'd been squeezing them together. "Considering what I've been through lately, you wouldn't think this would be so nerve-racking."

"It's the unexpected that always gets you," Asher said, moving to the leather chair and taking a seat.

She followed his cue and sat in the chair next to him, crossing her legs and bouncing the one on top. "How did you get us in here so fast anyway?" she asked, trying to fill the unbearable silence.

"A perk of being a cop," Asher explained, seemingly totally at ease in his chair. "I called in a favor."

"Does she know what's going on?"

Asher shook his head. "She knows I wanted to marry you this morning. She didn't need to know more than that."

A knock on the door had Remy glancing over her shoulder. The blood drained from her face as Boone and Rhett entered the room. That last thing she wanted was an audience. She was barely managing all this as it was. Asher nudged her knee, dragging her attention back to him. "We needed two witnesses."

Remy nodded, sure she couldn't get any words out, let alone any that made sense.

Boone moved inside the room and leaned against the desk. "How are you two holding up?"

"Good." Asher nodded.

Remy just shrugged.

"Well, if you were going for zero emotion at all, I'd say you've gotten it," Rhett said, frowning. "This place looks like somewhere I'd get married."

"Rhett," Asher warned.

A burst of nervous laughter bubbled up and Remy couldn't fight it. "You know, you're right, this is totally up your alley."

Rhett winked.

Asher visibly relaxed then, obviously realizing that Rhett was only lightening the mood.

Curious now, though, Remy turned to Rhett and asked, "What would you do if you were in my situation?"

Rhett gave Asher a long look, then dropped into the leather couch. "I'd do exactly what you're doing."

*Liar.* He thought this was a huge mistake, and maybe it was. But she needed a fix, and a marriage certificate was it. Didn't mean that made any of this easier. The room suddenly began to feel small, and the air stuffy. She rose and began pacing in front of the desk, her thoughts beginning to run wild with doubts, when the judge strode back into the room carrying a file folder.

"Ready to begin?" the judge asked.

Remy glanced back at Boone. He gave her a tight smile and a firm nod. Then her gaze fell to Rhett. He held her stare with his usual hard expression, revealing not much of anything. God, what was she doing? How had all the shit in her life led her to this moment, where she was finally marrying the love of her life, and the marriage was a total sham?

"Remy."

Asher's strong voice pulled her attention to him. She got lost in that steady gaze that could make her feel better on the worst of days. "Do you need a minute?" he asked, sliding his fingers gently down her arm.

She desperately wanted to melt into that touch, but her mind pulled back, protecting her. "No. No, I'm okay." She moved in front of the judge's desk and Asher joined her. After a deep breath and reminding her heart that she was the one who got herself into all this trouble, she took Asher's hand and said, "Make me Mrs. Sullivan."

* * *

Today was the worst day of Asher's life. He'd felt more emotion from Remy ordering pizza than when she'd agreed to be his wife. More than once he nearly called the marriage off, desperate to explain all the shit filling his head since he woke up this morning. But every time the words nearly left his mouth, he stepped back, seeing that he was the reason she was in this mess in the first place. Everything he touched, he tarnished. Over and over again, he hurt her.

Knowing the best thing he could do was continue to do right by her to get her free and clear from the situation that *he* put her in, he had left Remy with her lawyer at the bank right after they signed the marriage certificate. And while they squared the finances, Asher went to the station for some peace and quiet. She'd pay the money back and she'd still have her shop. All of that should have made him feel happy. That's what all this was about. Giving her back the life that he selfishly stole from her when he took her innocent heart and shattered it.

But then why did he have this sudden emptiness in his chest? This feeling that everything suddenly seemed all wrong when everything should be right. Why did none of this make him feel good? He finally protected her fully and completely, and yet, he suddenly felt like he was drowning.

And that's where he'd been for the last half an hour, while he'd waited for Remy and her lawyer to join him in his office. He leaned back in his chair and stared at the photograph of when he'd made Remy *his*. He tried to get a grip on his thoughts, but the web was so tangled now, Asher wasn't sure how to unravel it all.

"Congratulations."

Asher shut his eyes, breathed deeply, and then faced the evitable. "You only say congratulations if there's a reason to celebrate." He turned to Hank standing in the doorway. Boone's dad had been as close to a father as Asher had ever known, considering his father was no longer in the picture.

"You've been dealt a blow," Hank said gently, leaning a shoulder against the door, arms folded. "Doesn't mean what you've wanted hasn't happened. Just means you need to finagle all this a little bit to settle things into where you want to go from this day forward. You've still got Remy. That was the hope in all this, wasn't it?"

Hank never missed much. "I don't know what the hope was. To make her happy? To protect her?" He thrust his hands into his hair. "I don't even know anymore." He felt deep in the thick of it without a clear way out. He'd seen what love did to people. He didn't want that. And yet...*and yet*...everything felt wrong.

His chest felt worse than it had when he'd first returned home to Stoney Creek and she'd barely look at him.

Hank gave Asher a long look, then offered, "Start small, all right? Get this settled for Remy, then go from there." Of course he'd look out for Remy. Hank had loved her as a second daughter for nearly her entire life.

"Probably the only place to go," Asher muttered.

Hank agreed with a nod. "I'd like a call immediately after Remy hands over the money and this matter is concluded."

"Yes, sir." Boone had informed his father of Remy's situation. The DA didn't care much about the money at Remy's house, but was greatly interested in Lars. Now they were all in cleanup mode, ensuring this thing with King went away nice and neatly without any laws being broken.

Hank suddenly straightened and then said to Asher seriously, "And that's my cue to leave. Good luck this afternoon." He was gone from the doorway in less time than it took Asher to blink.

And in his place was a handful of women pushing themselves into Asher's officer. There went Asher's peace and quiet.

"Oh, Asher," MaryJane said, hurrying to place flowers on his desk. "We heard the news and just needed to come by right away."

He arched an eyebrow, wondering exactly what the gossip train had gotten a hold of, considering there were a couple of things they'd clamor over. "The news?" he repeated.

"Your marriage to Remy," Annie, the retired teacher, said, holding on to the strap of her purse, beaming from ear to ear.

"That news traveled fast," Asher said, leaning back in his chair and folding his arms.

"Well," MaryJane drawled, "Louise's sister works at the town office."

Louise stood next to Annie, giving him a blinding smile. "She does."

MaryJane nodded too. "Her sister issued the license, and hinted you were there, and then you know, Georgia, she works at the courthouse and saw Remy and Boone and Rhett and—"

Asher raised a hand, having had quite enough. "You are master investigators."

Cute laughter filled his office.

He rose and moved to his door. "Thank you, ladies, for dropping by with the flowers and for thinking of us. It's very sweet of you all."

"We're just so happy for you, Asher," Georgia said. "Your mom would have been so happy."

He felt like he'd been throat-punched. Georgia had known Mom—all the ladies had. She would have been right in the middle of this group had she still be there. Maybe not as nosy, but certainly there for friendship. "Thank you, Georgia. You're right, she would have been very happy." She also would have never let this get all fucked up and backward. She'd most certainly have a way out.

"Of course, we're all a little confused why you're back at work and not with Remy," MaryJane said, eyes narrowed thoughtfully.

Asher laughed and began gently ushering them out the door. "Sadly, ladies, when the job calls, the job calls. I'll be sure to bring your flowers to Remy and say you all stopped by to congratulate us."

After waves and smiles, Asher sat back behind his desk, welcoming the silence again. The mothers of Stoney Creek were mothers to everyone. Most times Asher didn't mind. Today he wanted to be alone.

*Silence.*

But then Boone said, "I thought they were never going to leave."

"Thanks for bailing me out," Asher said, glancing toward the door.

"Yeah, right," Rhett said, taking the first client chair. "Like hell I'd throw myself in that pile of gossip."

Asher snorted a laugh as Boone dropped down into the other chair.

Rhett's head cocked as he regarded Asher. "I didn't think you could possibly look more like shit since you put the ring on Remy's finger, but you do."

A ring that she took right off after the ceremony and threw in the garbage. "I want silence." He glared at his friend. "You're not helping with that." He thrust his fingers into his hair, tilting his head back and breathing deeply.

When heavy silence drifted into the room, Asher straightened, finding Rhett watching him closely. "What?"

Rhett lifted his brows.

Boone frowned. "Talk."

Asher leaned back in his chair, pressing his fists to his head. "I don't know how the fuck we got *here*."

"Married?" Boone asked.

Asher nodded. "I had a plan. Fix my mistakes. Make her happy. Protect her. Let her go."

"But?" Rhett asked.

Asher sighed. "We were never supposed to be married like *this*. I thought this was the best choice, and now, I think I've only hurt her more. I keep trying to fix all this shit, and the more I try to make things right for her, the more things unravel."

"Maybe you're not supposed to fix anything," Rhett said with a shrug.

Asher leaned forward, resting his arms on his desk as a

rookie strode by his office door. "Are you of all people giving me relationship advice?"

Rhett nodded with a serious expression for a long moment, then burst out laughing. "Nah, I tried. Didn't work. I wouldn't know what the hell to do in your situation. You're knee deep in it, and as far as I'm concerned, I'd run to avoid any more of a mess." He hesitated, then grinned. "Actually, no, I'd probably tell you to go screw that redhead who's been eyeing you at the bar, but I'm guessing that's not helpful either?"

Asher snorted. "Not particularly helpful."

"He's not exactly wrong, though," Boone said. "Maybe it's time to stop trying to fix everything and just let the cards fall. You've both been through a lot. It's time for some damn happiness in your lives."

Asher started at Boone. It was similar to what Remy had said last night. "I don't want to hurt her again."

"Then don't," was Boone's hard answer.

Asher looked at Rhett for his input.

Rhett gave an easy shrug. "I'm no expert here in all this shit, but it seems to me that you've been making her quite happy lately. Just keep doing what you've been doing. Seems pretty damn simple. Stop being a pussy, and go get your girl."

A frown tugged at Asher's mouth. "Has anyone told you lately you're a real fucking prick?"

Rhett grinned. "Yup, Cindy told me last night." He cocked his head. "No, wait, her name was Amanda."

Boone laughed.

Asher didn't. Tension ached in his muscles. All Asher knew was that when she threw that ring in the garbage, it was a direct hit to his chest. But Remy was still in danger. That had to be his priority. For now, he shoved that tension in his chest deep in his gut to deal with later. He stretched out his arms and then worked at the tension along his shoulders, glancing back at Remy's cell on his desk. He'd been putting this off, knowing the last thing he wanted to do was send Remy anywhere near Lars or King, but it would be worse for Remy if she involved the cops.

To keep her safe, Asher needed to let this play out.

He lifted the phone. "We ready to do this?"

Boone nodded. "Always ready."

Rhett gave a quick flick of his chin.

Asher unlocked Remy's cell phone with the password she'd given him before she headed off to the bank. He fired off the text to the number that had texted Remy's last night with just the words "three days."

I've got what you requested. Let's meet downtown.

Not even a couple seconds passed before he got a text back.

Meet at the square. Five o'clock.

"King's smart, I'll give him that," Asher said, confirming the place and time. "He picked the square to meet at rush hour." The square was in downtown Whitby Falls, full of restaurants and pubs.

"He's better than smart," Boone said with a frown. "He's well connected. That has proven to give him an advantage time and time again."

"Then we'll need to be smarter," Asher countered.

Boone's gaze lit up, and he gave a slow building smile. "I've seen that look before. What do you have planned?"

Asher had been over it all last night while Remy slept tucked safely in his arms. He'd thought out every scenario and every outcome. He'd considered the danger, the risks, and everything in between, until all he had left was a solid plan. "The *only* plan that I think will keep Remy safe."

Rhett leaned forward with interest. "Tell me—"

"Sorry to interrupt," Josh Silver, Remy's lawyer, said with a knock on the door. "I thought I'd come let you know we're all done at the bank. Just wondered if you needed me for anything else before I head off?"

Asher quickly rose and offered his hand. "Thanks for coming in so quickly, Josh. Appreciate it." They'd all gone to school with Josh's older brother, who looked nearly identical to Josh with his amber eyes and blond stylish hair.

Josh shook his hand. "No worries, glad to help."

Asher peeked out into the hallway, discovering it empty. "Where's Remy?"

"She left."

A beat. "What do you mean she left?"

"She said she had somewhere to go," Josh said slowly, looking between the men, obviously realizing he'd messed up. "Sorry, was I not supposed to let her leave?"

Boone rose. "Did she have the money with her?"

"Ah…"—Josh scanned the faces in the room—"yeah, it's her money, I didn't think to not let her leave."

"Call me if you find her," Asher barked the order. He didn't wait for Boone's or Rhett's response. He booked it through the station, hoping to hell that his new wife didn't do anything stupid.

# Chapter 22

Beneath the sunny sky on Remy's rooftop garden, she sat in between her raised flowerbeds and sipped her Quick Luck tea made of one part orange peel, one part rose hips, and one part camellia. She already knew that Asher was arranging the time for the money drop later today, and right now, she needed a little peace in all the madness. She regretted not grabbing Salem on the way, wishing for some feline love, but her heart and head felt too jumbled to have even thought of anything at all but her need to come to her garden. Her one place of total peace. She reached out next to her, touching the leaves of the devil's claw that had been dying. Now the plant thrived. The leaves were bright green and perky. Not much of a shock. After today, there was no danger around Remy anymore. At least none that didn't involve her heart.

"Everyone is looking for you."

Remy sighed. Of course the peace wouldn't last. She glanced up to see Kinsley approaching while Peyton waited by the ladder, a cell phone pressed to her ear. A call to Boone, no doubt.

"Figured as much," Remy replied with a shrug. "I didn't want to worry everyone. I was going to call Asher and let him know I came home, but I just needed a minute alone before everything got even crazier."

Kinsley dropped down, sitting cross-legged in front of Remy, her eyes fraught with worry. "Sweetie, you look so sad. What's wrong?"

Remy's heart felt like it had gone through a cheese grater. "I married Asher this morning."

Kinsley's mouth dropped open, but it was Peyton who sputtered as she sidled up to them, "Okay, that happened fast."

"Too fast, I think," Remy admitted, realizing she should have thought harder about what the wedding would do to her heart.

Peyton took a seat next to Remy. "So, if Asher agreed to the plan, what's wrong?"

"Nothing should be wrong," Remy said, giving the plant one last stroke. "I've got the money. I'll pay back Joaquin later today. I should be happy."

Kinsley reached for Remy's hand. "But you're not?"

She heaved a long sigh, glancing down at her mug between her legs. "But I'm not," Remy agreed.

Silence spread out between them until Kinsley said softly, "Why would you not tell us about this? We're your best friends. We could have been there for you today."

"I didn't want to talk about it," Remy admitted. "Maybe because if I talked about it, then it made it all real."

Peyton took Remy's other hand. "It's us, Remy. Talk to us."

The breeze blew through the garden and Remy caught the scent of the slightly musky vanilla-smelling hibiscus. "I just don't know how I got here. It's like I keep thinking it can't possibly get worse and then it does. Today, I thought I could totally marry Asher. I'm this new strong version of myself. This is my mess, and I'll clean it up. I don't need Asher. But…" Her voice hitched.

"But you do need him," Kinsley said.

Remy gave a soft nod. "I dreamed of my wedding day with Asher. The dress. The ceremony. The way he would smile at me. The love we had for each other. I had that whole day planned out in my mind for so long." Her throat constricted, and her eyes welled. "Today I was good, strong, and then when the judge declared us husband and wife, it was like the guards around my heart fell." Kinsley squeezed her hand tight as a tear dripped from Remy's eye and landed on her leg. She couldn't look up, face anyone. All she wanted to do was move on, and it seemed impossible. "I've been lying to myself. Pretending that I've got control of everything. I love him. I *only* want him, and when I can't have him, I look in terrible places trying to pretend I'm over him. I love him so much, and it makes me so sad that he doesn't love me back. That today wasn't real. That today will never be real."

"I wouldn't say that."

Remy's gaze jerked up to Asher standing a few feet away, his intense gaze locked onto her. The air suddenly thickened, electricity pining in the space between them.

"And that's our cue." Kinsley whistled and then gave Remy a tight hug. "Call me when all is said and done so I know you're okay."

"Make it a three-way call," Peyton said, kissing Remy's cheek before following Kinsley to the ladder.

Asher nodded at them and then approached with his long strides until he dropped down in front of Remy, one arm resting on his knee. He arched an eyebrow. "I'm listening, Remy."

She glanced down into her mug, butterflies filling her belly. "Well, I'm not exactly prepared for this conversation."

He tucked his finger under her chin, lifting her gaze to meet his intense stare. "You're the strongest person I know. You're prepared."

She drew in a long, deep breath, staring into his eyes that looked so different from the boy she used to know. Darker. Jaded. And somehow that made this conversation suddenly easier because Asher didn't deserve those ghosts as much as she didn't deserve them in her soul either. "I've been sitting here by myself, and thinking about everything, and it's all made me realize that ever since you left for Washington, I've been on autopilot. It's like for a long time I was thinking you were going to come back for me and our lives would go back to normal."

"I should have come back immediately."

Her breath caught at the raw emotion in his eyes. "No, you shouldn't have," she told him softly, cupping his face. "You needed time to recover and to heal from your mother's death, and that's okay. It's all right that our lives took us in two different directions. I was young—"

"I was a coward to leave you."

She slowly pulled her hand away, surprised by his answer. "How were you a coward? Moving away couldn't have been easy."

"It wasn't easy," he said, glancing off into the distance with years of pain etched into his expression. Until he looked back at her, then he was only steady. "Leaving you was the hardest thing I'd ever done in my life, but…I…" He drew in a long breath before blowing it out slowly and hanging his head. "When Mom killed herself, life stopped then. I could not trust that the dark shit I felt would not spill out and affect you. I thought leaving protected you from all that."

She scooted closer until her legs pressed against his. "I know that."

He took her hand in his, watching his fingers graze over hers. "Marriage terrifies me, Remy. Love is very hard for me. My parents were not good at it. And clearly I keep getting it fucking wrong." His haunted gaze flicked to hers. "I'm scared of letting go and unknowingly becoming my father. I'm terrified of loving too much and losing myself like my mother did. I don't know how to do any of this. I'm afraid if I let go of my control for a second, I'm going to destroy you, and that's the very last fucking thing I want."

*Her Asher.* His pain. God, her heart broke a thousand times for him. "Well, the good thing is, you're not your parents, and I'm not mine. Let's do the one thing that they never got right." She pulled her hands away to cup his face again, feeling the rough scruffiness of his five-o'clock shadow. "I know you're scared. But let's stay. Let's fight for this. Let's stop running."

He held her gaze for a beat, then placed his hands over hers. "I can't say I'll be perfect at this and not fuck up, but damn, I really want to try."

"I don't need perfect. I just need *you.* I love you, Asher. I've always loved you," she said softly, melting in the way his touch brushed across her skin.

"Remy, I love you too," Asher said when her eyes grew teary. "I'm going to make mistakes, but I want to build a life with you. You're all that I have. All that I need. The *only* woman I have ever loved." He went quiet, his eyes searching hers. "Today was real for me. But I absolutely want the real deal. To see you in the dress. To make you happy." He got up and went on one knee. "Remy Brennan, will you marry me...*again*?"

She laughed, and squeaked yes through the tears, throwing her arms around him. "Yes, of course!"

Asher's smile was real and honest and took her breath away. She tasted the sweetness between them in his kiss, and suddenly years of pain and heartbreak spilled out. She cupped his face as his kiss turned urgent with the same intensity she felt burning inside. An intensity that was better than new, happy love. What they had was love that was built through pain and memories. Real love. Honest love. Connected, touching, she knew this was where life began and ended for her. Always.

She'd run and hid and pretended that she moved on, but there was no denying the truth anymore. Remy could exist without Asher; she simply didn't want to. Life lost its flavor. Colors were duller. The air less breathable. And to live without him would be to live in a world that didn't make sense, where everything fell apart. Asher was the glue that made life make sense. And she knew she was that for him too.

Always and forever.

# Chapter 23

Fifteen minutes before five o'clock, Remy grabbed the duffel bag off the passenger seat of her car and then locked the doors with her key fob. She was only a two-minute walk from the square. Her throat constricted, even though she knew this was what she'd been waiting for. Soon, Lars and Joaquin King would be behind her and she and Asher could settle into a new normal.

She felt the weight of a stare on her back long before she turned around. It came as no surprise to find Asher frowning with his hands shoved in his pockets, scowling at her. "I've never seen you look so miserable," she said with a laugh, adjusting the bag on her shoulder to slide her arms through his until she pressed herself tight against him.

"I *am* miserable." He glowered down at her. "I don't want you doing this alone."

She wiggled against him a little, hoping to make him feel better. "I *need* to do this alone," she told him for the hundredth time today. "Besides, I'm in the middle of the square and surrounded by hundreds of people. Joaquin just wants his money. We all know that. I hand over the money, then this is done."

Asher stared hard a moment longer, then sighed and wrapped his arms around her neck, bringing her in close and kissing her forehead. "I still don't like it. I don't want you anywhere near King."

"Believe me, I don't want to be near him." She stood on her tiptoes, then pressed her mouth against his. "But I'll be back before you know it and then we can put this all behind us." Before she chickened out and changed her mind, she stepped out of his hold, and without looking back, headed down the street.

Remy was no cop, no detective, no FBI agent, and the last thing she wanted to do was hand off money to anyone. Especially Joaquin King. It took a lot of people's help to get her here, but she needed to take this last step alone. And as much as Asher hated that Joaquin had seen Remy's face, Remy didn't want Joaquin to see Asher's either. They were on opposite sides of the law. Remy didn't want those two squaring off.

When she reached the corner of First Avenue, she nearly bumped into a couple walking hand in hand. Remy held the bag a little tighter. Two hundred grand was in this bag, and was also her path forward. String lights hung over the street from one side to the other that would light up the square once the sun went down. Each bar or restaurant had their own eclectic style, desperately trying to outdo the other with the best patio in the square. From elaborate lighting to gorgeous floral displays to gas fireplaces, there wasn't a place that didn't invite Remy in.

She slowed when she reached the northeast corner of the square. When Asher told her how this would all play out, he picked this corner specifically because of the busyness of it. The thought that Joaquin could easily find her wasn't very settling.

She breathed deeply against the sudden surge of adrenaline pumping through her veins, trying not to let her mind run wild with the danger today presented.

Though soon, every set of eyes felt like they landed on her.

Her heart began pounding in her ears and sweat coated her flesh when her cell phone rang. She glanced at the screen seeing an unknown number. It didn't take much to know who was calling. "Hello," she said, answering the phone.

"You brought the cops with you," Joaquin said.

"No, I came alone," she replied, glancing around the street as the cars slowly drove past here. "I swear, it's just me."

"Then you just don't know they're there," Joaquin said. "Look down the street from where you are, they're there."

An icy shiver raced down Remy's spine as she realized she was currently being watched by Joaquin from *somewhere*. She turned in the direction he indicated, and sure enough she spotted Boone. He leaned casually against a street post, looking down at his phone, with his sunglasses on, which obviously was a ruse and he was looking straight at her. "I told them not to come. I don't want anyone else involved in this. But they love me and want to make sure I'm safe."

"Ah, but that's our problem, Ms. Brennan. They are involved in this now," Joaquin said.

Remy cringed, her eyes scanning the crowd until she found Rhett. "Tell me what to do to keep them out of it," she said.

"I've got a car coming up. Thirty seconds out. If you want to put this matter to bed, you'll get into that car. Do not hesitate. Your new husband is close."

Remy glanced around and couldn't see Asher anywhere...*and yet*, she shut her eyes and concentrated. She could sense that electric pulse whenever Asher came near, and her body hummed with his closeness. "I'm ready," she told Joaquin, opening her eyes. Because she'd made her bed, and now she had to unmake it, without somehow making everything even messier. Her happiness was so close, she could taste it. She'd have Asher and her shop, and nothing would get in the way of that. Not anymore.

"Five seconds," Joaquin said.

Remy blinked once, and then a black SUV stopped next to her and the door swung open. Remy took the breath she needed for bravery and then jumped in. With a squeal of the tires, the SUV sped away. She couldn't be certain, but she swore she heard Asher yell her name before she slammed the door behind her.

A quick look through the back windshield told her that she wasn't wrong. Not only was Asher chasing the SUV, but so were Boone and Rhett. She turned back in her seat, realizing that both of Joaquin's guards were in the front seat wearing bullet-proof vests and earpieces. She swallowed deeply.

"We've got her," the guard in the passenger seat said into his earpiece.

Remy noted the shaking of her hands while she fastened her seat belt. She kept the duffel bag on her lap, but then realized the seat belt was pointless considering the SUV pulled into an underground garage a few seconds later. The driver parked and then exited, so she followed. Before she could even shut the door, the taller bodyguard opened a door to a limousine next to them.

"Go," he told her.

She hurried inside, not all that surprised to see Joaquin sitting across from her. He wore a tailored suit, the jacket unbuttoned, as were the first couple buttons of his white dress shirt. "Here's your money," she said, offering him the bag, ready to get the hell out of his limo.

"Good." He knocked on the window.

The door across from Remy opened. Her muscles tightened and heart raced as Lars slid onto the leather seat next to her. She felt the weight of his stare and she looked him right in the eye.

"Ms. Brennan has cleared her debt with me," Joaquin said, gesturing toward the bag. "That concludes our business, Mr. Violi."

Lars smiled. "Excellent news."

Joaquin's cool and calm eyes flicked to Remy. "Now, before you go, I want you to understand that in a show of good faith, I am now offering you my protection."

Remy had to force her mouth not to fall open.

"Her." Lars snorted. "Why?"

Joaquin glared.

That's it. No words. No sound. Just a single look had Lars hanging his head.

"I'm going to ask you a question, Mr. Violi," Joaquin said. "Lie to me and you won't leave this car alive."

Remy felt the truth of his statement in the power of his voice. She forced herself to exhale through her nose when the car spun a little, reminding her she needed to breathe to get out of the car alive too.

"Are you planning on killing Ms. Brennan tonight?"

Remy jerked her gaze toward Lars, feeling the ground drop under her as Lars nodded and said, "Yes, sir. That was the plan."

"That plan is aborted," Joaquin said easily, like they were discussing the weather. "Ms. Brennan is under my protection now and cannot be touched. Call off your men."

Lars reached into his pocket and had his phone to his ear. "The chick is under King's protection. It's over." He ended the call, lifting his gaze to Joaquin.

"Let me make this very clear to you, Mr. Violi. I do not appreciate the heat you bring to me," Joaquin said. "Had you succeeded with your plan and killed Ms. Brennan, you would have implicated me."

"No, man—"

Joaquin narrowed his eyes. When Lars went silent, Joaquin continued, "Here is the only plan going forward. You're going to get out of this car and forget my name. Do we understand each other?"

Lars's skin lost all its color. "Yeah...ah, yeah."

"Good." Joaquin gestured at the door. "Get out."

Remy stared with her mouth now hanging open. She watched Lars run away like a coward. Though, when she glanced back at Joaquin, she realized that now she sat alone in a car with a man who had scared the scariest guy she'd ever met.

Joaquin tapped the window again, then the bodyguards were driving them out of the parking garage and down the road. "Your debt is clear," Joaquin said. "Our business here is done. When the limo stops, get out and go home, Ms. Brennan."

She let out a nervous laugh. "You won't hear me argue with you there."

She could have sworn his mouth twitched.

"Boss, we've got a problem."

Remy glanced out the front window and saw the *exact* problem.

Asher stood in the middle of the road. His weapon was aimed at the driver's head.

\* \* \*

Asher felt the slow steady beat of his heart as he stood in the middle of the street. Any pedestrians that were on the street were gone the second he pulled his weapon. But Asher could feel the cell phones trained on him, the watchful eyes of the public making sure they did their job right. He never minded an audience. They did good police work in Stoney Creek. He trained his weapon straight for the windshield, ready to take out the driver if he made a move.

Boone closed in from the back, weapon aimed at the car. Rhett had tackled Lars to the ground when he'd run out of the parking garage, and already had him in cuffs behind Asher. They'd stayed a step ahead of King. Asher had lost Remy once. That wouldn't happen again.

He kept his weapon aimed at King's bodyguard in case he hit the gas. "We have no business with you, King," Asher called. "I want Remy. Let her exit and you can leave."

A long moment passed as the breeze rushed across the street, swirling the leaves in front of the limo. The door closest to Boone opened and Remy jumped out, then hurried to Asher's side. Everything that had been wrong was suddenly right again. Asher lowered his weapon, seeing Boone do the same. The limo drove away without further incident, and Asher hoped that was the last time he saw King and his men.

When they moved farther down the road, Asher holstered his weapon and took Remy by the shoulders, scanning her from head to toe. "Are you hurt at all?" he asked.

"You weren't supposed to get involved!" she snapped, poking his chest. "I didn't want you involved with King. This was my mess, my problem. You had a gun aimed at him!"

Asher dropped his face into her neck, inhaling the sweet scent of her. The one scent he could recognize anywhere. "I didn't get involved with King. Rhett got Lars. That's who the DA wanted. That's who I needed to bring in to keep you out of trouble. As you saw, King drove off without any interference from us."

"Oh." She immediately softened and stepped into his arms.

He chuckled and then kissed her forehead. "So, now can we agree that we're a team? From here on out, we do this together. I won't get overly protective. And you won't completely shut me out and jump into the bad guy's SUV?"

"Okay, I can make that deal." She laughed softly and then added, "You know, I actually don't think he's a bad guy at all."

Asher leaned away. "What do you mean?"

"He saved my life," she said, sending Asher reeling, and went on. "After Joaquin said my debt was clear to him, Lars got into the car. That's when things got weird. He had Lars admit that he planned on killing me tonight after I paid the debt." She paused to shake her head. "He must still believe that I was in on all this with Damon from the start."

Asher's nostrils flared. "Lars would never have gotten close to you before his life ended."

She gave him a sweet smile. "I have no doubt that's very much true."

He wrapped his arms around her, realizing himself how much they'd grown since he left her. Maybe that was the takeaway in all this. They fought for their happiness after coming from pasts that nearly drowned them. "Out of curiosity, what exactly did King say to Lars?"

"Joaquin said I was under his protection and not to be touched." She stared at him for a long moment, probably at the confusion racking him, and then she shrugged. "Yeah, it surprised me too."

"Under his protection?" Boone asked, sidling up next to Asher, his eyes wide with the same shock Asher felt rushing through him. "Why would he put you under his protection? That makes no sense."

Again, she shrugged. "I don't even know if I can explain it right, but through all this, I kind of got the feeling that he was looking out for me."

"I think that's just your kind heart, Remy," Rhett said, closing in on Remy's right. "This man is dirty."

Remy considered that and then shook her head. "I know it seems that way, believe me, but that's just how it felt. Even his bodyguards were almost…professional with me." She hesitated, then laughed softly. "I know it sounds insane, but honestly, I felt like he was trying to keep me safe."

Asher exchanged a long look with the guys. There was more to King, Asher would bet on it, but it also wasn't his problem. And right now, all he cared about was Remy. Only *her*.

"And what of Lars?" Boone asked.

"I kind of…sort of…got the feeling that Lars was a giant pain in the ass," Remy explained. "Like, he brought more annoyance than anything else."

"That's not surprising," Asher muttered. "He's been a royal pain in my ass and I've barely had to deal with him."

"Good thing we got him into custody, then," Rhett said. He turned to Asher. "DA confirmed Lars's fingerprints matched the ones found in Remy's house after the break-in, and without a doubt, he'll serve time for harassing Remy. That will give the investigators in Whitby Falls time to get a case together on him for conspiracy and likely the murder of Fanning."

"Damn glad to hear that." Asher sighed a breath of relief.

So did Remy. "It's over, then? All of this? It's done?"

Asher gathered her in close, noting Boone and Rhett heading toward the awaiting cruiser, where Lars still sat in the back seat. "It's over. All of this. It's done."

# Chapter 24

One week later, life had actually become the dream Remy imagined for herself. Her shop was back open again and sales were climbing. And the best dream of all came true: She had Asher. She'd moved into his place the very night they'd taken Lars into custody.

And it felt good to be here. Damn good.

"There, you're perfect," Kinsley said, her minty breath brushing across Remy's face as Kinsley applied makeup.

Remy opened her eyes, finding both Peyton and Kinsley smiling at her. Salem had found a place on her lap a half hour ago and clearly had no plans on leaving. "You know, the last time you were both in a bedroom with me," she pointed out, "I was hiding under the blanket and refusing to leave."

Kinsley laughed, reaching for the curling iron, then began to curl Remy's hair. "I like you this way so much better."

Peyton agreed with a nod. "I told you that everything would work out. Good things happen to good people."

"Well, it's nice to actually believe you," Remy said, leaning away from the heat in the curling iron. Kinsley had a habit of forgetting how hot a curling iron was. And the last thing Remy wanted was a burn mark at her wedding.

Well, her *real* wedding.

A sudden knock on the door had them all glancing toward it. Asher peeked his head in and gave a soft smile. "Sorry to interrupt, ladies, but can I have a moment alone with the bride?"

"You should be sorry," Kinsley snapped, holding the curling iron like it was a knife ready to gut Asher. "You're not supposed to see the bride on the wedding day!"

Asher frowned. "Might I remind you that I woke up with the bride this morning."

Remy smiled. He also gave the bride multiple orgasms.

Asher pushed the door open a little wider and then held up a dress bag. "I come with gifts. I won't be long."

Kinsley's eyes widened and gleamed. "Okay, well, since that looks like it has a dress in it, and since I was the one unhappy that Remy was wearing a white summer dress instead of a proper wedding dress, I'll forgive you."

Peyton laughed. Kinsley might have been bummed about the dress, but Remy was just excited to start her life with Asher. She didn't need the fancy wedding she'd dreamed of all those years ago. "Just let us know when you're done," she said to Asher. "We need to finish her hair."

Asher gave a firm nod. "I'll be quick. Promise." He wore jeans and a gray T-shirt, and Remy couldn't wait to see him in the suit he'd bought. Asher rarely dressed up, but the man could pull off a suit like a big-time CEO when he wanted to.

Asher waited for Peyton to leave and shut the door behind her before he turned back and smiled. "I've got a surprise for you."

Remy studied the bag with a smile. "I like surprises."

"I know you do." He hung the bag on the long mirror on the wall, then gestured to it. "Well, your surprise is waiting for you to open."

A short giggle burst from her chest as Remy jumped to her feet to place Salem on the bed and unzip it. Though the moment she got the dress free, she froze, sure she had to be seeing things wrong. She blinked. Twice. The dress didn't change. The ivory bohemian wedding dress had delicate lace on the top, a flowy chiffon skirt, and a scallop open back. "How did you?" she barely managed, turning back to a grinning Asher, her voice all but a whisper.

"How did I buy you the wedding dress of your dreams?"

Speechless, she nodded.

His gaze filled with emotion, as did his voice. "I bought you this dress one week before my mother died. You didn't know it then, but I had originally planned to propose to you on the day that we had Mom's funeral."

Remy moved to him immediately and pressed her hands against his chest, feeling the steady beat of his heart beneath her touch. "You never told me that."

He placed his hands on top of hers. "I never told you a lot of things back then."

God, *this man!* "You bought me my dream dress?" She couldn't believe it.

"I remember when we walked by the shop and you showed me the dress. Your eyes lit up. The dress was meant to be yours." He cupped her face and pressed his lips against hers. She melted into him. First there was love and then there was pain, and now there was something better. A happiness that had been fought for and earned.

When he broke the kiss, he kissed her nose. "I love you, Remy."

"I love you too." She smiled up at him, then turned back to the dress, running her fingers across the soft chiffon. "God, Asher," she gasped, "I can't believe you kept this all this time."

"That's not the only thing I kept."

She turned back just in time to see Asher holding up a vintage square diamond ring surrounded by smaller diamonds. "This was my grandmother's ring," he told her gently, reaching for Remy's hand. "And her mother's before that. My mom gave this to me to propose to you. I had to size it to your finger, which is why I didn't give it to you when I proposed...*again*." He slid the ring on her finger. "You should have seen Mom that day, Remy, she was so very excited about you officially becoming her daughter. It had been a bright moment in her depression."

Tears welled in Remy's eyes and she fought them not to mess up her makeup. "It's so beautiful, Asher."

He glanced into her eyes. "It's perfect on you." He kissed her forehead, then hugged her so very tight. "I better let the girls back in here before they kill me."

When he turned away, she grabbed his hand. "Your mom is with us today, you know. I dreamed of her last night." Remy hadn't wanted to say anything when they woke up this morning, thinking that maybe mentioning his mother would have been too hard for him.

"What did you dream?" he asked softly.

Remy smiled. "The dream was of her and two mourning doves. She looked so happy petting them. Peaceful."

Asher returned the smile, but he looked full of emotion. "Thanks for telling me that, Remy. I hope you're right." He moved to the door, then glanced over his shoulder. "Did you know that mourning doves were her favorite birds?"

She shrugged. "No, but after last night's dream, I figured as much."

Asher laughed softly, then left. He may never believe in all the things Remy did, but he never discounted her either.

Kinsley entered the room again, with Peyton in tow. "Holy shit," Kinsley said, rushing toward the dress. "That is...no, it can't be." She glanced over her shoulder at Remy, wide-eyed. "Is it?"

"What am I missing?" Peyton asked, studying the dress intently. "This is a seriously gorgeous dress."

"A really long time ago I saw this dress in a store and fell madly in love," Remy explained, moving back to her spot on the bed. She tucked in her robe when she sat cross-legged, and Salem promptly climbed back onto her lap. "I was with Asher when we walked by the store and I don't think I stopped talking about it for weeks." She hesitated, then realized something she hadn't before. "Actually, the old dress shop store was where my shop is now."

"Oh, my God, you're right," Kinsley said, reaching for the curling iron and getting to work on the curls again. "I totally forgot that dress shop was there. That's kind of cool."

"It's perfectly right," Peyton said, grabbing the blush brush and getting back to work on Remy's makeup.

Remy's gaze fell to the dress again. Okay, so maybe fate sometimes did get things right.

Forty-five minutes later, wearing the dress that was a tad too tight but thankfully fit, Remy followed the girls down the staircase, with her hair in flowy waves around her face. When they reached the kitchen that led to the outside, Peyton smiled. "Ready?"

"Beyond ready." Remy nodded.

Peyton left through the back door and then a beautiful feminine voice filled the silence. Remy made a note to make sure to thank the regular singer at Whiskey Blues for lending her voice to the ceremony.

"I'm so happy for you, Remy." Kinsley gave Remy a quick kiss on the cheek. "Let's go get you married...*again.*" She laughed as she headed out.

Remy followed, immediately greeted by every cop in Stoney Creek and some even from Whitby Falls. The rest of the people in the yard were friends that both she and Asher had gained over the years, and, of course, MaryJane and her gossip crew were there to witness something they could talk about for the next month, even though they all seemed confused there was a second wedding.

Remy carefully made it down the wooden stairs of the deck and then her focus narrowed on Asher. He looked slick and sexy in his black suit and a light green tie. He stood between his mother's flowerbeds, which looked alive again with the green plants that Remy had bought, and the girls had gotten planted. Boone and Rhett stood off to the side, standing up for him. Judge Mulroney was in front of Asher.

With each step Remy took, Asher's eyes warmed. Right as she passed the first flowerbed, nearly reaching him, two mourning doves suddenly flew out of the flowerbed closest to Remy and then rested on the white wooden arbor.

"See, she's here." Remy smiled when she reached him.

Emotion danced in his eyes as Asher took her hand and kissed her palm. "You brought her back here." He tugged her forward until she pressed against him and his hand sprawled along her back. "You brought life back here...and to me."

She smiled up at him, not caring they weren't following

wedding protocol. Life was on their terms now. "If these are your vows, you're off to a good start."

He chuckled and arched an eyebrow. "Baby, I've had years to think of what I'm about to say to you."

She slid her hand up to cup his face. "Just promise me forever, Asher. That's all I need."

His mouth brushed across hers. "Don't kid yourself, Remy. Me and you, we've always had forever."

# Epilogue

*Five months later...*

The heat didn't seem to quit. Sweat dripped down Remy's back as much as it had earlier this evening when Peyton and Boone became husband and wife. The trip to the tropics had been six days of pure bliss and relaxation, but today had been all about Peyton and Boone and their love. They'd been married on the beach at sunset, had a private dinner with just the six of them, plus Hank, and then Boone and Peyton returned to their honeymoon suite, while Asher and Remy strode the beach, the sand squishing between her toes.

"What if we never go home?" Asher asked as the waves crashed up on the rocky shoreline.

She hugged his arm and leaned into him. "I'd lose my shop. You'd lose your job. And we'd never see our lifelong friends again."

"Shit. Good point." Asher chuckled and winked. "This has been nice, though. We need to do this vacation thing more often."

"Definitely." Over the past five months, everyone kept wondering if Joaquin would make contact again, considering his unusual behavior in the end, but he never did. And Lars was in jail. Life had returned to easy days filled with love and happiness and everything in between. "You know, I really hate to disappoint you, but taking another vacation might soon be hard for us."

With the moonlight shining down on them, Asher stopped and glanced at her, brows drawn together. "Why is that?"

"Well…" She took his hand and placed it on her belly, giving him a smile she hoped answered his question.

His head cocked and eyes searched hers for a long moment. "Are you…?"

"Pregnant?" She smiled, tears filling her eyes. "I am."

He kept one hand on her belly, with the other he cupped her face. "But you've been drinking this week?"

"No, you thought I was drinking this week," she countered. "I've been ordering virgins all week."

It felt like he stared at her for another full minute before he asked, "How long have you known?"

The breeze rushed by, a blessed break in the heat. "I took the test the first day we got here."

His expression was in full detective mode, revealing nothing. "Why didn't you say anything?"

"Because it was really early when I took the test. I didn't want to say anything until I took the test again." She moved a little closer, feeling the warm pull Asher exuded. "But this morning, I took another test."

"Shit," Asher exclaimed, grabbing her and lifting her up and swinging her around. "A baby." He grinned, full of manly pride before he dropped to his knee and kissed her tummy. "Our baby."

Remy smiled, happy tears in her eyes. She slid her hands in his hair, holding him close when he hugged her belly. "Our family."

He eventually rose and gathered her in his arms. "Our family." He scooped her up in his arms. "Damn. Let's get back to the room. I'm going to show you just how happy I am."

She laughed, dropping a kiss on his neck, shivering at his low moan.

When they reached the path lit by lights, he let her back down on her feet. They walked along the path of lush tropical forest until they reached the block of rooms. Heading down the hallway toward their room, Remy quickly realized they weren't alone. "Am I seeing this?" she whispered, freezing on the spot.

"You are," Asher managed. "What. The. Fuck."

What they were seeing was Kinsley and Rhett going at it. Hard-core. Rhett had Kinsley pressed against the wall, nearly ripping at each other's clothes, kissing each other like they'd been starved of each other's flesh. Kinsley managed to get Rhett's shirt off right as he opened his suite's door and then the door slammed shut behind them.

Sure, Remy hoped that maybe Rhett and Kinsley would get together one day, but she certainly wasn't expecting it to *ever* happen. Or happen like *this*. She slowly glanced at Asher. "Are we ever going to talk about what we just saw?" she asked him in a whisper.

Asher barked a loud laugh. "No. Never."

"Is Boone going to kill them?" Remy cringed.

Asher glanced down at her and grinned. "Yup."

Are you ready for Kinsley and Rhett's story? Keep reading for a preview of RUTHLESS BASTARD, available in early 2020.

# Chapter 1

*The sun began to set over the forbidding mountains, giving a slight reprieve to the brutal heat soaking Rhett West in sweat, but the constant screaming and echoing of gunfire remained. As part of the Army Rangers, they'd been deployed on a top secret mission to capture a high-value target, but upon arriving to the town tucked away in the treacherous mountains, they were surrounded by enemy forces and immediately under rapid gunfire. He kept his gun aimed, his focus steady, and fired bullets, watching bodies drop. He never looked at their faces. Never made it personal. This was a job.*

*His fellow Rangers stayed close, tucked safely behind boulders while they fired.*

*Rhett felt a body fall next to him, heard the roar of pain. He reached out, grabbing his buddy Matthews by the vest and yanking him back behind the boulder. After a quick assessment, he grabbed Matthews's hand. "Got shot in the thigh." He squeezed his hand around Matthews's leg. "Don't let go."*

*Matthews nodded quickly. "Yeah. Fuck. Yeah."*

*Rhett took aim again and saw the enemy forces moving higher up the mountain. Hundreds of them, compared to ten of Rhett and his men. He shut his eyes, knowing perhaps this time, death had come calling.*

*Until he heard the sound of fighter jets overhead, followed by explosions rocking the ground beneath him.*

Rhett shook himself out of the dream. He had gotten out of Afghanistan alive. That was what he needed to remind himself. After serving twelve years in the military, he retired from the Army Rangers with a medical discharge after an M-60 machine gun, 7.62 NATO caliber tore into his shoulder, and he brought home every single dark memory of grounds littered with bodies. Men. Women. Children. War was war, and it wasn't pretty. He ran his hands through his hair and drew a deep breath.

For the past three years, he worked as a detective for the Stoney Creek Police Department, and he took pleasure where he could take it. Most times that happened in bed with a lithe woman back home in Stoney Creek, Maine. But he'd come to the tropics to watch his childhood friend and fellow detective Boone Knight marry Peyton Kerr, the newest member to their group. Also on the trip was his other buddy and detective, Asher Sullivan, as well as his wife, Remy Brennan… along with Boone's sister, Kinsley Knight. Rhett shook his head. His plan had gone accordingly, until he got into the whiskey earlier.

After that, he couldn't quite piece together coming back to his hotel room or how the gorgeous brunette got into his bed.

Not just any woman. Kinsley, Boone's little sister.

Dehydrated, naked, and with a mother of all headaches, Rhett stood up and looked down at the biggest mistake he'd ever made lying in his bed. He glanced down to the floor, finding three open condom wrappers.

Fuck.

Sure, he'd wanted to kiss her since the day he suddenly looked up and realized she was a beautiful woman and no longer the kid that used to drive them crazy. Yeah, they had passion that was hot and addictive and totally off-limits. But it was this damn tropical island, seeing her strutting around in a string bikini with barely anything covering her ass. He wanted a taste of her sun-kissed skin, and apparently, he'd done just that last night.

"Why are you staring at me?" Kinsley groaned, her face buried in the pillow.

"Did we fuck last night?" No beating around the bush. He needed answers. Now.

She turned her head a little and peeked open an eye. "Ugh. There's two of you, and both of you look really pissed off."

"Kinsley, answer me," Rhett said sharply. "Please tell me this is a nightmare and we actually didn't sleep together last night." But every moan, every hot kiss was there burned in his memory.

She rolled over then, and Rhett caught a full view of her incredible breasts. At the sight of them, he remembered sucking on those while she rode him until they both orgasmed. *Jesus Christ.* He quickly turned around. "Get dressed."

"You're naked too, you know," she said with a smile in her voice. "And it's quite clear you still want me."

He glared at her over his shoulder and then scowled at his hard cock. "Get dressed. Right now." He moved to the dresser and then took out a pair of shorts. He slipped into them and then turned to find her sitting up in bed with the blankets up, covering her chest. His mind stuttered at the sight of her. Dark, rustled long hair, gorgeous blue eyes, both were a stark contrast against the white pillows and sheets. "Jesus Christ," he said aloud, moving to the chair, as far away from her as possible, considering he was contemplating climbing back into bed with her. "What the fuck have I done?"

"Me," she said with a laugh. "And damn, it was good."

He dropped his hands. "Kinsley," he said in a warning tone.

Instead of responding, which was what he expected, she pushed away the sheets and rose. Rhett's cock went from hard to rock hard so fast, he grunted. She was perfect. Every single inch of her. Curves in all the right places. Her skin smooth and creamy. But those eyes of hers—filled with heat and sass and something he couldn't put a name on—unraveled him. "What are you doing to me?" he grumbled.

"Making this as painful as possible." She laughed, then moved to her panties and bra on the floor. When she reached for them, she turned her heart shaped ass to him and bent over.

"It's working." He groaned.

She quickly dressed in her sexy thong panties and black lace bra, then slid back into her slinky bridesmaid dress, reminding Rhett that they were there at the resort for her brother's wedding. He was a fucking terrible friend.

When she turned back, she gave him a soft smile. "You can relax. Boone will never know about this." She moved closer and stared down at him, her pretty hair curtaining her face.

Rhett clenched his fists, fighting against his desire to tangle his fingers in their strands and to bring her right back onto his lap. "This shouldn't have fucking happened." He rose. He saw the way her pupils dilated. The same way they always did when he got close. It was why he kept his distance. She deserved better than him. Kinsley was sunshine and light, and radiated warmth. He was darkness.

Boldly, like she always was, she took a step forward, closing the distance. "We both knew eventually this would happen. Now it has, and we can finally get over this push and pull we've had going on for years." She gave him a smile that didn't reach her eyes. "Don't worry, you can go back home and let everyone keep thinking you're a ruthless bastard."

"I am a ruthless bastard," he called out to her as she headed for the door.

Her hand froze on the door handle and then she turned back to him. She didn't need to say a word. All the guards he felt like he had up against the world suddenly broke and fell apart. Kinsley did that to him. She slayed him. "Rhett," she said. "We both know that's complete and total bullshit." And then the door shut behind her.

# Acknowledgments

To my husband, my children, family, friends, and bestie, it's easy to write about love when there is so much love around me. Big thanks to my readers for your friendship and your support; my editor, Lexi, for believing in me and my small-town shop owners and their hot detectives; my agent, Jessica, for always having my back; the kick-ass authors in my Sprint group for their endless advice and support; the entire Forever Yours team for all their hard work. Thank you.

# About the Author

Stacey Kennedy is an outdoorsy, wine-drinking, nap-loving, animal-cuddling, *USA Today* bestselling romance author with a chocolate problem. She writes sexy contemporary romance full of heat and heart, including titles in her wildly hot Dangerous Love, Kinky Spurs, Club Sin, and Dirty Little Secrets series. She lives in southwestern Ontario with her family and does most of her writing surrounded by lazy dogs.

Learn more at:
www.staceykennedy.com
Twitter @Stacey_Kennedy
Facebook.com/authorstaceykenne

# You Might Also Like…

her quiet, anonymous existence is instantly destroyed. To make matters worse, Boone—a police detective—is assigned to the case, and Peyton knows she can't keep him at arm's length any longer. She's resisted the simmering heat between them—but now this gorgeous man is promising to keep her safe—and satisfied...

Boone Knight doesn't want the complications of a relationship. But when he volunteers to protect his town's newest—and sexiest—resident, he finally admits he'd like to explore their sizzling attraction. And after one incredible night, everything changes for Boone. Peyton is sweeter—and braver—than anyone he's ever met, and with her in his arms, everything makes sense. He just needs to convince her to trust him enough to reveal her secrets, or risk losing her to a merciless killer who seems to grow bolder with each passing day.

**In this compelling, fiercely emotional debut, childhood sweethearts have a second chance at true love—but can they overcome the past that tore them apart?**

I've been a fighter all my life, even before I made it my career. As a kid in the foster system, I didn't have any other choice.

But I've never fought for something--for *someone*--as hard as I fought for Lucy. I was her protector, her hero—and she was my everything. From the day we met, she made our grim days in Atlanta's notorious Brighton Park fade away—leaving only us.

But we broke each other's hearts, and we did a damn good job of it. A decade has passed since I last saw her, but not a day goes by that I don't think of her clear blue eyes or easy smile. So when I see her at one of my matches—and find out that she's engaged—I need to understand why she turned her back on me all those years ago. Because no matter what I do, no matter how many guys I knock out in the boxing ring, I can't forget her.

So I'm not giving up on her. I'm not walking away.

I'm going to fight for Lucy one last time.

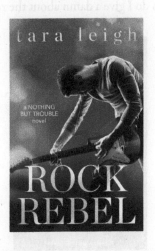

**He's a rock star with a secret, she's a pop princess with a painful past - can their forbidden romance survive, or will their lies destroy them both?**

I've earned my bad reputation.

A few years ago, I was New York City's hottest classical music prodigy. But I wanted something else, something *more*. So I chased my real dream, and now…I'm rock royalty. Dax Hughes, lead guitarist of Nothing but Trouble. But to my family and former Juilliard classmates, I'm an outcast. A misfit. A rebel.

They're not entirely wrong. I *don't* give a damn what other people think, and I'm all for breaking the rules…except when it comes to our new opening act, Verity Moore.

Rock gods don't tour with pop princesses.

It's not personal. Actually, under that fallen diva reputation, Verity's incredibly talented. And her fiery redheaded personality is…intriguing. But I'm convinced the skeletons in Verity's closet are as scandalous as my own, and when we're not sparring, she has a way of drawing out all those secrets I'm determined to keep hidden.

Yeah. Verity Moore is definitely off-limits…

But since when do I give a damn about the rules?

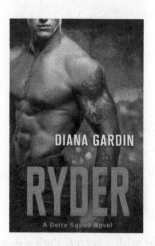

**This Navy SEAL is putting his life—and heart—on the line to protect a woman on the run, but her dangerous secret threatens to destroy them both in this high-octane novel that proves "no one does romantic suspense like Diana Gardin" (Susan Stoker, *New York Times* bestselling author).**

I'm a Navy SEAL and a member of the elite Night Eagle Security team, so you better believe I take every one of my missions seriously. But this one is different. I'm protecting Frannie - she's beautiful, fiercely independent, and on the run from her criminal ex-husband. I know he's dangerous, that he'll do *anything* to get Frannie back. But there's no way I'll ever let that happen...

Trouble is, I can tell Frannie is hiding something from me. Something big. Since she barely got away from her ex alive, I understand that she's wary, but I can't help her if she doesn't let me in. And no matter how badly I want a future with her, I swore I'd never allow myself to be with someone who doesn't trust me. But when Frannie's secret comes out, I have to decide whether her betrayal is enough to make me walk away...or if I'll protect the woman I love no matter the cost.

9 781538 746943